DEATH
AND THE
DUTCH UNCLE

THE HENRY TIBBETT MYSTERIES
BY PATRICIA MOYES

DEATH AND THE DUTCH UNCLE

Patricia Moyes

An Owl Book

HOLT, RINEHART and WINSTON
New York

Death and the Dutch Uncle has appeared previously
in the New York *News* under the title *The Dutch Uncle*.

There is, of course, no such organization as PIFL, nor
are there any such states as Mambesi, Galunga, or Northern and
Southern Bimbasi. All the characters in this book are imaginary,
as are The Pink Parrot and Dominic's Hotel. By contrast, however,
the American and Amstel Hotels in Amsterdam and the Hotel Moderne
in Rethel are, I am glad to say, very real indeed, and I can warmly
recommend a visit to any or all of them.

Published by Holt, Rinehart and Winston,
383 Madison Avenue, New York, New York 10017.

Library of Congress Cataloging in Publication Data
Moyes, Patricia.
Death and the Dutch uncle.
(An Inspector Henry Tibbett mystery)
"An Owl book."
I. Title. II. Series: Moyes, Patricia. Inspector
Henry Tibbett mystery.
[PR6063.09D4 1983]   823'.914   82-23259
ISBN 0-03-063543-8 (pbk.)

First published in hardcover by Holt, Rinehart and Winston in 1968
First Owl Book Edition—1983

Printed in the United States of America
3 5 7 9 10 8 6 4 2

ISBN 0-03-063543-8

For Jonk Mouton, in grateful and affectionate memory.

DEATH
AND THE
DUTCH UNCLE

1

The hospital was exactly like any other hospital—green and white and hygienic and profoundly depressing under a veneer of brisk jollity. The London traffic, swirling and hooting around the building's austere walls, had no more power to penetrate them than it had to invade the cloisters of Westminster Abbey. The hospital was an island, a small enclosed unit which bore toward the world outside something of the relationship of anti-matter to matter.

In a green-painted cell in the heart of this anti-world, Detective Sergeant Derek Reynolds sat on a hard, upright chair and stifled a yawn. The man in the white bed did not stir. Outside in the corridor nurses' footsteps clicked busily on the linoleum; trolleys clattered importantly; occasional masculine voices cracked jokes. It occurred to Sergeant Reynolds that men seemed to take hospitals less seriously than women did. He supposed that it was because they did not have the responsibility of running them. Men in hospitals were either the infinitely superior doctors and surgeons or the cheerfully inferior porters. Both could afford to laugh irreverently in the sacred groves.

The door of the room opened and a nurse looked in. "No sign of life?" she asked with a professional smile.

"Not so far."

"Ring at once if his breathing changes, won't you, Sergeant?"

"I'll do that."

The smile flickered on and off again, like a flashlight, and the nurse disappeared. Beyond the double-glazed window of the small room, Reynolds could see the traffic moving noiselessly, as on a television screen with the sound switched off. It was a warm evening in early April, and as the twilight deepened to violet the streetlights sprang suddenly to life, threading necklaces of light along London's thoroughfares. The conscientious buses put on their sidelights, like fireflies.

The man in the bed moved uneasily and murmured, "One forty-five, one forty-five . . ."

And a fat lot of help that is, thought Sergeant Reynolds. He sighed, picked up his notebook, glanced at his watch, and wrote, *"1948 hours. One forty-five, one forty-five."*

Around the bed complicated machines and bottles and plastic pipes dripped and bubbled and hummed. The whole panoply of modern medicine had been mobilized to save the life of "Flutter" Byers, small-time crook, burglar, gambler, and occasional gunman. Sergeant Reynolds could not help wondering whether it was worth it.

Ten minutes later the man on the bed said, "Madeleine . . ." He said the name twice, quite distinctly. Then he murmured, "One forty-five" again, and after that he sounded as though he wanted to say "Phyllis," but he didn't quite make it.

Sergeant Reynolds made another careful note and then yawned again.

The change in breathing came suddenly. A change from a deep, steady rhythm to a harsh, irregular snorting. Reynolds leaped to the bell, and within seconds the room was full of people in white.

An hour later Detective Sergeant Reynolds was walking down the long hospital corridor with Superintendent Henry Tibbett of the C.I.D. "Flutter" Byers lay in the mortuary, having disdained all efforts to persuade him to stay in the world, even in the anti-world of the hospital. He had died of gunshot wounds, which had patently not been self-inflicted. So the case had become murder, and Henry Tibbett had arrived to take charge.

Beside Reynolds, who was a dark, strongly built six-footer,

Henry looked small and unimpressive in his crumpled mack-intosh. His promotion to superintendent had not changed him in the least particular. His sandy hair, quiet voice, uninsistent manner, and blue eyes, which could appear positively vague if required—all these added up to an impression as far removed from that of a great detective as can conveniently be imagined. Henry had always denied strenuously that he cultivated this harmless air as a pose; but to himself he admitted that it had been useful on more than one occasion. For a man in Henry Tibbett's position, it could be an advantage not to be taken too seriously by the opposition.

Reynolds was saying, "Just the sort of case I hate, sir, if you don't mind my saying so. The world's no worse off for the loss of 'Flutter' Byers, and you and I are going to have one hell of a job pinning it on anyone. As if it mattered. One small, nasty crook shoots another small, nasty crook, and look at the trouble everyone's put to." Reynolds was thinking of the doctors and nurses, not of himself. He had been there when Byers died. He knew the trouble that had been taken.

"It happened at The Pink Parrot, I understand," said Henry.

"That's right, sir. Reported by the landlord at 1356 hours today, by telephone. It's all written down in my report. You know the place, sir?"

"The Pink Parrot? Only by repute, as the drinking haunt of a lot of minor villains. It's not a club, I gather."

"No, no. The Major's too shrewd for that. A club would mean lists of members, names and addresses. An ordinary pub doesn't have members, and every single patron can be a complete stranger to the guv'nor, if the need arises. Much more convenient, if you follow me."

"It's in Notting Hill somewhere, isn't it?"

"Corner of Maize Street and Parkin Place, sir. Just on the edge of respectability, if you know what I mean. And it has a perfectly respectable clientele as well as the others. Businessmen who drop in for a drink in the saloon bar on the way home from the office, and working chaps who use the public for a pint or so. Nothing wrong there. It's the private bar—upstairs—that's where the hard lot meets. You don't get outsiders in there. Or if you do, they don't stay long."

"And Byers was shot in the private bar?"

"Where else?"

"What about the landlord?"

"Nothing against him personally, sir." Reynolds sounded regretful. "Keeps his nose clean. *He* can't help it if some undesirable characters choose to drink in his pub. It's a free country. That's his line, and it's a hard one to crack."

"I see." Henry was thoughtful. "You say he phoned the police just before two. I suppose our friend in the morgue had been in for a lunchtime session."

"That's right, sir."

"Him—and who else?"

"Ah." Reynolds sighed. "That's just it, sir. Talk about see no evil, hear no evil. You get a shoot-up like this, and you'd be surprised at the characters that turn temporarily blind, deaf, and dumb. Nobody saw anyone, recognized anyone . . ."

"I presume the pub was empty when you arrived?"

"But for the Major and poor old 'Flutter.' "

"And Byers himself was no help?"

"None at all, sir. He had quite a lucid spell when they first got him to the hospital. But he'd seen nobody, heard nobody, recognized nobody. They're all the same."

"What exactly was the landlord's story?"

"Ah well, sir, for that you'll have to ask Sergeant Roberts. He stayed at The Pink Parrot, you see, while I rode in the ambulance with 'Flutter,' hoping he might talk. Some hope. All I gathered before I left the pub was that he'd been found by the Major in the gents, lying on the floor more dead than alive."

The two men had reached the big swinging doors of the hospital. As Reynolds pushed them open, the sounds and smells and sights of the world crowded in from outside. Cars, buses, taxis, trucks, people—real people, some dirty, some highly perfumed, some in a hurry, some drunk—but all real, all with names. Not a sterile collection of puppets labeled "Patient," "Nurse," "Porter," "Doctor," or even "Corpse." Reynolds heaved a huge sigh of relief.

"Nice to be out of there," he said.

Henry grinned at him. "I quite agree with you." Then he looked at his watch. "It's nearly half past nine. We'll pick up Sergeant Roberts' report, and then I'll go on to the Pink Parrot and have a word with this Major of yours. What's his name, by the way?"

"Weatherby, sir. Or so he says."

"Is he really a major?"

"Heaven help the British army if he is," said Reynolds.

In the police car, threading its way through the glittering, untidy mass of London, Henry said, "Tell me more about Byers."

"Nothing much to tell that isn't in his record," said Reynolds. "His name, of course, was a sort of pun in reverse on butterfly—and 'Flutter' was appropriate because he was a compulsive gambler. Funny how the underworld goes in for nicknames, isn't it? Like schoolboys. Anyhow, to judge by his record, it was simply to get money for gambling that he took to crime in the first place. Quite a decent background, no broken home or any of *that* jazz," added Reynolds, conveying eloquently his opinion of modern psychiatric theories about the causes of criminal behavior.

"What was his particular line?" Henry asked.

"Anything and everything. Small stuff mostly. A sort of hired help to the big boys. He hadn't the initiative to plan jobs on his own. His heart wasn't really in it, you see. Now, your big-time crook, he really cares. It's a profession to him. But men like 'Flutter' steal and cheat and even kill sometimes strictly for the money, money to gamble or to spend on women. In his case, both." Reynolds stopped suddenly. In the darkness of the car he had gone very red. "I'm sorry, sir."

"Sorry, Sergeant? Why?"

"Well—shooting my mouth off like that about criminals to you. As if you didn't know them better than . . ."

5

"But I don't, Sergeant," said Henry. "Murderers are seldom criminals, you know, not in the professional sense. It's quite some time since I had to do with the regular small-time mob. Tell me more. What form did Byers' gambling take? And what about his sex life?"

"It was horses mostly," said Reynolds, and added hastily, "the gambling, that is." Henry smiled to himself in the darkness, as Reynolds went on. "He'd play the tables from time to time, but horses were the thing. As for women, his tastes were expensive, very expensive. The latest was a very classy bit, name of Madeleine."

"You seem to know a great deal about his private life," said Henry. "Do you keep tabs on all your clients' girl friends, just in case?"

"Well, you see, sir, she was there at The Pink Parrot when we arrived to answer the 999 call. That's how I know. I'd forgotten about her when I said there was only the Major. I was thinking of the mob. She was sitting there at the bar, cool as you please, drinking gin. Never even looked at 'Flutter' when they took him away. Never came to the hospital either, even though they called her."

"Called her?"

"He was asking for her, you see. Pathetic, really."

"What exactly *did* he say in the hospital before he died?"

"It's all down here in my book, sir, the exact words and times. But it doesn't amount to much. The first bit, while he was conscious, I asked him questions, as you'll see. His answers were like I told you. Nobody in the pub he recognized. No idea who shot him. He was having a pee, he said, when he was shot in the back. That's all he knew. Then he got worse, sort of delirious. That's when he started on about Madeleine—repeating her name over and over. That, and racing."

"Racing?"

"Yes, sir. 'One forty-five,' he kept saying. That'ud be the one forty-five race at Sandown Park today, I suppose. Over and over he said it, with the name of a horse. Phil—something. I couldn't catch it properly. I suppose he'd put a big bet on this horse and wanted to know if it had won. He never did know, poor sod. That's about the lot, sir. It's all written down."

"Thank you, Sergeant," said Henry.

He felt profoundly depressed. Like Reynolds, he had no taste for this sort of investigation. The petty feuds of the underworld were about as boring as anything Henry could think of, and when they erupted into violence they brought nothing but a great deal of unrewarding work.

At the local police station Henry dropped Sergeant Reynolds, picked up Sergeant Roberts' report, and telephoned his wife, Emmy, that he would be home late and she must expect him when she saw him. Then he set off with very little enthusiasm for The Pink Parrot.

On the way Henry stopped the car to buy a late paper, and out of curiosity turned to the racing results. The 1:45 race at Sandown Park had been won by Paddy's Fancy at 100 to 8, with Sunspot second and Minstrel King third. So. "Flutter" had lost his last bet. Perhaps, Henry reflected, it was just as well that he never knew.

The black police car pulled up smoothly in Maize Street. On the corner a curiously old-fashioned inn sign swung in the light breeze. It depicted, crudely, a pink parrot. There were no other cars in the street. The news of Byers' death had not yet broken—if broken was the word. It would hardly cause a furor in Fleet Street when it did. So far, the wounding of a minor crook in a pub lavatory in Notting Hill had rated no more than a two-line filler paragraph, if Henry's evening paper was anything to go by.

The police experts, the photographers and fingerprint men, had done their work and departed long since. Lights shone from the windows of the bars. It was obviously business as usual at The Pink Parrot. Henry got out of the car, told the driver to wait, and began to look for the private bar.

There did not appear to be one. The swinging doors opening onto Maize Street were clearly labeled PUBLIC BAR. Around the corner, in Parkin Place, similar doors were

7

marked SALOON BAR. Then Henry remembered that Sergeant Reynolds had said "upstairs." He looked up. In a room above the saloon bar lights were burning behind carefully curtained windows. Henry went into the saloon bar.

It was an unnecessarily ugly room, which seemed to have been expressly designed for the discomfort of its patrons— peeling veneered chairs, tables topped with dirty green oil-cloth, harsh overhead lighting, cream paintwork darkened to a hideous yellow by dirt and neglect, a dartboard so placed that only dwarfs could have enjoyed a game. Hardly surprisingly, there were no customers. Behind the bar a thick-set man in a grubby white coat was reading a lurid magazine.

Henry walked up to the bar. "Mr. Weatherby?" he asked.

The man did not even look up. He gave his head a curious sideways jerk and said, "Upstairs."

It was then that Henry saw, in the corner of the big bleak room, the steep staircase and the yellowing notice which read PRIVATE BAR. An arrow pointed unenthusiastically heaven-ward beside it.

Henry smiled to himself. There was no law against it, of course. Licensed premises could be on any level, and plenty of pubs still retained a private as well as a saloon bar, even though the fine Victorian distinction between the two had long since disappeared. But here the combination of the word "private" and the narrow stairway winding upward into ob-scurity were quite sufficient to discourage any casual custom-ers. As an added advantage, anybody visiting the private bar had to approach it through the saloon. As he moved away from the bar, Henry was not in the least surprised to notice that the barman was pressing a small bell push under the counter. Major Weatherby would be expecting his visitor. And yet, as Reynolds had pointed out, The Pink Parrot pos-sessed all the advantages of not being a club.

Henry was impressed. He began to climb the stairs.

2

It came as a surprise to Henry to find the private bar so full, not because he doubted the ability of the underworld to bluff out a little matter like a shooting affray behind a façade of blank unconcern; but for a more interesting reason. Outside, on the dark landing at the top of the stairs, there had been no noise at all, and yet, as soon as he pushed open the door of the bar, a wave of voices spilled out. That meant that the room was efficiently soundproofed. It also meant that nobody outside the private bar would have heard the shots.

The private bar was private in every sense, even as to its privies. Downstairs Henry had noticed the usual doors marked "Ladies" and "Gentlemen" leading off the saloon bar. Here they were repeated on the floor above. It was, presumably, behind the door labeled "Gentlemen"—which now had an "Out of Order" notice hung on its handle—that Byers had been shot down. His murderer must have walked out into the private bar, down the stairs, through the saloon bar, and out into the street. If the bar had been half as full at lunchtime as it was now, at least a dozen people must have seen him, and probably recognized him. It needed only one honest man among them and Henry's case would be solved; but honest men, as he knew well, were rare in the private bar of The Pink Parrot.

The décor of the private bar was markedly different from that of the saloon. It was almost opulent, in a brash and tasteless way, running to a lot of chrome fittings and an irritating wallpaper sporting an endless array of feebly drawn hunting and racing scenes. The chairs were deep and comfortable and upholstered in real leather, and the tables, topped with imitation marble, were well beyond the scope of an ordinary pub. Everything about the place had a horsy motif, from the

9

ashtrays shaped like saddles to the horseshoes painted on the gin glasses. It was obvious that the clients of the private bar were deeply interested in horseflesh, although Henry thought it unlikely that any of them had actually touched a horse, much less mounted one. To them, horses meant lists of names—and money. As if to underline this point there were no less than three telephones at the far end of the room, each screened in a soundproof cone resembling an eggbox. This was, presumably, for the convenience of customers who wished to place their bets without interrupting their drinking.

There were more than a dozen men in the bar when Henry walked in, and not one of them as much as glanced in his direction. They had been warned of his approach by the barman in the saloon, and they were playing it cool. They sat in groups of three or four in the leather armchairs around the mock-marble tables, drinking gins and Scotches and trying to look like members of the Jockey Club. Henry recognized several faces from the Criminal Records Office files, and felt reasonably sure that he would find the others in the same repository, if he looked.

Behind the bar a square man in tweeds, with a florid face and a stiff gray mustache, like a nailbrush, was reading *Sporting Life*. He put the paper down on the bar as Henry came in and bared his yellow teeth in a caricature of a smile.

"Good evening, sir. And what may we have the pleasure of doing you for this fine evening?" The voice was a parody of a country squire. At closer range Henry could see that the man was wearing a tattersall-check shirt and a tie printed with foxes' masks and riding crops. His cuff links were in the form of silver stirrups.

Henry sat down on a stool at the bar. He said, "Mr. Weatherby?"

"I'm Major Weatherby, yes, at your service, sir."

Henry flipped his official identity card out of his pocket and laid it on the bar. Weatherby barely glanced at it. He had seen such things before, and in any case he had expected Henry.

Henry said, "Byers is dead."

A ripple of silence ran over the room, like wind over a cornfield. Then the men started talking and laughing again. Weatherby stared at Henry in owlish solemnity. His pale blue eyes were unhealthily bloodshot.

"That's a bad business, sir, very bad. Sorry to hear it." He sighed. "Nice fellow, Byers. Quiet, inoffensive. Yes, it's a bad business, the sort of thing that could get this house a bad name."

"I'm sure you wouldn't want that," said Henry dryly. "Where can we talk?"

The Major glanced around the bar. Nobody was paying any attention to Henry. "Well, old man," he said, "as a matter of actual fact, it's a spot difficult for me to leave my post just now." He turned around and flicked a switch on a small radio which stood on a shelf behind the bar. At once a wave of fairly inoffensive light music blanketed the other sounds of the bar. "That should make it private enough for us to chat in here, what? In any case," the Major added, "it'll be closing time in a quarter of an hour. We'll have the place to ourselves then."

"Very well," said Henry. "I want you to tell me exactly what happened at lunchtime today."

"But, my dear fellow, I made a complete statement to your sergeant chappie . . ."

"Byers wasn't dead then," Henry pointed out. "And in any case, that statement isn't viable."

"Not—viable?"

"According to Sergeant Roberts' report," said Henry, "you saw nobody you recognized, except Byers, in the bar at lunchtime today. You heard nothing; you noticed nothing unusual, until you happened to visit the gentlemen's lavatory, for the usual reason, at ten minutes to two—when you found Byers lying on the floor, wounded, and dialed 999."

"That's right."

Henry noticed with satisfaction that Major Weatherby was looking just slightly uneasy.

"It won't do, I'm afraid," said Henry. "This is a murder case now. You'll have to think again."

"I told the Sergeant all I knew." The attempt at bluster was not convincing, and the Major was patently relieved when a diversion occurred in the form of a customer, who came up to the bar and ordered four double Scotches. The man was tall, dark, and dangerous-looking, and Henry recognized him as an accomplished confidence trickster who had served several terms in prison. It was known that he was not averse to violence and that he usually operated on or around race tracks. He gave Henry no flicker of recognition, but paid for his drinks with heavy deliberation and carried them back to his table.

Weatherby said, "I'm really sorry I can't help you more, old man. I liked Byers . . ."

"But you can help me," said Henry gently.

"I've already told you . . ."

"There must have been quite a few people drinking at the bar at lunchtime, surely?"

"I didn't . . ."

"You didn't recognize any of them. I know that. But they must have been here, because one of them shot Byers. Unless, of course, you were here alone with him—in which case I presume that you shot him yourself."

This time the Major's smile was even more of a parody. "Of course, you're right, sir. Yes, we were quite full, for a Wednesday lunchtime. A lot of coming and going."

"Especially going," said Henry.

"I don't quite . . . ?"

"When the police car arrived at five past two, you were the only man in this bar. Or in the pub, for that matter."

"We close at two," said Weatherby.

"Oh no you don't. Half past two on weekdays. In any case,

when you discovered Byers, you should have prevented anybody from leaving the premises."

"That's a tall order, Inspector. Superintendent, I should say. My congratulations, sir."

"Never mind about congratulations."

"Well, as I was saying, sir, I'm only a poor publican. I have to think of my customers. I didn't want to alarm them by telling them about Byers."

"Oh—so you didn't tell them?"

"No, I didn't. I just slipped the 'Out of Order' notice on the door of the gents and went straight to call the police."

"You called them from here?" Henry's question was so nicely casual that Weatherby had already replied before he saw his mistake.

"Yes," he said, "from one of those . . ." He stopped, but it was too late.

"From one of those soundproof telephones," said Henry. "So, if you are telling the truth, nobody heard what you said. And yet, by a strange coincidence, there was a general exodus just at that very moment. All these strangers happened to leave in a body half an hour before closing time."

There was a pause. Weatherby said nothing.

Henry went on. "In fact, every man in this bar knew that Byers had been shot. I imagine that they heard the shots, but even if they didn't, you told them. What's more, they all knew who was responsible for the attack. So they all just melted away and left you to call the police with a story that a child of two could rip to pieces." Henry grinned. "Come on, Major. Have a Scotch and tell me what really happened."

The Major hesitated for a moment, then turned to the racks of bottles behind the bar and poured two stiff measures of whisky into a couple of squat glasses, one of which he placed on the bar in front of Henry. Then he looked at his watch and, without warning, grabbed the hanging rope of a ship's bell, which—incongruous among the horsy impedimenta—was suspended above the bar. In the silence that followed the

13

strident clanging the Major shouted, "Time! If you please, gentlemen! Time!"

Henry looked at the clock behind the bar and also at his own watch. The latter told him that it was twenty past ten, while the clock, with the customary impatience of public-house timepieces, insisted on twenty-five past. By neither reckoning was it half past, closing time. Rather surprisingly, however, the patrons of the private bar raised no objections. They did not hurry, but neither did they loiter. They finished their drinks and got to their feet, still chatting. Most of them came over to the bar to say good night to the landlord. And then they clattered off down the stairs and out into the street. None of them paid the faintest attention to Henry.

It was very nearly faultless, but not quite. There was an element of too-good-to-be-true about it, like amateur dramatics too carefully rehearsed, or like schoolchildren planning deviltry. Nothing, Henry reflected, that one could even mention in a court of law. He poured water into his glass of whisky and drank, as the door closed behind the last customer.

Major Weatherby downed his drink neat and said, "Now we can talk, sir."

"Your flock," said Henry, "is very well behaved."

The Major looked at him unblinking. "Yes," he said. "We get a good type of patron in the private bar. Quiet. Gentlemanly. No trouble."

"One of them caused trouble at lunchtime today," Henry pointed out.

"That's true," said the Major, "that's very true, alas. But it wasn't one of our regulars."

"Of course not," said Henry. "None of your regulars were here, were they? Or you'd have recognized them." There was a silence, and then Henry said with a carefully judged rap of impatience, "Come along, Weatherby. I'm waiting."

The Major was not to be ruffled. He had been expecting this moment and he knew just how he intended to handle it. He grinned—a grin that was intended to be whimsical, but was in fact wolfish. Then he said, "You won't believe me."

"That's quite possible," said Henry politely, "but try me."

Major Weatherby poured himself another drink. Then he said, "It was about a quarter to two."

"One forty-five." Henry was talking to himself, but the Major reacted sharply.

"What's that, Superintendent?"

"Nothing. Just another way of expressing the time of day. A quarter to two. One forty-five. What happened at one forty-five?"

"This character walked in here, into the private bar."

"What character?"

"This is what you're not going to believe, Superintendent."

"I'm the judge of that. Get on with it."

Weatherby took a deep breath. "Well, here goes. He was a medium-sized man in a medium-sized overcoat, wearing a medium-sized Trilby hat well down over the eyes, and medium-sized black kid gloves. He was also wearing medium-sized dark glasses and a medium-sized false black beard and mustache."

For a moment Henry considered losing his temper; then he thought better of it. If this mob had decided to mock him, he could at least give as good as he was getting.

He pulled a notebook out of his breast pocket and carefully wrote down what the Major had said. Then he looked up and asked, "Did you have any reason to suspect that this man might have been trying to conceal his identity?"

The Major's mouth dropped open. It took him quite a few seconds to comprehend that he was being taken seriously. Then he pulled himself together and said, "Well, naturally, I thought it was a bit odd, old boy. I mean, false whiskers and dark glasses went out of fashion thirty years ago."

"They still make an effective disguise," said Henry.

"Exactly. So they do. But between ourselves, Superintendent, I had decided that this bearded character was just one of the boys playing a practical joke."

"One of the boys?"

"One of our regular patrons, I should say. I mean, the disguise was so obvious."

"Was it obvious who was behind it?"

"No, no. Indeed, no. It could have been anybody."

"Very convenient," said Henry. "So, what happened?"

"Well, the bearded type came up to the bar and I asked him what I could get him to drink. I felt sure I'd recognize him as soon as he opened his mouth."

"But you didn't?"

"No, no. He was too clever. He answered me in a thick foreign accent, like a third-rate repertory-company spy character." The Major took a deep breath and embarked on an imitation. " 'I 'ave rendezvous mit Bayers.' That's what he said," added the Major in his normal voice. Then, lapsing into stage-Middle European again, he went on. " 'Vich off dese mens iss Bayers?' "

"He said that?"

"His very words," said the Major solemnly. "So I said, 'You're out of luck for the moment, chum. Byers is in the gents.' He said, 'Vot iss dis gentz?' " Major Weatherby paused. "I was beginning to suspect," he added seriously, "that my leg was being pulled."

"You still couldn't recognize the man?" Henry asked.

"No. In fact, I'd swear I'd never seen him before."

"I bet you would," said Henry under his breath. Aloud he said, "Well, what happened then?"

"I—I gestured toward the back," said the Major. He did not demonstrate the gesture. "The bearded chap seemed to understand. He nodded, ordered two whiskies, and put money down on the counter. I turned around to pour out the drinks, and when I looked back he had gone and the door of the gents was swinging shut behind him." The Major paused, looking slightly uneasy. Then he said quickly, "A minute or so later the bearded man came out. He didn't come back to the bar. He went straight out of the door and down the stairs. I never saw him again."

"Leaving his drinks and money on the bar?" Henry asked.

"Yes, yes. Leaving everything."

"And you didn't hear the shots?"

"Nothing at all, Superintendent."

"And yet, just at that moment, everybody else in the bar decided to leave."

"Well . . ." The Major tried hard to produce another smile, but his stock was running low. "You know how it is. Most of the chaps were in one large party, and when that broke up there were only a few isolated patrons left. People don't like drinking in an empty bar, Superintendent," the Major added with the air of a philosopher. "That's one of the first things you learn in this trade. Once you're down to three or four you may as well put the shutters up for the evening."

Henry looked at him, half-smiling, but the Major was giving nothing away. He regarded Henry with a carefully deadpan expression on his square face. However preposterous, this was his story and he was sticking to it.

"So," said Henry, "the bar emptied. Sheer coincidence. Go on."

"When you say 'emptied,'" said the Major, "we mustn't forget Madeleine."

"I wasn't forgetting her," said Henry. "She was 'Flutter's' girl."

"That's putting it rather strongly, old man," said Weatherby. "She was having a drink with him at the time certainly. But that proves nothing."

"Right," said Henry. "The bar is empty, except for Madeleine. The bearded stranger has gone, and so have all the other strangers who happened to be here. What happens then?"

"Well, now—as far as I remember—Madeleine said to me, 'Flutter's' taking a bl . . . a very long time in the gents.' And I said, 'If you'll mind the shop for me, my dear, I'll go and see how he's getting on.' So I went in—and I found him. I called the police and the hospital at once."

Henry made another note in his book. Then he said, "So Madeleine also saw the bearded stranger?"

"She certainly did," said a voice from behind his left shoulder.

The girl who had come into the bar was strikingly beautiful. More than that, she was elegant. Her thick, shining golden hair was either that color by nature or had been tinted by a master. Her make-up was discreet and faultless. Her dress and shoes looked as if they came from Paris, and her slender, supple bracelet was real diamond and platinum. She would have looked perfectly at home in an Italian palazzo, a French château, a Park Avenue penthouse, or an international hotel anywhere. She pointed up the tawdry vulgarity of The Pink Parrot in the same merciless way that a sudden shaft of sunlight exposes the dusty corners of a neglected room.

"Ah, Madeleine, my dear," said Weatherby. "We were just talking about you."

Madeleine swung herself gracefully onto a bar stool. "I realized that," she said. "I'll have a double gin."

As he poured the drink the Major said, "This is Superintendent Tibbett from Scotland Yard, dear." He turned to Henry with another of his unpleasant grins. "And don't get any ideas about booking me for serving drinks after hours, Superintendent. Madeleine is my niece and she's staying here."

Madeleine took a long drink, looking seriously at Henry as she did so. Her eyes, above the rim of her glass, were the color of violets. At last she put down her glass and said, "Scotland Yard. So poor old 'Flutter' is dead." There was no emotion in her voice.

"I'm afraid so, my dear. You must try not to distress yourself too much."

The Major was doing his best to give a convincing performance as a gruffly comforting uncle, but Madeleine did not make it easy for him. Henry thought that he had never seen anybody less distressed.

She sighed, with what sounded more like relief than sorrow. "He was no good, poor little bastard," she said in her beautifully modulated voice. "Couldn't keep his money. I should never have wasted my time on him."

The Major cleared his throat noisily. "Now, now," he said. "*De mortuis . . .*"

The girl ignored him. She said to Henry, "You were talking about the man who shot him."

"The man with the beard," said Henry.

"False beard," amended Madeleine. She smiled at Henry. "Ludicrous, isn't it? Of course, you don't believe a word of it. That's why we decided that it wasn't worth even trying it on your sergeant this afternoon."

"I'd like to hear your version of what happened," said Henry.

She smiled again. "Be your age," she said. "We've had plenty of time to synchronize our stories. You surely don't expect to trip me up, do you?" Without giving Henry time to answer, she went on. "At a quarter to two, or thereabouts, this man walked into the bar. Great black bushy beard and mustache—you could see the elastic behind his ears. Dark glasses. Hat pulled well down. Thick foreign accent. Small to medium height. I was just going to say, 'Come out from behind those whiskers, Oscar, we know you,' when I realized that we didn't. Know him, I mean. He looked around the bar and asked which was 'Flutter,' as if he had a date with him. My uncle told him that 'Flutter' was in the gents. Whereupon he ordered a drink—the bearded wonder, I mean—and then marched off into the gents. He was out again a minute later, and he simply walked off downstairs, leaving his drink on the bar."

"And you didn't hear the shots?" Henry asked.

"Oh no, Superintendent." She was laughing at him. "Of course not."

"And yet, by chance, everyone else in the bar suddenly left?"

"Yes—wasn't it surprising? And then the Major went in and found 'Flutter.' And there you are."

Henry said, "Do you live here all the time, Miss—er . . . ?"

19

The girl and Weatherby exchanged the briefest of glances. Then she said, "No. On and off. When I'm in London. I travel a lot, you see."

"With friends?"

"Of course." Teasing again. "Traveling alone is no fun."

"How long do you plan to stay in London this time?"

"You are inquisitive, Superintendent. I really don't know. Not very long." She swung a ravishing leg, pensively. "I think I shall go to Amsterdam. I haven't been there for a long time, and the flowers will soon be at their best."

"I'm afraid I shall have to ask you not to leave this country without letting us know," said Henry. "You are a key witness and this is a murder investigation."

The violet eyes opened very wide, mocking. "Dear me. How very solemn and official. You're sure you wouldn't like me to report to you personally every three hours at Scotland Yard, Superintendent?"

"I should like it very much," said Henry, "but it won't be necessary. What is necessary is to know your name."

"Madeleine."

"We need a surname as well."

"Never satisfied, are you? Miss Madeleine La Rue."

"Is that," Henry asked, "your real name or a—professional pseudonym?"

The girl laughed with genuine merriment. "It's the name on my passport, Superintendent. That should be good enough for you. As I told you, I travel a lot."

Henry stood up. He said to Weatherby, "I'll take a look at the lavatory now, if you don't mind."

"Certainly, sir, a pleasure."

The Major seemed relieved that Henry's conversation with Madeleine was over, at least for the time being. Henry sympathized with him. The Major was a predictable knave, cunning enough but far from brilliant. The girl—who, whatever else she might be, was certainly not his niece—was in a different category altogether. Henry did not know, although he intended to find out, what had brought these two incongruous characters together. He did know that the girl was playing her hand coolly, almost contemptuously, with a dizzy disregard for danger that reminded Henry of an expert tightrope walker. He was not surprised that the Major should be having spells of vertigo.

There was nothing at all spectacular about the gentlemen's lavatory. Byers' statement had apparently been strictly accurate. Users of the urinal stood with their backs to the door, and from the chalk marks conscientiously sketched on the floor by Sergeant Roberts, it was plain that Byers had been so engaged when he was shot down. Henry knew from the medical reports that he had been shot at close range three times. The first shot had presumably felled him. The second and third were just to make sure. The whole thing would not have taken more than a few seconds. It was, of course, just possible that the killer had used a silencer, but Henry did not believe it. A gun with a silencer is too bulky to conceal.

When Henry came back into the bar he had the impression that Major Weatherby had not moved a muscle. Nervousness had turned him into a grinning puppet. Madeleine, on the other hand, was completely relaxed. She was examining her exquisite features in the mirror of a small, heavy gold compact, humming lightly to herself. She greeted Henry with a dazzling smile.

"Did you find the murderer lurking in the cistern, Superintendent? Such an undignified place to die, but so like the poor little man." She shut the compact with a snap, as if closing the final chapter of Byers' small, sordid life. . . .

In the car, as the driver threaded his way expertly through the maze of West London, Henry deliberately shut his mind to the case. Madeleine's personality was a potent, disturbing element, and Henry was tired. A night's sleep would help to sort out his thoughts; meanwhile there was no more he could do before the morning. He switched on the small reading light and diverted his mind with the trivia of the evening paper, which was still in his overcoat pocket.

By the time the car reached Chelsea Henry had read, without any marked interest, an account of how the boys of Burke Green Secondary Modern School had won a brass-band contest at the Albert Hall; had snorted sardonically at a judge's remarks concerning a divorce case in which the parties, in a misguided attempt to be honest, had slipped up over a piece of legal jiggery-pokery and must therefore remain married; and had nodded over the Greater London Council's plans to open another mile of subway in 1990. Half asleep, he absorbed the fact that Miss Candida Simple, the film star, had flown in from New York with her sixth husband; that the American jurist Mr. Justice Findelhander had died of a heart attack at his London hotel at the age of eighty-nine; that a group of back-bench M.P.'s were threatening to abstain in the vote on armaments; that . . .

"Here we are, sir," said the driver cheerfully.

Henry jerked himself into wakefulness to find that the car had pulled up outside the ugly Victorian house in west Chelsea where he and his wife, Emmy, occupied the ground-floor apartment. He thanked the driver, climbed out of the car, and went in.

Emmy was in bed and asleep. As Henry switched on the bedroom light the lump under the bedclothes stirred resentfully and the dark mop of hair buried itself deeper into the pillow. Then a blurred and sleepy voice said, "Is that you, darling?"

"It is," said Henry. "Were you expecting somebody else?"

"Idiot," murmured Emmy. After a moment she added, "Got something to tell you . . ."

Henry had already taken off his coat and was loosening his tie. He found a hanger, slipped his jacket onto it, and then said, "Have you? What?"

But there was no answer. Emmy was sound asleep again.

3

The next morning Henry woke at seven feeling fit and re-
freshed and not particularly enthusiastic about spending the
day in pursuit of the murky career of 'Flutter' Byers. Even
Madeleine seemed to have lost a lot of her glamour in the
cold, clear light of the April morning, and on reflection,
Henry decided that her air of supreme self-assurance was
probably due to nothing more than sheer innocence, combined
with a certain obtuseness. Innocence as far as Byers' death
was concerned, that is; outside that limited sphere Henry felt
that innocent was not the word for Madeleine La Rue. Of all
the fool, phony names to choose. Almost as silly as the mythi-
cal stranger in the false beard.

And yet, both had the merit of being so unlikely as to be
possibly true. Henry considered how Dr. Klaus Fuchs, for instance, might have set the table in a roar at Harwell by calmly
announcing, "Actually, of course, I'm a Soviet spy." Or what
would have been the reaction of one of Christie's lady friends
if he had said, "Do drop in for tea. I have several murdered
women buried in my garden." Or . . .

"Oh, you're awake," said Emmy from the doorway. She was
wearing a lemon-yellow terry bathrobe and carrying a tray
of early-morning tea. Her short, dark hair was tousled, but
her fine, honey-colored skin had the clean-scrubbed, peach-
bloom look that Henry had loved for years. She put the tray
down beside the bed. "You look very solemn. What are you
thinking about?"

"Nothing," said Henry. He had, in fact, been comparing
Emmy mentally with Madeleine La Rue, and finding to his
satisfaction that he preferred Emmy.

"Did you get home very late?" Emmy asked. She sat on the

edge of the bed and began pouring tea. "I never heard you come in."

"You did. You woke up and spoke to me."

"Did I really? I don't remember a thing about it."

"You even said that you had something to tell me, but when I asked you what it was, you'd gone out again like a light."

Emmy wrinkled her brow. "Something to tell you? Oh yes, of course. You'll never guess who telephoned yesterday evening." She paused hopefully.

"You're right," said Henry, "I never will."

"Don't you want to have a guess? The most unlikely person you can think of. Someone we've never met."

"Oh, really?" said Henry. "General de Gaulle? Elizabeth Taylor? Prince Philip?"

"Don't be silly."

"Well, I've guessed. Now you can tell me."

"All right." Emmy sipped her tea. "You remember when we were in Geneva and poor John Trapp was killed?"

"I'm not likely to forget it," said Henry feelingly.*

"Well, you remember, too, how the consulate gave us the name of his next of kin, his young brother, Gordon?"

"That's right," said Henry. "I wrote to him afterward. It seemed the least I could do."

"Well," said Emmy, "last evening Gordon Trapp called!"

"Good Lord. What did he want?"

"He wanted to speak to you, but of course you were out."

"But—wait a minute. He was in Africa, somewhere. I remember having to write to some extraordinary address—in Mambesi, I think it was."

"Well, he's in London now," said Emmy. She tucked her bare feet up on the bed under her dressing-gown. "And he's coming to dine with us tonight."

"Oh, really, Emmy." Henry was annoyed. "You know I hate social functions when I'm working on a case. Anyhow, I never know what time I'm going to get home . . ."

* See *Death on the Agenda.*

24

"I can't help that," said Emmy. "For a start, when Gordon Trapp telephoned, I didn't know you were on a case. You only called to tell me just before ten o'clock, if you remember. And to go on, it sounded urgent."

"What sounded urgent?"

"I don't know. Whatever it is that he wants to see you about. After all, he wouldn't have called otherwise, would he?"

"He was probably just being polite. Feels he ought to thank me or something—and there's nothing I like less. If this is the first time he's been to London since John's death, he may feel that he has an obligation to . . ."

"No," said Emmy quite sharply.

Henry looked up from his teacup, surprised.

Emmy grinned. "You're not the only person in this family with a nose." She was referring to Henry's legendary power of intuitive detection, of which he was secretly rather ashamed. "I *know* this is important. Otherwise I wouldn't have asked him here. He's arriving at eight, so do try to be on time. If you're done with your cup, I'll wash it up and get breakfast."

Sergeant Reynolds had not been idle. While Henry had been visiting The Pink Parrot the night before, he had been getting on with the less attractive job of a routine check in the Criminal Records Office in order to establish the *curriculum vitae* of the late Mr. Byers.

Henry arrived at the imposing glass-and-gray-marble building of the new Scotland Yard soon after nine and took the elevator to the fifth floor and the "C" (for Crime) Department. He still felt slightly overwhelmed, both by the new building and by the new nameplate on his office door. Superintendent Tibbett still seemed to Henry to be a bit of a myth, not quite real. Promotion was rather like changing out of a well-worn, comfortable pair of shoes into gleaming new riding boots. So far, the new boots had not pinched. But the unfamiliar feeling still lingered. The sight of Sergeant Reynolds' dossier, laid out neatly on the desk, was reassuring. Henry took off his coat, settled himself in his chair, and began to study the life and times of "Flutter" Byers.

It seemed that he had been one of those inconsequential characters whose progress through life is maddeningly difficult to chart, owing to its erratic nature. Like many gamblers, he had swerved dizzily between opulence and penury. When opulent, he had dressed like a dandy and spent money freely at the most expensive haunts, both in London and abroad. When penurious, he had apparently been content to take on the most menial of jobs—criminal or otherwise—while he waited hopefully for the pendulum of chance to swing him back into luxury.

A few hard facts emerged. Byers had been born thirty-five years before, the only child of eminently respectable parents, to be precise, a suburban bank clerk and his wife. They had made considerable sacrifices to send him to a good school. He had repaid them by embarking on a career of gambling, petty larceny, and car stealing when only seventeen. He was caught and sent to jail. His parents had been prepared to have him home again after this first sentence, but he had refused to go back. He apparently considered a steady job in the suburbs as lacking in adventure and unworthy of his talents. Thereupon, the father had become extremely angry and had severed all connection with his son.

Sergeant Reynolds' report ended: "I finally contacted Mr. and Mrs. Byers at 11:40 P.M. on the 4th. Mrs. Byers is now a branch manager of the bank, and the couple live at 68 Chestnut Avenue, Southam, S.E. 19. Although they stated that they had not seen or heard from their son for nearly fifteen years, they were obviously distressed at the news of his death. They have expressed a wish to be responsible for the funeral arrangements."

Henry sighed, full of compassion at the quiet tragedy of these two worthy people. And yet, he could not suppress a stab of sympathy for the young man who had been so determined to break away from suburbia. Nobody could ever know what had gone on behind the lace curtains of Chestnut Avenue, or its equivalent, fifteen years ago.

Sergeant Reynolds appended details of Byers' police record, together with the latest available information on his most recent activities. After his period of training in jail, he had kept out of trouble for several years, which is to say, no charges had been brought against him. His first slip-up had occurred when he was twenty-three, when he had been convicted of demanding money with menaces—in plain language, of blackmailing an extremely wealthy man whose love life was allegedly irregular. Byers had been convicted, but at the time the police had felt reasonably certain that he was not the brains behind the scheme; he had been working for somebody else. However, Byers had kept his mouth shut, gone to prison, and been remarkably prosperous when he came out. Later, he had been convicted for smuggling gold watches out of Switzerland. Once again there was a strong suspicion that he had been employed by a master.

Although these were his only convictions, it was clear that Byers would have stood in the dock many more times if the police had been able to back up their suspicions by proof. Meanwhile, he was known by the company he kept. He had a reputation in the underworld as a discreet and efficient hireling who would undertake any sort of job as long as the money was right.

As Reynolds had pointed out the previous evening, Byers was not a professional crook in the true sense of the word. Gambling was his passion, and to gamble he needed money. So, when going through a tough time financially, he was prepared to hire out his talents to the more dedicated members of the criminal fraternity. When he had funds, he disdained crime; dressed, ate, and drank in style, and lavished money on the most expensive women he could find. When he was broke, he would return to the only permanent base he had—a shabby bed-sitting-room in northwest London. If there was no call for his illegal services, he lived by taking casual jobs, usually in the kitchens of the very same hotels which he patronized as a guest when affluent. He must, Henry reflected, have been something of a philosopher. Certainly he had taken Kipling's advice, not only the bit about risking all his winnings on one turn of pitch and toss but also the injunction, when faced with triumph or disaster, to treat those two impostors just the same.

Recently, it appeared, Byers had been in the throes of a typical swing of the pendulum. A few months previously he had made a considerable killing at the races and had enjoyed a spell of high living. It was at this time that he had met Madeleine La Rue, and not surprisingly, she had disposed of his winnings with impressive speed. In consequence, he had been forced to return to his bed-sitting-room and had taken a job as a kitchen porter at Dominic's Hotel in Knightsbridge, a position which he still occupied at the time of his death. He had continued to hang around The Pink Parrot, where Miss La Rue was staying with her so-called uncle. Sergeant Reynolds' report described Madeleine, with commendable understatement, as a young lady of expensive tastes. Nothing was known against her. In fact, nothing was known about her at all. Reynolds would endeavor to find out more. Between the lines of officialese, Henry could sense the Sergeant's dislike of Madeleine. He remembered how she had refused to come to the hospital.

Next came the report of the ballistics expert. Three bullets had been recovered, one from the body and the other two—having passed clean through Byers—from the plaster of the cloakroom wall. The spent cartridge cases had also been found. The bullets were of .38 Special caliber, and the cartridge cases suggested that they had probably been fired from a Smith and Wesson lightweight revolver. If this was so, the weapon was one which could easily be slipped into an overcoat pocket.

Henry read the reports twice through and then sent for Sergeant Reynolds and regaled him with an account of the previous evening's visit to The Pink Parrot.

"A total stranger with a false beard." Reynolds laughed

with bitter amusement. "You have to hand it to them, don't you, sir? I mean to say, it takes a bit of a joker to think up a tale like that. And all they've got to do is to keep a straight face and stick to their story, solemn-like . . ."

"We'll make them do a little more than that," said Henry. "Tomorrow I want you to get both of them in here and take down proper, signed statements from them. Make it as impressive as you can. You won't make any sort of dent on the girl, but I don't imagine that Major Weatherby will enjoy himself. And before then, if we humanly can, we've got to find another witness to confute them with."

"Somebody else who was in the Parrot's private bar at the time, you mean?" Reynolds had stopped smiling. "I'll do my best. I'll let it be known, discreetly, that we'd be uncommonly grateful if anyone would come forward. But it's hopeless, if you ask me. Nobody's going to admit he was there."

"You know the regulars?"

"Most of them, yes, sir. But . . ."

"Then put on all the pressure you can. I must have some way of breaking that story."

"I'll try, sir," said Reynolds gloomily.

"Well, I'll have to leave it in your hands for today, Sergeant," said Henry. "I've got to appear in court, the Buster Jones case. I'll get back as soon as I can, but you know how these things go."

It was, in fact, after five o'clock in the evening when Henry finally got back to his office, exhausted after a day in the courtroom but satisfied at having obtained a conviction against a particularly unpleasant robber-with-violence. Ten minutes after he got in, Sergeant Reynolds telephoned.

"Well, sir, I've found your witness."

"You have? Good work, Sergeant. Who is it?"

"Young chap, name of Peterson. Been in jail, but going straight now, as far as we know. Getting married next month. He telephoned about an hour ago, and luckily I was in the office and spoke to him, if you can call it lucky."

It occurred to Henry that Reynolds was sounding extraordinarily subdued for a man who has just come up with important evidence. He said, "This man Peterson, he's admitted being at The Pink Parrot?"

"Oh, yes, sir. He's admitted it, all right."

"And what's his version?"

In the pause that followed Henry could hear the Sergeant taking a deep breath.

Then Reynolds said, "He's coming in later to make a proper statement, sir, but he gave me a detailed description of the murderer over the phone. A tall man wearing a large, false black beard and dark glasses. Trilby hat pulled down over the eyes. Thick foreign accent. All exactly as Weatherby and the girl said. The only useful thing he's admitted is that everyone in the bar heard the shots and cleared out; but we knew that already. Even if Weatherby admits that much, it won't get us any further." There was another pause. Then Reynolds added, with a sort of desperation, "Peterson is trying to help us, sir. He's trying to make a fresh start and get into our good books. I believe he's telling the truth, sir. I hate to say it, but I believe him."

"How much," said Gordon Trapp, "do you know about piffle?"

"I've been hearing an uncommon amount of it recently," said Henry feelingly.

Gordon, tall and fair and uncannily like a younger version of his dead brother, stretched his long legs and took another sip of coffee. "Really?" he said. "You surprise me. Our activities don't make the headlines, as a rule."

"I'm sorry," said Henry. "You must have thought I was being facetious. When you said 'piffle,' I thought that you meant 'piffle.' Obviously, you don't."

"I asked for that," said Gordon with a grin. "I meant the institution for which I have the honor to work. The Permanent International Frontier Litigation people—P-I-F-L. Therefore, of course, piffle for short."

"In that case," said Henry, "I know nothing about it whatsoever. Is that what you wanted to see me about?"

The dinner had been excellent. Emmy, plagued by feelings of guilt for having landed Henry with a dinner guest in the middle of a case, had spent more than her usual allowance of time and money on preparing a meal that would have won stars in any good-food guide. Gordon Trapp had been charming, amusing, and talkative. Quickly and gracefully he had thanked Henry for his investigations into the murder of his brother John in Geneva and for the subsequent letter of explanation and condolence. Then, dismissing the subject, he had gone on to talk about his experiences in Africa, the current political and economic scene, the London theater, and other equally fascinating topics. Now it was ten o'clock, and Emmy had served a second pot of coffee. Still Gordon Trapp had failed to mention the real reason for his visit. Henry had enjoyed the evening, but he had a tiring day behind him and another one ahead, and he was beginning to feel that it was time for bed.

"See you about?" Gordon echoed. He sounded a little uneasy.

"Emmy had the impression," said Henry, "that there was some rather special reason why you wanted to . . ."

"I'm in the same line of business as John was, you know," said Gordon Trapp. Henry could not be sure whether he was changing the subject or not. "Interpreting. We both read modern languages at the university. Of course, he had a full-time job with the United Nations in Geneva. That seemed to suit him, but I've never liked being tied down. I free-lance."

"And at the moment you're interpreting for PIFL?" Henry tried not to sound bored.

Trapp put his coffee cup down on the table, sat up straight, and said, "I'm well aware that I'm beating about the bush, Superintendent, but the fact is that—well—now it comes to the point, it sounds so damned silly."

"Whatever you have to say," said Henry, "it can hardly be sillier than some of the stories I've been hearing recently.

Yours doesn't concern a character in a false beard, I hope?"

Trapp looked startled. "A false beard? Good heavens, no. It's just that—oh, well—now that I've gotten this far, I may as well get it over and give you your big laugh of the week. You say you know nothing about PIFL?"

"I've heard of it vaguely, now that I think about it," said Henry, "but quite honestly . . ."

"There's no earthly reason why you should know anything about it," said Gordon. "It's just about the least important or sensational international institution in existence. It was set up ten years ago, a permanent commission to settle frontier disputes, especially in the case of newly independent countries."

"I should have thought that could be pretty sensational," said Emmy.

"It could be," said Trapp, "if any nation ever referred any matter of any possible interest to PIFL. But they don't. All the sensational disputes go before the International Court of Justice at The Hague."

"So what does PIFL . . . ?"

"The things PIFL decides," said Trapp, "are usually not even disputes, in any real sense. It's like—like golfers in a friendly match consulting the rule book. Both states must agree to bring the problem to PIFL and to abide by its ruling. It's generally a question of deciding where a frontier line shall be drawn on a map, probably in uninhabited country which neither side wants anyway. What they do want is to get the matter settled, neatly and legally. You see what I mean?"

"It doesn't sound wildly exciting," said Henry. He stifled a yawn.

Trapp laughed. "You can say that again. The commission consists of eleven members, and their combined ages can't be much short of a thousand. They're nice old boys, most of them, and all highly distinguished, of course—ex-diplomats and judges and so on—but you'd never call PIFL a throbbing center of international intrigue. The commission sits in a dingy Victorian office in a back street off Whitehall, and how we all manage to keep awake through the hearings is a small miracle."

"And yet," said Henry, "you've come here to tell me about it."

"Yes." There was a long silence. "The commission is a permanent body, you see."

"So you said before. But . . ."

"That means that no member can be replaced during the hearing of a dispute. If a commissioner should be—incapacitated—then his chair simply remains vacant and the case proceeds without him. So long as there's a quorum, of course."

"How many make a quorum?" Henry made a gallant effort to sound interested.

"Seven. Seven out of the eleven. Decisions are reached by a majority vote. In the case of a tie the chairman has a casting vote."

There was another silence.

Then Henry said, "I don't want to hurry you, but I do wish you'd get to the point."

"It sounds so bloody silly."

"Then get it over and you'll feel better."

"Well—I told you there were eleven commissioners, didn't I?"

"You did, several times."

"Well—there aren't."

"What does that mean?"

"At the moment there are only nine."

"Why's that?"

"Because two of the members have died recently. Pereira and Findelhander."

Henry put his cup down. "Are you trying to suggest that there was something suspicious about their deaths?"

Trapp gave an embarrassed little laugh. "Oh, no. Goodness me, no. Pereira was eighty-seven and Findelhander was eighty-nine. Pereira tripped over the curb in Oxford Street one evening and was run over by a bus. Findelhander died of a heart attack—he'd had a dicky heart for years." Trapp looked at Henry. Then he said, "And yet, I am quite convinced that they were both murdered."

"Why?" said Henry. Suddenly he did not feel tired any longer.

Gordon Trapp didn't answer directly. Instead he said, "The current dispute before PIFL concerns Mambesi and Galunga. You know where they are?"

"I should," said Henry, "but quite frankly, I can't keep pace with the map of Africa these days. And what with all the new names . . ."

Gordon Trapp smiled. "I can't say that your ignorance surprises me," he said. "They are two of the newest, poorest, and least desirable territories on the whole continent. Both became independent three years ago. They have a common frontier about a hundred miles long, and that's what the argument is about. The question is, should the frontier be marked by the watershed of the Blue Smoke mountain range, which runs along the southern side of Mambesi, or should the whole range belong to Mambesi, with the River Lunga, which flows through the valley on the Galunga side, as the dividing line? Really, the point is purely academic. Apart from a tiny strip of sandy plain between the river and the foothills, the disputed territory consists of the southern slopes of the least attractive mountains I have ever seen in my life."

"You know the area then?" said Henry. And, answering himself, added, "Of course. You were working in Mambesi when John was killed."

"Yes. I was out there interpreting at the pre-independence conferences, and I did quite a bit of traveling around. And I can tell you that nobody in his senses would want that land. It's nothing but rocks and scrub, can't even graze a goat on it. Between ourselves, when the matter was referred to PIFL two years ago my personal opinion was that each side really wanted to lose, except from the point of view of prestige, of course."

"I see," said Henry. "Well, go on."

34

"Sure I'm not boring you?"

"On the contrary. It makes a pleasant change from the sordid sort of case I'm working on at the moment."

"Well, I'll probably bore you now," said Trapp with engaging frankness, "because the whole thing hinges on the interpretation of international law. How much do you know about that?"

"We work very closely with Interpol . . ."

"No, no, no. That's quite different. International law is concerned only with states, not with individuals. It's a vast subject, of course, and very complicated. Even the learned members of the commission argue like mad about the interpretation of various aspects of it, and each case can make legal history."

"That sounds like our English system of legal precedent," Emmy remarked.

"It may sound like it, but it isn't," said Trapp, "because international jurists aren't bound by precedent, the way English courts are. Naturally, it may influence them if one side can point to, say, a previous decision of the International Court of Justice in a roughly similar case; but it wouldn't compel a commission like ours to come to the same conclusion itself."

"But the members must have *something* to go on," Emmy objected, "otherwise . . ."

"Oh yes, they do," said Gordon, "and that's what I'm getting around to. Mind you, I'm no lawyer, and I can only give you a layman's simplified idea of the matter—and pretty garbled at that, I expect. But as I understand it, there are two main schools of thought among international lawyers. One takes the view that decisions must be guided entirely by the provisions of treaties entered into by states, even if it subsequently can be demonstrated that the treaty is foolish, outdated, impractical, or unjust. The other maintains that treaties needn't always be sacrosanct; for example, that a newly independent nation should not necessarily be bound by agreements entered into on her behalf by the ex-colonial power."

"And how does all that affect the Mambesi-Galunga situation?" Henry asked.

"Actually, it's a very good illustration of the two points of view," said Trapp. "You see, it's clear to any reasonable person that the mountain range makes a natural barrier between the two countries. The language is different on the northern side of the range. The people belong to different tribes. The southerners, the Galungans, are nomadic herdsmen, while the plainsmen of Mambesi, in the north, live in villages and cultivate farms. On the face of it, it's absurd to set the frontier anywhere except along the line of mountain peaks."

"But . . . ?" Emmy prompted.

"But, as you have so rightly guessed, there is a treaty. It was signed in 1876, when Mambesi was a British colony and Galunga was French. This treaty defined Mambesi as extending 'as far as the River Lunga in the south.' The fact of the matter is that the whole territory was virtually unexplored at the time and the river was a convenient landmark that everybody knew. The mountains had never been climbed, and precious little was known about the region at all. In practice the Galungans have always felt perfectly free to cross the river with their herds if they wanted to, while, as far as we know, not a single Mambesian has ever set foot on the southern side of the mountains.

"Galunga, quite naturally, says that she's not bound by a treaty which was signed not by her but by the ex-colonial power. She also pleads usage and—well—common sense. Nevertheless, the strict letter of the 1876 treaty quite clearly gives the wretched strip of land to Mambesi. Frankly, nobody cares much either way except the legal eagles, and they've been having a ball, arguing happily for two years and giving employment to deserving interpreters like myself."

"This is all very interesting," said Henry, "but you spoke about two men being murdered."

"I did, didn't I? I dare say you think I'm drunk."

"On one whisky and half a bottle of Burgundy? You must have a very weak head, Mr. Trapp."

"That," said Trapp seriously, "is what everybody will say. That's why it's so damned difficult to put this across to you. And yet, I know that I'm right."

"Well, get on with it," said Henry. "Then I'll tell you whether or not I think you're weak in the head."

"Very well. For two years now this case has dragged on. First of all there were the written submissions by both sides. Then the public hearings—not that anybody came to listen to them, but technically the proceedings were public. Recently we've been having the private deliberations of the commission. Any moment now the vote will be taken and the decision announced. Now, in the course of these private deliberations it became clear very early which member was going to vote which way. This particular case looked like a pushover for Galunga. Seven of the eleven members were clearly going to vote for her, because they felt particularly strongly about the invalidity of pre-independence treaties. That left only four pro-Mambesi members, including the chairman. And then Pereira fell under a bus."

"At the age of eighty-seven," said Henry.

"Agreed. On a filthy evening when there had been a frost and the pavements were slippery. Oh, I know. It never crossed my mind to be suspicious at the time. But he was a Galunga man. That left the score at six to four."

"But I don't understand," said Emmy, "*why* anybody should want to . . . ?"

"Findelhander was the next," Trapp went on, interrupting. "The day before yesterday. Found dead in bed at his hotel. Heart attack."

"I read about it in the paper," said Henry.

"So then there were five. Five to four, and the chairman has a casting vote. There's only got to be one more fatality in the pro-Galunga ranks and Mambesi wins." There was a short silence, and then Gordon added, "Well?"

"Well, what?"

"Am I weak in the head?"

Henry considered. "On the whole," he said at last, "I'd be inclined to say—yes, you are."

Trapp shrugged. "I might have known it," he said. "Still, it was worth a try."

"It would be quite reasonable—your suspicion, I mean—if there was the faintest reason why anybody should want to kill these old gentlemen," said Henry. "But you've said yourself that the land in question has no value whatsoever. So unless you know more than you are prepared to say . . ."

Trapp stood up. "Very well," he said. "Your common sense is irrefutable. I shall go back to my interpreter's booth like a good little boy and wait for the next member of the commission to have a heart attack. If you like, I can tell you who it will be."

Henry said, "You've no personal interest, have you, Mr. Trapp, in the outcome of this hearing?"

"Personal interest? Of course not." Gordon Trapp turned to Emmy and held out his hand. "Good night, Mrs. Tibbett. Thank you for a delicious dinner. And please forgive me for keeping you up so late with profitless nonsense."

When the front door had closed behind Gordon Trapp, Henry walked into the kitchen, where Emmy was washing the coffee cups. He said, "What a curious evening. He's a nice young man though."

"You didn't believe a word of it." Emmy was not asking a question, but stating a fact.

"My dear Emmy, how could I, on that evidence?" Henry felt irritated. "I have enough solid, open-and-shut murder cases without getting involved in fantastic flights of fancy. Young Trapp is obviously a highly imaginative character, and I dare say his brother's death has made him . . ."

"If you're going to stand there, you might as well dry," said Emmy.

Henry picked up a tea towel and applied himself to a coffee

cup in silence. Then he said, "So you took Trapp's ideas seriously, did you?"

"Of course not. How could I, on the evidence?" Emmy gave the sink a last wipe around and pulled up the plug. As the soapy water gurgled away down the drain, she added meditatively, "It would be funny, though, wouldn't it, if one of them did have a heart attack? One of the five, I mean."

"It would prove nothing, one way or the other."

"No. No, of course it wouldn't. But it would be funny, all the same. . . ."

4

Milburn Road, North Hampstead, was a street which had known better days. Built in the mid-nineteenth century for prosperous merchants, the houses must always have been gaunt and ugly, but a hundred years ago they had represented solid comfort and respectability. Now their red brick was stained and dirty, their areas and backyards were unkempt, and their paintwork was peeling. As Henry climbed the worn steps of number 17, he wondered how many Londoners had, at one time or another in their lives, lived in a room in just such a street as this in Hampstead or Pimlico or Fulham or Battersea—and how many lonely souls still did so.

The front door of number 17 stood open, revealing a drab corridor of yellowing paint and thin brown linoleum. The door jamb sported a vertical row of twelve doorbells, each with a grubby card of identification beside it. One of these read BYERS 2ND FLOOR. There was nothing to indicate that any of the bells communicated with the owner of the house.

Sergeant Reynolds said, "It may be the basement we want, sir. They often keep the basement for themselves, the landlords. Difficult to let, you see. Damp, often as not."

"Let's go and see," said Henry.

The basement door was firmly shut, and there was no name card beside the black bell button. Henry pressed it and heard the shrilling of the bell. After a moment of silence there was a brisk clattering of footsteps from inside and a key was turned in the lock. Then the door opened, and Henry found himself looking into a pair of heavily mascaraed black eyes.

"Can I help you?" The black eyes flickered, sizing up first Henry and then Reynolds. "I'm Mrs. Torelli. I expect you're looking for a room. Do come in."

Mrs. Torelli must once have been, if not beautiful, at least very pretty, and, Henry thought, she might still be so if only she had the sense—or perhaps the courage—to acknowledge the fact that she would never see forty again. As it was, there was a distinct element of the grotesque about her skinny figure decked out in teen-age gear, and her sharp little face hardened by layers of Pancake make-up which emphasized rather than disguised the crow's-feet and frown lines. She minced up the dark corridor ahead of Henry and the Sergeant and opened a door at the far end. The room beyond was light, in contrast to the gloomy hallway, for it had large windows opening on the small yard, which a house agent would certainly have described as a garden. The room was brightly furnished with cheerful bad taste, and a couple of painted gnomes leered in through the French windows.

"My little nest," announced Mrs. Torelli coyly. "Come in and sit down. Can I get you a tiny little drink?"

"Not at the moment, thank you," said Henry. It was just 10:00 A.M. "As a matter of fact . . ."

"Was it one room you were wanting or two?" Like radar beams, Mrs. Torelli's sharp eyes scanned the two men, assessing permutations and possibilities. "I couldn't manage two, not just at the moment, but I do have a lovely one free, third floor, overlooking the garden, ever so quiet and cozy. Two beds. The last couple what had it were *very* happy there. Two charming boys."

"We don't want a room, Mrs. Torelli." Henry was having some difficulty in keeping a straight face. He carefully avoided Sergeant Reynolds' outraged stare.

"Oh." She sounded disappointed. "Two rooms. I see. Well now, if you'd be prepared to share just for a day or two, I've another free, as it just so happens, but it'll have to be cleared out. The previous tenant—left rather unexpectedly. I haven't had a chance to clean up yet."

"Mrs. Torelli," said Henry, "we don't want any of your rooms. We are police officers."

"Police?" Mrs. Torelli gave a shrill little laugh. "Well, fancy

41

that now. You naturally wouldn't want to share a room then, would you? Not being police. I can see I'll have to mind my P's and Q's."

"There's no need to be frightened or upset, madam," said Sergeant Reynolds unnecessarily. Mrs. Torelli was clearly neither. "Just a few routine inquiries."

Enlightenment seemed to break upon Mrs. Torelli. "Oh, but of course. How silly of me. You'll have come about poor Mr. Byers, I dare say. I should have been expecting you, shouldn't I? Silly little me. Well, what a terrible thing to happen. I was quite upset when I read it in the paper." She paused and added, "He is dead, isn't he? I mean, it said in the *Evening News* 'died in hospital,' but you never can tell with newspapers, can you? And I naturally wouldn't want to re-let his room and then have him come back. He was my oldest tenant, you know. Six years—on and off, of course—but six years all the same. Yes, it really has upset me."

"He's dead all right, madam," said Reynolds; "that's why we're here."

"Well then, you'll be wanting to see his room, won't you? It was his I meant, the one I haven't cleared out yet. I was rather thinking that somebody might have come for his things. I hardly know what to do with them, but I can't have the room standing empty, can I? Quite a dilemma for poor little me," added Mrs. Torelli with a gruesome ripple of laughter.

Henry said, "After we've looked at the room, Mrs. Torelli, I think you can set your mind at rest. Mr. Byers' parents will arrange for his things to be collected."

Mrs. Torelli looked shocked. *"Parents?"* she said, as if she had never heard the word before. "Father and mother, do you mean?"

"That's right, madam." It was Sergeant Reynolds who answered. "A very nice lady and gentleman from Southam."

"Well, whoever would have thought that Mr. Byers had *parents?"* said Mrs. Torelli. "It just shows you never can tell, doesn't it? No, I had been thinking that one of his lady friends might . . ." Her voice trailed off into silence. Then she laughed again. "Oh, dear. Naughty of me. I shouldn't have said that, should I?"

"Byers had a lot of girl friends, did he?" Henry asked.

"There now, you see, you've taken me up all wrong, officer. No, if I'm to be honest, he had more *boy* friends—ooh, now what have I said?" Another shrill of laughter. "Not what *you* mean, officer! I mean, he always had a lot of gentlemen callers—when he was here, that is."

"I gather," said Henry, "that he didn't live here all the time."

"Oh, dear me no, officer. He used it as a sort of peederterry, if you know what I mean. So nice for a gentleman, I always think, to have a peederterry in town. He paid for it all the year around, of course."

"And when he wasn't here . . . ?"

"That I can't tell you, officer. He traveled a lot, I believe, abroad and all over the place."

"What did he do for a living, do you know?"

For the first time Mrs. Torelli looked a little put out. "I certainly have no idea, officer," she said, bridling a little, as though Henry had made an indecent suggestion. "I always assumed that he was a gentleman of independent means."

"You have a lot of lodgers like that, don't you?" Henry asked.

"Like what?"

"Gentlemen of independent means."

Mrs. Torelli decided that this had gone far enough. "I must make it clear, officer, that I *don't* pry into my tenants' lives. I keep myself to myself. I respect their privacy and they respect mine. So long as the rent is paid prompt, I always say, it's no business of mine where the money comes from. Of course," she added, on a more human note, "there's some you can't mistake, like the group on the fourth floor. I had to ask them to leave. And then there's number twelve, with his typewriter. An author he is, and *don't* we all know it! But at least he

43

doesn't go on all night, like the group did. The Woodworms, they called themselves. I gave them woodworm, all right. Now, Mr. Byers, he was quite different, a very quiet, refined gentleman. No trouble at all. He was often out late, that I will admit, but he'd let himself in as quiet as a mouse. Of course, he moved in what you would call caffy society. Out at the best hotels up West till all hours."

This, Henry knew, was true. Mrs. Torelli did not add, because she presumably did not know, that it was a toss-up on any particular evening whether Byers had been dining in the restaurant or washing up in the kitchens. He said, "What about these men friends who visited him?"

Mrs. Torelli simpered. "What about them, officer?"

"Can you describe them? Would you recognize them again? Do you know their names?"

"Names? No. Indeed not. And I wouldn't recognize them, I'm sure of *that*."

Much too sure, Henry reflected gloomily. Mrs. Torelli might put on a show of innocence, but she obviously knew enough about her late lodger not to recognize any of his friends.

"All right," said Henry. "Let's forget the men. What about the girls?"

"I never . . ."

"You said you thought that a young lady might come to collect his things."

"Well . . ." Mrs. Torelli hesitated. "It was only just recently. To tell you the truth, I had the impression that Mr. Byers wasn't one for the ladies, if you follow me. I mean, it's not natural, is it, officer? A nice-looking young man like that and never a young woman to visit him. I felt ever so sorry for him. I even asked him once or twice if he'd like to come down here for a little drinkie, when I wasn't busy. But he never would. Well, *that* shows you, doesn't it? And then, just a few weeks ago, when he came back, this young lady started to visit him. Several times. A model, I shouldn't wonder. Blond. Not my type, I must say, but I can imagine her appealing to some,

44

I suppose." Mrs. Torelli sniffed, full of envy. "Madeleine, he called her. High and mighty, *I* called her. Looked right through me, as if I was dirt. Not a very nice thing in one's own house."

"You say 'when he came back.' He'd been away, had he?"

"Oh, yes. Like I said, this was only a . . ."

"I know. A *pied-à-terre*."

"A what?"

"Never mind," said Henry. "When was the last time he went away?"

"Well now, let's see. Where are we now?"

"April sixth, madam." Sergeant Reynolds sounded bored.

"That's right. Goodness me, and it's Easter next week. How the time does fly, doesn't it? Now, it must have been early in the New Year that he left. Abroad, I think it was. St. Moritz, I dare say. He was *that* sort of gentleman, you see. January tenth or thereabout, it would have been. And he came back in the middle of March."

"And since then, this girl called Madeleine has visited him several times?"

"Well—once or twice. I wouldn't like to say more than that."

"And men visitors?"

"I don't remember any, not recently." Mrs. Torelli's thin mouth clamped into a firm line.

Henry said, "Very well. Perhaps we could see his room now."

Standing in the middle of "Flutter" Byers' peederterry, Henry was aware of a sense of profound depression, not because of what the room was but because of what it was not. It was not, in any sense, a home. It was not a refuge or a camouflaged hideout. It had not even the impersonal comfort of a hotel room. It was even more discouraging, in Henry's view, than the hospital morgue which had been Byers' last resting place, for that at least fulfilled a useful, if gloomy, purpose. This room was nothing, like an empty, punctured paper bag.

"Nice little place he had here." Sergeant Reynolds' voice sounded unnaturally loud to Henry. "Snug."

"Empty," said Henry.

"Empty?" Reynolds was surprised. "I wouldn't have said that, sir. Not badly furnished, not at all. Clean, too. And I like the picture." He indicated a reproduction in misty colors of a Connemara landscape.

"I'd rather have seen a racing calendar," said Henry.

"You would, sir?"

"Yes, or some pin-ups."

Sergeant Reynolds cleared his throat. "Yes—well—I like a nice landscape, myself. Always have. Matter of personal taste, I suppose."

Henry grinned. "I didn't exactly mean," he began, and then thought better of it. "Right, Sergeant. Let's take a look around."

There was very little to see. The closet contained a selection of extremely smart suits bearing the label of a reputed tailor. The chest of drawers revealed rows of clean white shirts and handkerchiefs, carefully rolled socks and neatly folded underpants, and a pile of pure-silk scarves. "Flutter" had been a dandy, all right.

A cabinet beside the bed contained half-full bottles of gin and whisky and several glasses. There was no trace of any reading matter whatsoever; in fact, it at first appeared that the room did not contain a single scrap of paper of any sort. It was only when Henry climbed on a chair to pull down the large suitcase from the top of the closet that the documentation of Byers' life was revealed. For the suitcase was not empty. It had, in effect, been used by its late owner as a combined desk and filing cabinet. Henry brightened a little.

"We'll take this with us," he said. "There's far too much to go through here and now. Explain to Byers' parents, will you, Sergeant? And tell them they can collect his clothes any time they like. The sooner the better, I should imagine. Mrs. Torelli will certainly charge them for the room until it's been cleared."

* * *

Back in his own office at Scotland Yard, Henry sorted through the contents of the suitcase with minute care and growing discouragement. The papers could hardly be called personal, in any real sense. They represented a detailed statement of Byers' gambling activities, and apart from the fact that it was useful to know through which bookmakers he had placed his bets, nothing very worthwhile emerged. It was interesting, though, to trace "Flutter's" financial ups and downs, for he had recorded meticulously the sums staked, the odds, and whether or not the various horses had been placed. This information was, of course, duplicated in the statements of account from the bookmakers. It certainly emerged that he had struck a vein of bad luck recently. The last substantial win had been early in January, which would have coincided with the date when Mrs. Torelli remembered his going away from Milburn Road. Since then, loss had piled on loss. "Flutter" evidently worked on a "doubling-up" scheme, and this had inevitably led him deeper and deeper into the red. What with Madeleine's expensive tastes and this record of losses, Henry was not at all surprised that by the middle of March Byers had returned to North Hampstead and a humble job in the kitchens of Dominic's Hotel.

Apart from these records, however, there was nothing to interest Henry, no diary, no private letters, not even an address book. Henry sighed. If he had not known already that Byers belonged in criminal circles, this blank anonymity would have given away the fact. Byers might not have been a mastermind, but he had had sufficient common sense to follow the basic law that the successful criminal never puts anything in writing. The big-time crooks who employed him to do their dirty work would have insisted on such elementary caution.

The telephone on Henry's desk rang and Reynolds said, "I've traced his bank account, sir."

"Good work, Sergeant. Not in his own name, I presume?"

"No, sir. Not very imaginative either. John Smith, he called himself."

"Quite good protective camouflage, I suppose," said Henry. "How did you get on to it?"

"It was the Major, as a matter of fact, sir. I've just been taking his statement, like you said."

"You mean Weatherby from The Pink Parrot?"

"That's right. Byers slipped up there. He was short of cash one evening, it seems, and he persuaded Weatherby to cash a check. It was made out to cash, signed by John Smith and endorsed, and Byers told the Major it had been given to him by a friend. Weatherby's no fool; he knew well enough it was Byers' own check, and he made a note of the name, the bank, and the account number, in case it should come in handy, as he put it."

"Blackmail, you mean? Or fraud?"

"Neither would surprise me, sir," said Reynolds. "But as a matter of fact, I think the Major was just storing up a scrap of information, like a woman hoards pieces of string and snippets of material in case they may be useful one day."

"I wonder," said Henry, "why Weatherby told you this?"

Reynolds chuckled. "Because I put the fear of God into him, sir. Not nearly so cocky, he wasn't, out of his own bar and in an office here at the Yard. It went just as you said. No dice, as far as the girl was concerned. Talk about an iceberg—*and* nine-tenths out of sight, too, if you ask me—but I couldn't shake her. I had the feeling all along that she was laughing at me."

"I know just what you mean," said Henry.

"But the Major was a different proposition altogether. When I threw Peterson's statement at him, he went all to pieces. He's always kept in the clear himself, you see, and he aims to stay that way. So he started being helpful."

"But Peterson confirmed his story about . . ."

"Not all along the line, sir. Not about everyone in the bar hearing the shots and scarpering. That didn't match with the Major's evidence, and you can be sure I made the most of it."

"So he told you about the check. Which bank is it?"

"London and Northern, sir. Hampstead branch, 97 Gold-hanger Road. Not too far from Byers' room."

"Good," said Henry. "Send me along the details of the account and a photograph of Byers, will you? I think I'll pay a call on the bank manager before he goes off to lunch."

The bank manager was a large, round-faced character on whose affable countenance the credit squeeze had imprinted a permanently pained expression. He looked like a rosy apple under the cider press. He greeted Henry warmly, and almost at once began to expound his tale of woe.

"It's heartbreaking, Superintendent," he said, his multiplic-ity of chins quivering with the pity of it. "One wishes to help one's clients. One wants the nice young families to be able to buy new houses and the nice old ones to be able to keep up their family homes and gardens. In the old days, Superintend-ent, one's work was a pleasure. But now, having to say 'No' a dozen times a day . . . My doctor says he thinks I'm getting an ulcer, and I'm not surprised."

"You take a very personal interest in your customers then, Mr. Bingham?" said Henry.

"Oh, indeed, yes. Indeed, yes. My friends, I prefer to call them." Mr. Bingham sighed deeply. "Although how many will remain my friends after all these years of austerity—some of them understand my predicament and sympathize with me, but others seem able to think only of their own problems. . . . Understandable, of course. . . ."

Henry decided he must break the flow. He pulled the pho-tograph of Byers out of its envelope and pushed it across the desk. It was the official photograph from the police files and not flattering.

Henry said, "I believe you know this man."

Bingham picked up the photograph, adjusted his spectacles, and said, "What a very unprepossessing face, Superintendent. He looks like a criminal."

49

"He was a criminal," Henry said.

"Dear me. You're not suggesting . . ." Mr. Bingham peered more closely at the picture. "It's strange, you know. There's a look, a definite look—of one of my customers. Ridiculous, of course . . ."

"He was one of your customers," said Henry.

"Oh, surely not. You tell me that this man is a criminal. Whereas Mr. Smith . . ."

"Smith?"

"That's right. This unhappy young man bears a vague resemblance to a Mr. John Smith, who is an old client of ours. Just a coincidence, naturally."

Henry referred to Sergeant Reynolds' notes. "Account Number 39715. Address: 17 Milburn Road."

"I fear I cannot tell you offhand the number of Mr. Smith's account; indeed, it would be improper of me to do so. But I admit that the address has a familiar ring. However, I can assure you that there is no possible connection . . ."

It took five minutes of hard talking before Mr. Bingham would as much as agree to check the facts, and another five to convince him that John Smith and "Flutter" Byers had been one and the same person. By the time he had assimilated the fact that Mr. Smith had not only been a man with a criminal record but was also the "gunman's victim" of whom he had read in his morning paper, the manager was bordering on apoplexy.

"But Superintendent, Mr. Smith was such a gentlemanly person . . . Always so beautifully dressed and very well spoken. . . . I cannot but believe that there has been some dreadful misunderstanding. . . ."

Authority won in the end, of course. With numerous protests and reservations, Mr. Bingham produced records of Mr. Smith's account. They made interesting reading.

For a start, it appeared that Mr. Smith dealt strictly in cash. That is to say, the credit entries in his statement consisted entirely of sums in cash deposited personally across the counter of the bank; the only exceptions were checks from bookmaking firms. Similarly, the withdrawals were all in the form of checks made out to cash. Never, at least during the past two years, had he made out a check to another person.

The state of the account had varied briskly from several thousand pounds in credit to meager balances of ten or twelve pounds. At no point had he ever been overdrawn, and for this reason he had never had cause to wring Mr. Bingham's generous heart with requests for loans. He was the type of customer who, while "a bit rum," as the chief cashier admitted, caused the bank no trouble whatsoever and was therefore popular with the staff.

The most intriguing entry in the account book occurred just a week before Byers' untimely death. This showed that on a day near the end of March Mr. Smith had deposited—in cash, as usual—the sum of two thousand pounds, thus bringing his credit balance up to two thousand and eleven pounds, six shillings, and ten pence. Henry knew very well that this had not been a gambling win. "Flutter" must have been hired to do a job, had done it, and been paid.

And a week later he had been shot dead. And at the time of his death he was still employed as a kitchen porter at Dominic's Hotel.

Henry left the badly shaken Mr. Bingham gulping down stomach pills and made his way to Dominic's Hotel.

5

"The manager?" The blond receptionist gave Henry a haughty look, which he recognized as her first line of defense. "The manager?"

"If you please," said Henry.

"If it's about a reservation . . ."

"It's not about a reservation."

"Mr. Holcroft deals with complaints."

"It's not a complaint either."

"Mr. Epstein arranges the banqueting. I could . . ."

"Not banqueting either."

"And you don't want to contact any of our guests?"

"No," said Henry patiently. "Just the manager please."

"Oh, well." Having exhausted her standard repertoire of discouragements, the blond seemed resigned. "Whom shall I say?"

"Superintendent Tibbett of Scotland Yard."

The blond did a double-take. "Did you say Scotland Yard?"

"I did."

"*Well.*" The blond put down the telephone receiver which she had just picked up. "Who would have thought it? Don't tell me there's been a murder at Dominic's? Like in that Agatha Christie I was reading." She giggled.

Henry said, "We do deal with other things besides murder, you know. I wonder if you'd be kind enough to get through to the manager for me."

"Leave it to me, Superintendent." The blond had decided to play Della Street. "Am I to say who you are?"

"If you would, please," said Henry patiently.

The blond looked disappointed, but she picked up the telephone again. A few minutes later Henry was ushered with some ceremony into the beautifully furnished office of the manager of Dominic's Hotel.

Dominic's was not listed among the largest hotels in London, nor among the most spectacular. Gossip writers were never invited to lavish press receptions at Dominic's, because Dominic's had no need of the press. It was a medium-sized hotel of unsurpassed excellence situated in an old-fashioned part of London on the border of Knightsbridge and Kensington. The décor was unobtrusive, but the chairs were extraordinarily comfortable. The menu was not large, but every dish was lovingly and superbly prepared. The prices were enormous.

Dominic's was the sort of place which, above all, shunned publicity. It was patronized by people who really knew what was what, and word of mouth—passed discreetly from client to client—was all that Dominic's wanted or needed in the way of advertisement. Of recent years, to the alarm and despondency of the management, the name of Dominic's had begun to creep into fashion. Henry knew all this very well, and he also knew that a visit from Scotland Yard would be anything but welcome. He took a deep breath and prepared for battle as he entered the manager's office.

The man who rose to greet him might have walked straight out of an advertisement enticing the public to enroll the services of a friendly bank manager. On the other hand, he could hardly have looked less like the flustered, red-faced Mr. Bingham, who really was a friendly bank manager. This character was so smooth that he seemed to have been enameled and polished. He was just the right age for a manager—somewhere between forty and fifty-five; just the right height for a manager—between six-foot and six-foot-two; his hair was just the right color for a manager's—chestnut brown, slightly silvered at the temples. It hardly needs to be said that everything else about him was just right—the impeccably cut dark gray suit, the well-cared-for hands and nails, the shoes which had been polished with a bone. In the midst of so much perfection, the face scarcely seemed to matter. It was, of course, the right color—pale bronze—and it wore just the right, neatly clipped mustache. It took quite an effort for Henry to penetrate this elaborate shell and observe the shrewdness behind the eyes. He decided that he would not enjoy asking this man for an overdraft.

At the moment, however, the face was smiling and the manner just short of effusive. A perfectly manicured hand was extended to Henry across the polished expanse of desk and a beautifully articulated voice said, "Superintendent Tibbett. What a very delightful surprise. May I introduce myself? My name is Nightingale."

"I'm sorry to intrude on your precious time, Mr. Nightingale," said Henry. He sat down in one of the leather swivel chairs. "I'm afraid I have to make a few inquiries at your hotel."

"I understand perfectly, Superintendent," Mr. Nightingale assured him. "Do allow me to offer you a glass of sherry —or perhaps you would prefer something else?"

"Not just at the moment, thank you."

"A cigarette then? Or a cigar? Are you a cigar smoker, Superintendent?"

"No, I'm not."

"A pity. I would have liked your opinion on some rather special Havanas I have been lucky enough to get hold of. No matter. Please help yourself." Nightingale pushed a tooled-leather box across the desk, flipping it open to reveal serried ranks of cigarettes of all kinds.

Henry gave in and took one.

"I dare say," Mr. Nightingale went on, "that you will want to inspect our register of guests. Naturally, everything is at your disposal. If you would just tell me which of our guests it is . . ."

Getting a word in with some difficulty, Henry said, "I'm not interested in any of your guests. I've come to talk about a member of the staff."

The relief which crossed Mr. Nightingale's face would have

escaped a less well-trained observer, for it was no more than a fleeting shadow.

"The staff?" Mr. Nightingale sighed. "Of course, we try to screen people as well as we can, but with the labor shortage these days one has to take what one can get. If one of our staff is under suspicion, Superintendent, I can only thank you profoundly for bringing it to our attention. With our clientele . . ." Mr. Nightingale waved the hand which now held a gold-and-ebony cigarette holder. The gesture was obviously meant to imply that crowned heads were a commonplace at Dominic's, as indeed they were. "With our clientele, we simply can't be too careful in the selection of our senior staff. The slightest breath of suspicion . . ."

"Not one of your senior staff, Mr. Nightingale," said Henry. "I want to talk to you about a man called Byers."

"Byers?" Nightingale leaned forward, puzzled. "I'm afraid there must be some mistake, Superintendent. We have nobody here of that name."

"I know you haven't," said Henry. "He's dead."

"One of our staff? Dead? I really think there must be a misunderstanding . . ."

Henry said, "Frederick Byers, known by the nickname of 'Flutter,' was working in your kitchens until the day before yesterday, when he was shot in a pub in Notting Hill. He died later in the hospital. It's a murder case and I'm investigating it."

Enlightenment had dawned on Mr. Nightingale's immaculate features. "Kitchen staff?" he echoed, "temporary kitchen staff?"

"That's right. Washing up, preparing vegetables, and so on."

"My dear Superintendent." Nightingale was tolerant now, benign and infinitely condescending. He was making it clear, without rudeness, that Henry should have applied at the tradesmen's entrance. "As I told you, there has been a misunderstanding. I don't wish to give myself airs"—he laughed with unconvincing self-deprecation—"but I'm afraid I simply don't have the time to concern myself with the kitchen staff. They come and go, you know. Come and go. Go more often than come, alas. It's perfectly possible that this—what did you say his name was?"

"Byers."

"That this Byers was working in our kitchens, but I'm afraid that's not my department at all. I appreciate the fact that you came to see me personally, of course, and I've enjoyed our little chat. But for the moment, the best thing I can do is to pass you over to Mr. Wardle. He is in charge of the kitchen staff, and he will certainly be able to help you. You say the poor fellow was shot? Of course, Notting Hill has become a—well—a somewhat dubious neighborhood of late . . ." His hand was on his desk telephone. "I'll ring Mr. Wardle and ask him to come up."

"If you don't mind," Henry said, "I'd rather go down to the kitchens and talk to him there."

"To the *kitchens?*" repeated Mr. Nightingale. "Are you sure, Superintendent? You could talk to Mr. Wardle far more comfortably up here . . ."

"The kitchens, if you please," said Henry flatly. He stood up.

"Oh, very well, my dear fellow, if that's what you want." Mr. Nightingale had lost interest in Henry. He picked up the telephone and spoke into it. "Miss Minster? Come to my office, please, and show Superintendent Tibbett to the kitchens. . . . Yes, I said the kitchens. . . . He wishes to speak to Mr. Wardle. . . ."

A couple of minutes later Henry was walking down the richly carpeted corridor in company with the blond from the reception desk.

She looked at him with frank curiosity. "Something sinister going on in the kitchens, Superintendent? I don't often go down there myself."

"I'm just making a few inquiries about someone who used to work there," said Henry.

"You get all sorts of riffraff down there, so Mr. Wardle

says," remarked the blond disdainfully. She led the way into the main foyer of the hotel.

The reception desk was now under the care of a sweet-faced girl who could hardly have been older than sixteen. She gave an evident sigh of relief as she saw Henry and his escort.

"Oh, Miss Minster . . ."

"I can't stop now, Sandra."

"But, Miss Minster, please . . ."

"The kitchens are inclined to be rather warm, Superintendent," said the blond. "May I suggest that you leave your coat up here? Let me help you . . ."

"Miss Minster, please . . ."

"*There* we are."

Henry would have preferred to have kept his raincoat, but Miss Minster was being Della Street again, and he thought it easier to submit. The coat slid off his back and Miss Minster handed it across the desk to Sandra.

"I'll see you later, dear," she said with a firm smile; and to Henry, "This way, Superintendent. We'll take the elevator down."

The basement was a world quite divorced from the hotel above. As Henry stepped out of the elevator into the echoing, subterranean corridor, he was reminded of the hospital. One could frequent and even live in Dominic's Hotel for years without ever having the remotest conception of what went on beneath the surface.

The comparison with the hospital grew more meaningful as Henry followed Miss Minster down the passage. Both places were bustling, dedicated, and hygienic; but the kitchen was a grisly parody of the other. In the hospital white-aproned nurses wheeled human patients on aluminum beds; here, white-coated porters wheeled sides of raw beef on aluminum trolleys. In the hospital stainless-steel containers hissed steam as nurses opened them to remove sterilized instruments; in the kitchens they disgorged soup or coffee. Indeed, the long, shining electric range could have been an operating table, with the white-coated chefs doubling for surgeons, while the dumbwaiters with their colorful loads of hors d'oeuvres were, at a casual glance, indistinguishable from the trolleys of disinfectants, dressings, and medicaments which Henry had noticed in the hospital corridors.

Miss Minster knocked briefly on a closed door and preceded Henry into what he involuntarily designated the matron's office.

"Superintendent Tibbett to see you, Mr. Wardle," she said briskly and stood back to let Henry enter.

The room was like any small office. The walls were hung with charts and stacked with filing cabinets and there were three telephones on the desk. One of these was in use. Mr. Wardle—a tall, thin, spiky individual in a striped blue suit—was speaking into it in a high-pitched, petulant voice.

"Yes, Mr. Nightingale, I understand. But . . ." He waved a skinny arm at Henry, making a complicated gesture which was apparently intended to convey that his visitor should sit down. "Yes, he has just come into my office, Mr. Nightingale . . . of course I will, Mr. Nightingale. . . . Yes, I remember the man perfectly. . . . No. . . . No. . . . Yes. . . ." The arm, which seemed to have a life of its own independent of the rest of Mr. Wardle's body, sprang into action again. This time it seemed to be offering Henry a cigarette.

Henry shook his head in a polite gesture of refusal, but this was, of course, wasted on the arm, which continued to extend hospitality. The rest of Mr. Wardle was fully occupied with the telephones, the second of which now began to ring insistently.

"Yes, indeed, Mr. Nightingale. . . . I will make a note of it. . . . He will be entertaining while he is here, I presume? If you can let me have as much notice as possible . . . Well, the staff position is *never* easy, is it?"

The arm had by now become so importunate that Henry felt he could no longer ignore it without rudeness. So he sat down and took a cigarette from the open box on the desk. At once the arm seized a table lighter, ignited it, and extended it in Henry's direction. Simultaneously the other arm replaced the first telephone receiver and picked up the second.

"Oh, yes, Mr. Epstein. . . . Yes, Mr. Nightingale has just told me. . . . You have? Splendid. . . ." The hand now began busily taking notes, having wedged the telephone receiver neatly between Mr. Wardle's chin and shoulder. "Tenth or eleventh—for thirty—the Garden Room . . . Quite a small party, considering . . . You will confirm the date? Thank you, Mr. Epstein. . . ."

The arm which Henry had by now begun to regard as his exclusive property extracted the telephone from beneath Mr. Wardle's chin and replaced the receiver on its stand. The other hand continued to scribble on the pad for several seconds. At last Mr. Wardle looked up and said, "Now, Superintendent. I understand you want to make inquiries about Byers."

"Yes," said Henry, "I do."

"You must forgive me for keeping you waiting. Mine is a very busy existence, I fear. We have a visiting prime minister arriving this afternoon, not to mention Scandinavian royalty, a Nobel Prize winner, and the usual assortment of film stars." Mr. Wardle smirked complacently. "I am surprised that you have not come sooner about Byers. The moment I read the report in the paper, I . . ."

"He only died on Wednesday night," Henry pointed out.

"Wednesday is Wednesday and today is Friday," said Mr. Wardle briskly. "Goodness me, if we conducted our affairs in such a manner—however, what do you want to know?"

"For a start," said Henry, "how long had he been working here?"

The arm shot out, opened a green-metal filing cabinet, and whipped out a dossier. "Let me see—here we are—March twenty-eighth, he started."

"Only about a week ago?" Henry was surprised. "And just what was his job here?"

"Kitchen hand. Unskilled. Casual labor. As a matter of

fact, Byers was a useful chap. Had obviously done this sort of work before. I'm sorry to lose him, but then, I'm sorry to lose anybody these days. We cannot get the people, Superintendent. We cannot get them."

"What's the procedure for getting a job like this?" Henry asked. "Would Byers have gone to the Labour Exchange and . . . ?"

"Most unlikely. We get very few people from the Labour Exchange. No, no. He would simply turn up at the kitchen entrance and ask for a job. We don't ask too many questions about our unskilled kitchen staff, Superintendent. We're too pleased to get anybody, anybody at all."

"Had Byers worked for you before?"

"Funnily enough, no."

"Why do you say 'funnily enough'?"

"Well, as I told you, he was clearly used to the work. That means that he probably belonged to what we call the floating pool of kitchen workers. They drift from job to job, from hotel to hotel, always doing the lowliest tasks. No ambition, you see. They're not interested in a job as a job, just as a means of making a little money before moving on. I thought I knew most of them, but Byers was new to me."

"I rather fancy," said Henry, "that he had, in fact, been working in another hotel before he came to you. He'd been doing this type of work since early in March."

"Oh, that's very likely, Superintendent. These fellows are shiftless and restless. I dare say he had a fight with one of the chefs or waiters and walked out. If I *told* you the trouble we have . . ."

"So he had only been here a few days," said Henry. "Do you know if he had any friends among the staff?"

"Not that I know of. I'm a busy man, of course. You might like to talk to some of his colleagues; they could tell you."

"I think that's a very good idea," said Henry.

Mr. Wardle led the way down the passage and into the big kitchen. Lunchtime was approaching and the tempo was quickening by the minute. White-coated waiters, high-hatted chefs, aproned kitchen boys and maids—all bustled and hurried and stirred and clattered. At the bottom of the hierarchy a group of grubby, nondescript individuals in dirty striped aprons busied themselves washing up in huge, steaming sinks, or flung kitchen waste into resounding metal garbage pails. These were the casual workers, the floating pool.

Wardle called one of them over, a sad-faced, middle-aged man with a deep scar on one cheek.

"Yes, sir, Mr. Wardle, sir?" The man spoke with the hopelessness of one who has long since learned to expect nothing from life.

"You remember Byers, Taylor?"

"Byers? Oh, you mean 'Flutter' . . ." Henry fancied he detected a wary note. "Poor old 'Flutter.' Bought it, so I read in the paper."

"You knew him?" Henry asked.

"Well, now, not so as to say knew him, sir. No, no. I'd *met* him, like. Seen him around. That's not the same as knowing, is it?"

There was no mistaking the fear now.

"This gentleman is a superintendent from Scotland Yard," pronounced Wardle with evident relish. Henry cursed himself for not having given Wardle the slip sooner. The man called Taylor went a delicate shade of green and swallowed hard. He said nothing and avoided Henry's eyes.

Henry said, "I'm just filling in a few details about Byers' background, Mr. Taylor." He considered trotting out the old cliché about "purely routine inquiries," but decided that it was too threadbare, even for Taylor. He could only hope that a friendly and reassuring manner would do the trick, but he doubted it. Most people in the world have something in their lives that they would prefer to conceal from the police, and members of the floating pool would, Henry felt, be especially vulnerable in this respect.

"I never knew him," said Taylor again. "Couldn't help it

if we worked together now and again, could I? Doesn't mean I knew him, not to say *know*."

"You'd worked with him in other hotels, had you?" Henry asked.

"I never said that."

"Where?"

"Well . . ."

"Come along, man. Answer the Superintendent. This information may be important."

With difficulty Henry resisted the impulse to hit Mr. Wardle over the head with a large copper frying pan which was conveniently at hand. Instead, he cooed like a dove. "Really, Mr. Wardle, I mustn't take up any more of your valuable time. I know how busy you are. I'll just have a short chat with Mr. Taylor and then I must be on my way."

Mr. Wardle hesitated. "Mr. Nightingale was most emphatic that I should assist you in every way, Superintendent. After all, this is a murder investigation, isn't it?"

Taylor was standing there, head drooping like a broken-spirited old horse. At the mention of the word murder he swayed, as if he might faint.

Henry said loudly and cheerfully, "Well, it's true that Byers was shot, but I'd hardly say I was conducting a murder investigation here at Dominic's, Mr. Wardle. I've really found out all I want to know, so I'll leave you to get on with your work. Good-bye to you." He held out his hand, smiling.

Surprised, Wardle shook it. "Well, if we really can't help you any further, Superintendent, I'll see you to the elevator. Just follow me—this way . . ."

He was halfway across the big kitchen before he realized that Henry was not with him. He turned, surprised and displeased. Henry raised his arm in a chirpy farewell salute. Two, he thought, could play at arm conversation. Wardle hesitated for a moment. Then he shrugged pettishly and went back toward his office.

Henry turned to Taylor, who seemed to have relaxed a little. "I won't keep you a moment, Mr. Taylor," he said, "just one or two questions. You were telling me where you'd met Byers before."

"Here and there. The Excelsior for a spell last year. The Olympic once. I couldn't help it if we happened . . ."

"Of course you couldn't, Mr. Taylor. You and he were doing the same work here, were you?"

"That's right, sir. We was both on trays."

"On trays? What exactly does that mean?"

"I'll show you, sir." Taylor was almost eager. Apparently he felt that Henry had been steered away from dangerous topics; as far as Taylor was concerned, the more Scotland Yard concentrated on the mechanics of the kitchen, and the less on individuals, the happier he would be. He led the way to the far end of the room.

The pandemonium was mounting. The impedimenta of a kitchen are among the noisiest objects in common use. As stainless steel struck china and aluminum crashed against cast iron Henry felt that he was in Vulcan's domain—except that the forge under the mountain was presumably free from the hysteria of human voices raised ever louder to compete with each other and with the mechanical din.

Taylor was an old hand. He did not even attempt to shout. He turned his face toward Henry and spoke slowly and almost silently, mouthing each word elaborately. Henry was no lip-reader, but he understood better than if the words had been yelled.

"It's the orders for the private rooms here," mouthed Taylor. "Room service sends through the orders, see? Then the chefs' assistants make up the trays. There. See, sir?"

Taylor had brought Henry to a long counter which divided the room—behind it was the kitchen proper, where the food was actually prepared; in front was the serving area and the rows of service elevators which bore the food upward and into the main body of the hotel. On the counter were rows of trays on which, as a result of considerable teamwork by different kitchen departments, were assembled the clients' individual choices of delicacies. Each tray bore, for the purpose of checking, the original order slip sent down by room service, listing the order and the number of the room for which it was destined.

The job on which "Flutter" Byers had been engaged called for no great intellect or skill. It consisted of carrying the tray from the counter to the service elevator, shoving it into the boxlike compartment, and pressing the button to send it upward to its destination. The first figure of the room number, Taylor explained laboriously, indicated the floor number, so that all the rooms on the second floor were two hundred and something, and likewise rooms on the third floor. . . . Henry thanked him and said that he had grasped the system.

Then he said, "Why was Byers doing this work?"

"Why?" Taylor's bewilderment appeared genuine. "He told Mr. Wardle he'd done trays before, so . . ."

"I mean," said Henry, "that he had plenty of money. Usually he only took these jobs when he was broke. Why did he come here to work last week?"

"I tell you, sir, I never knew him. Never. Anyhow, he didn't have any money."

"How do you know?"

"Well, he happened to mention it. Like you said. He told me he only took these jobs when he was skint. Seems he'd had some sort of a row at the Olympic . . ."

"So he was working at the Olympic before he moved on here?"

"He did happen to mention it. No harm in that, is there? Not that I ever knew him, not to say *know* . . ."

It was half past twelve. The milling, shouting, clanking bedlam was reaching its vortex. Kitchen hands dashing between the counter and the elevators with loaded trays swirled around Henry, as angry seas froth around a rock. He had already been buffeted nearly off his feet, and further conversation with Taylor was virtually impossible. The sensible thing to do, he decided, was to go and get some lunch himself. Taylor watched him go with undisguised relief

It was blessedly quiet in the elevator, and as Henry stepped out into the softly padded peace of the main foyer the subterranean chaos he had left behind seemed no more than a nightmare. Elegantly dressed men and women meeting at Dominic's for lunch greeted each other and chatted quietly over iced drinks. A small commotion at the main door heralded the arrival of an important personage; Henry caught a glimpse of a handsome, coal-black face surmounting a Savile Row suit, surrounded by a discreet entourage and many porters. Henry made his way to the reception desk. Miss Minster and the sweet-faced teen-ager were both there, conversing earnestly.

"You see, I simply didn't know what to do, Miss Minster," the girl was saying. "I mean, I simply didn't. This man said he'd come for Mr. Findelhander's luggage, and . . ."

"Ah, Superintendent. All through?" Miss Minster beamed at Henry, ignoring her young assistant. "Here's your coat."

"I mean," the girl went on, "I didn't know it was the poor gentleman who died in one-four-five. And then the man explained that he was from the embassy, but I didn't know where it was—the luggage, I mean. . . ."

"Aren't you lunching here, Superintendent? Mr. Nightingale said . . ."

"I have to get back, I'm afraid. Duty calls."

"Well, I hope you'll come and see us again. It has been a pleasure."

Henry returned Miss Minster's smile, put on his raincoat, and made his way into the street. He was halfway to the bus stop when he suddenly stopped dead, causing a certain amount of confusion to the rushing lunch-hour crowd. Then he hurried back to the hotel.

Miss Minster was surprised but very ready to be helpful. Certainly, she said, poor Mr. Justice Findelhander had been staying at the hotel at the time of his death. Such a nice old gentleman, but elderly and very frail, of course. They didn't see much of him, as a matter of fact. He took all his meals in his room. Yes, it had been a heart attack. The waiter had found him when he went in to collect his dinner tray. Miss Minster had telephoned for the doctor herself. Yes, he had been in Room 145. He was in 197 before, but he had asked for a change of room on the very day he died. Why? Well, 197 was in the front and he found it rather noisy, with the traffic. A lovely room, mind you, ever so much nicer than 145, really, but for an old gentleman like that—well—you could understand that he'd be happier in a quiet room at the back. Of *course,* 145 had been completely spring-cleaned since then and in fact it was now occupied again. Yes, the American Embassy had sent a man that very morning to collect Mr. Findelhander's luggage. Sandra hadn't been expecting him and that was why there was a little bit of a muddle. She was new, of course, Sandra was. Was Henry sure he wouldn't change his mind and take lunch in the dining room? Mr. Nightingale had said . . .

Henry thanked her, refused courteously but firmly, and went out into the street again. He stopped at the first unoccupied telephone booth, and made three calls.

A polite official at the American Embassy, who seemed to take Henry for a journalist, informed him that Mr. Findelhander's body had been flown back to the United States two days ago. He understood that the cremation had taken place in Washington that very day.

The kitchen manager of the Olympic Hotel was in a great hurry and clearly resented being worried at lunchtime by such a trivial query, but came through eventually with the news that Byers had been employed in the kitchen from March 10 to March 27. No, there had been no fight that he knew of; Byers had simply walked out, the way these people did. And now, if Henry didn't mind, he was a very busy man . . .

Finally, Henry looked up the telephone number of the Permanent International Frontier Litigation Commission, dialed it, and asked to speak to Mr. Gordon Trapp.

6

"Superintendent Tibbett, you astound me. Have you developed a craving for the society of the mentally unbalanced, or are you sending a plain van to have me quietly put away?" The light irony in Trapp's voice reminded Henry vividly of the man's dead brother.

"Neither," said Henry. "I was hoping we might be able to lunch together."

"Today? Now?"

"That's right."

"Well, well, well. May one ask to what . . . ?"

"No," said Henry, "one may not. Can you meet me in twenty minutes?"

"I suppose so, but there's no need to be such a bully." There was a little pause. Then Trapp added, "Is this an official call?"

"No," said Henry, "not yet."

"I see. So I could refuse?"

"Of course you could, but I hope you won't. I'm sorry if I sounded bullying. I'm in rather a hurry, that's all."

"Curiouser and curiouser. Where shall we meet?"

"Somewhere large and impersonal. You're quite close to Parliament Square, aren't you?"

"We are."

"Then I suggest the Third Class Buffet at Victoria Station. You'll get there before I do. Find yourself a table and I'll come and join you. It would be best if we appeared to meet accidentally."

"My God." Trapp was patently amused. "Should I wear my false beard and dark glasses?"

"Your—what?"

"Forget it. Just a pleasantry."

67

"I hope so," said Henry a little grimly. "See you in twenty minutes."

The buffet was busy, but not overcrowded. Most of the hungry travelers had decided to perch on stools at the bar to take their refreshment and several tables were unoccupied. Gordon Trapp was sitting by himself at one of them reading the midday edition of the evening paper and toying with a ham sandwich.

Henry approached the table. "Excuse me," he said, "is this seat taken?"

Gordon lowered the paper and gave Henry a sardonic look. "Help yourself," he said. "Why, if it isn't my old friend Tibbett. How astonishing to meet you. What an exceptionally small world it is, to be sure."

"Exceptionally," said Henry. He sat down. "What brings you here, Mr. Trapp?"

Trapp, who was in the process of taking a bite from his sandwich, appeared to choke slightly. "Forgive me," he said, "I was brought here by an urgent desire for a ham sandwich and a beer."

"I was intending to have a snack lunch myself," said Henry, "but now that we've met—well, are you in a great hurry?"

"*I'm* not," said Trapp. "I thought that *you* . . ."

"In that case," said Henry, "let's go somewhere together and have a decent meal. That sandwich looks pretty unappetizing."

"It is," said Trapp. "I relinquish it with no regrets. Lead on, Tibbett."

In the taxi Gordon Trapp said, "Was that charade really necessary?"

Henry glanced at the impassive back-of-the-neck of the elderly driver. The glass screen between the compartments was tightly closed and the cab had been called at random from the street. He said, "I dare say it wasn't, but it might have been."

"Cloaks and daggers," remarked Trapp. "Am I to deduce that you no longer doubt my sanity?"

"If you like," said Henry.

"What a coincidence—just as I am beginning to doubt yours. Dan to Beersheba," said Gordon Trapp. He settled back into the corner of the cab with evident enjoyment. "Where are you taking me, Superintendent? To a sinister dope pusher's hideout in Limehouse? Or to a discreet Mayfair mansion, from whose impeccable façade the casual observer would never suspect that . . ."

"I'm taking you back to my flat in Chelsea," said Henry. "Emmy is expecting us. I telephoned her."

Trapp looked disappointed. "At least I hope the joint is bugged," he said.

"We are having fish," said Henry gravely. He had the impression that Gordon Trapp did not trust himself to reply.

They finished the cab ride in pleasurable silence.

The fish was waiting for them and so was Emmy. She had been greatly intrigued by Henry's telephone call, but she knew better than to show her curiosity. She greeted Gordon warmly, remarked that she was sure both men were in a hurry, and quickly served lunch. Then she sat back and waited for developments.

Helping himself to beans, Henry said, "We haven't much time, Mr. Trapp, so I'll come straight to the point. I've changed my mind about what you said last night."

"*No*," said Gordon in mock incredulity.

Henry ignored the interruption and went on "How much can you tell me about Mr. Justice Findelhander?"

"About him personally, you mean?"

"Yes. And about his death."

Trapp shrugged. "I told you last night. He was eighty-nine and a widower. I think he lived with a married daughter in Washington. When he had to come to London for a hearing, he always stayed at Dominic's—you know, the hotel in Knightsbridge. Some of the members of the commission bring their families over here and rent apartments, but Findelhander's daughter had her own family to look after in the

States. So he did the sensible thing and lived in a hotel."

"And his bad heart?"

"My dear fellow, I'm not his doctor. All I can tell you is that on a couple of occasions we received telephone calls from the hotel to say that Mr. Findelhander would not be coming to the office as he had had a mild heart attack and must rest. And once he had an attack actually in the conference room. He'd been having a briskish up-and-downer with the chairman, Sir Bertram Clegg. The old argument—Clegg's a strong treaty man. If I remember rightly, Clegg had compared the Mambesi-Galunga dispute to a game of cricket and had accused Findelhander of the legal equivalent of throwing. Findelhander thought that he was being accused of dishonesty and leaped up to reply. Then he suddenly went quite gray in the face, clutched his heart, and collapsed. There was quite a to-do. Our secretary knows a bit about nursing, so she was called. Findelhander managed to mutter something about pills in his pocket, which she duly found and administered. He recovered quite quickly after that, although he had to go home for the rest of the day."

"So everybody at PIFL knew about his weak heart."

"Obviously."

"Do you know the name of his doctor—here in London, I mean?"

"Not a clue," said Gordon. "I presume Dominic's would know. Or I suppose Yvonne might remember."

"Yvonne?"

"The secretary I was telling you about. She rang Findelhander's doctor. I'll ask her this afternoon." Trapp looked quizzically at Henry. "Am I allowed to ask," he said, "to what we owe your dramatic change of heart?"

"Not for the moment," said Henry. "Now tell me about the others."

"What others?"

"You said yesterday that it would only need one more pro-Galunga member to die for the decision to go to Mambesi."

"True."

"Very well then, who are the men whose lives you think may be in danger?"

Promptly Trapp said, "Pasheda, Koetsveen, Bootle, and Svensen."

"Tell me about them."

"I'll do better," said Gordon Trapp, "I'll show them to you, if you like."

"Show them to me?"

"There's a meeting at half past three this afternoon. They'll all be arriving at the office a few minutes before that. If we were sitting quietly in a parked car . . ."

"An excellent idea," said Henry. "I'll call for the car right away."

"I can't take you into the meeting, of course," said Trapp, "because it's confidential. But you can see our offices, if you like, and very welcome too. I'm not actually interpreting this afternoon, so I'm at your disposal."

"Good," said Henry. "Now, tell me about Mambesi."

"What about Mambesi?"

"Emmy, darling," said Henry, "will you call Sergeant Reynolds for me and get him to send a car? And then you might make us some coffee. We haven't much time."

Reluctantly Emmy went out into the hall, as Gordon Trapp said, "There's not much to tell. You know, of course, that they have a virtual dictatorship. The present lot of big boys are a bunch of thugs in my humble opinion, and I know plenty of people who wouldn't be surprised if there was a classic military coup in the near future. . . ."

Emmy closed the door behind her and picked up the telephone.

The car was black and anonymous and Henry drove it himself. Following Gordon Trapp's directions, he parked in a gloomy side street not far from Parliament Square. The houses were Edwardian and busily decorative with the ponderous exuberance of the period. Decades of London grime

71

had not improved their appearance, but they had the solidity which promised stout walls, draft-free windows, lofty ceilings, polished brass banisters, and slow-moving elevators in wrought-iron cages.

In the case of the mansion which was designated numbers 17-23 in ornate figures on the door pillars, the polished brass extended to the exterior in the form of curly handrails on either side of the immaculately whitened entrance steps; also brass and as highly polished was the plaque which informed passersby that this was the seat of the Permanent International Frontier Litigation Commission.

Trapp glanced at his watch. "Twenty past," he said. "They should start rolling up soon. Ah, this'll be one of them."

A taxi had pulled up outside numbers 17-23. A very tall, thin man jumped quickly from it, paid the driver with no fumbling for the correct money, and ran lightly up the steps and into the building. Henry had the impression of an agile man in late middle age, although he had time to notice that the fair hair was liberally streaked with gray.

"Svensen," said Trapp.

"One of our candidates, in fact?"

"That's right. Finnish. He's seventy-one."

"I don't believe it," said Henry. "He looks about fifty."

Trapp laughed. "Tell him that to his face and he'll be your friend for life," he said. "He makes a fetish about health, actually, sauna baths and massage and regular exercise and all that."

"Is he married?"

"Yes indeed. His wife is over here with him, and they have a grown-up family and numerous grandchildren. Svensen used to be a legal adviser to the government, and he's the elder brother of one of Finland's senior diplomats."

"So we can virtually cross him off our list," said Henry. "He's obviously as fit as a fiddle, so he could only be removed by violence, and he has enough influential friends and family to make pretty searching inquiries if he happened to have an accident. Who's this?" he added as a red-faced old gentleman

72

with a huge white mustache came puffing around the corner from Victoria Street.

"Not one of ours," said Trapp. "That's Sir Bertram Clegg, the chairman."

"He looks like a caricature of Colonel Blimp."

"He is."

The next arrival, who turned up in a magnificent chauffeur-driven Bentley, was a Middle Eastern gentleman, grizzled but handsome, who wore a Savile Row suit with a small rose in his buttonhole. He paused to give instructions to his chauffeur before making his way up the steps with great dignity. Henry turned interrogatively to Trapp.

"Sir Abdullah Pasheda," said Trapp. "One of ours, but I don't fancy him as a serious candidate."

"He looks healthy enough," Henry agreed.

Gordon Trapp grinned. "That's not exactly what I meant," he said. "As a matter of fact, it's rumored freely that Pasheda has some rare liver complaint and might hand in his chips at any moment. No, what I meant was that he is an exceptionally well-organized character with many millions in oil wells behind him. His friends could and would make things *very* unhealthy for anybody who tried any funny business with Sir Abdullah."

"So that leaves Bootle and—what was the other man's name?"

"Koetsveen. Dutch."

"And which do you put your money on?"

Trapp said, "On the face of it, they're both suitable candidates for murder. You know Bootle, of course."

"No, I'm afraid I don't."

"Charlie Loudwater."

"Loudwater? The great trade-union leader of the twenties? Good lord, I thought he had been dead for years."

"Not dead," said Trapp lightly, "but kicked upstairs. He became Lord Bootle much against his will fifteen years ago. I believe that he planned to set the House of Lords by the ears and force it to swallow its own coronet as a final act of public life, but the poor fellow had a coronary thrombosis in the middle of his maiden speech, causing an abrupt retirement into private life. He's as tough as old boots, of course, and the doctors pulled him through, but by the time he emerged onto the public scene again it was five years later, and he'd lost a lot of his old fire. Physically, that is. Mentally, he's still as sharp as a needle, but he wouldn't have lasted this long if he hadn't been the same old Battleax Charlie that he always was. My bet is that the Prime Minister shoved him off to PIFL in an attempt to prolong his life."

"What do you mean?" Henry asked.

"Well, it gives the old boy something to do, makes him feel that he's not on the scrap heap, without putting any undue strain on his constitution. If you stopped Charlie Loudwater from working at all, you'd kill him in a week. All the same, he won't last long, I fear. He's seventy-eight, and he's had a couple more attacks since that first one."

"He sounds like the ideal victim," Henry remarked.

"Yes and no. You see— Ah, there he is. Look."

A small unpretentious family car had pulled up outside the entrance to PIFL. Henry could see that there were two people in it. The driver's door opened and a vigorous gray-haired woman in a hideous magenta coat got out. She went around the car, opened the other door, and, with most gentle firmness, helped the other occupant to climb laboriously out on the pavement.

Henry felt a sense of sadness and shock. The lantern jaw and bristling lock of hair, so familiar in every newspaper and newsreel in the early decades of the century, were unmistakable; but the jaw was haggard, the hair had turned from black to white, and the sturdy workman had shrunk into a stooping, emaciated old man. But as Bootle lifted his head for a moment to stare straight at Henry's car, Charlie Loudwater looked out of the clear brown eyes as uncompromisingly as the day when he had led his ragged union members into Downing Street fifty years before to do battle with the government and win. Then the old man lowered his head again and allowed the woman to lead him up the steps, one by one, as he leaned heavily on her arm.

"Who is she?" Henry asked.

"She's the snag," said Trapp. "Baroness Bootle in person. Annie Loudwater, née Cardwell."

"The suffragette?"

"The same. It seems that once female franchise had been achieved, our Annie felt acutely the lack of a good cause to champion. Then, in 1923, she met and married Charlie Loudwater. And got behind him and pushed with a vengeance. Went on pushing, year after year. I've heard it said that he'd never have had that coronary if she hadn't been whipping him along at such a pace. However, it seems that an invalid Charlie has given her a final good cause. She's turned herself into a sort of combined nurse, personal assistant, valet, chauffeur, and watchdog. Heaven help the assassin who gets to grips with that particular flaming sword. She keeps the old boy in a small house in Potter's Bar and literally never lets him out of her sight. Even when he has to come to a private meeting here, like this afternoon, she has a chair brought for her and sits in the corridor outside the conference room until he comes out. If I was—whoever it may be—I'd think twice before I tried to put Charlie Loudwater out of the way, coronary or no coronary."

"Which leaves your Dutchman. Is this him now?"

Trapp craned to look, as a taxi drew up at the entrance. "No, no," he said. "That's nobody of importance, just my colleague."

"Your colleague?"

"The English-French interpreter, Pierre Malvaux." Henry saw a neat, bespectacled man with dark hair, who had extracted a wallet from his breast pocket and was now paying the taxi, handling the carefully folded notes with precise, slightly fussy gestures.

"And the girl with him?"

"Oh, that's Yvonne. I was telling you about her. Our secretary."

It seemed to Henry that Trapp's unconcern was very slightly overdone. "I suppose they've been lunching together," he said.

The girl had alighted from the taxi and now stood waiting on the pavement, while the taxi driver searched his pockets for change. She stood with her back to Henry's car, but he could see that she was small, dark, neatly built, and soberly dressed. Even her backview suggested the perfect secretary. At last the change was produced. Malvaux gave a tiny, Gallic bow of thanks to the driver, pocketed the money, and took the girl's arm. They went up the steps together and disappeared into the building.

Trapp said, "Ah, here's Koetsveen now."

Mijnheer Koetsveen was returning to the conference on foot. He came briskly around the corner, a stout, pear-shaped man with a ruddy face and a wealth of chins. His hair was white, the fine, pure whiteness which suggested that it had once been very fair. Everything about Mijnheer Koetsveen was comfortable, rounded, and jolly, and Henry felt sure that he had met him before somewhere; it took him several moments to realize that it was not this particular elderly Dutchman with whom he was familiar but his innumerable forebears who beam stolidly from the canvases of Frans Hals, Jan Steen, and Rembrandt.

"He looks healthy enough," said Henry.

"Appearances are deceptive," said Trapp. "I have reason to believe that he has a weak heart or high blood pressure or both."

Henry looked at Gordon Trapp. "How do you come to be so well informed about all these people?" he asked.

Gordon smiled. "Since I first got suspicious, I've been making some discreet inquiries," he said. "But as a matter of fact, I got the inside story on Koetsveen some time ago, from a friend of mine, a KLM pilot. Dutch, of course. When he heard I was with PIFL, the conversation naturally turned to Koetsveen. It seems this chap's family was thick with the Koetsveens—his grandmother was a bosom pal of old Mrs. Koets-veen, right up to the time she died."

"Mrs. Koetsveen or your chap's grandmother?"

"Mrs. Koetsveen. The old man's a widower. Two sons in America and a daughter in South Africa. He has a married daughter in Holland, but they don't live together. Old Ko-etsveen lives alone in a service apartment in London at the moment. In Holland he has an apartment in Amsterdam and a converted farmhouse in Friesland for the summer."

"And this pilot friend also told you about his weak heart?"

"No, no. I found out about that for myself, quite by chance. You'd certainly never suspect it, to see him in action. He's eighty-three and he can work three secretaries off their feet from ten until six, and then breeze off to an official dinner as fresh as a daisy. But I have noticed that he gets short of breath sometimes, and a week or more ago I caught him hid-ing in the toilet, purple in the face and gasping for breath. I thought he was going to explode. When I came in he pulled himself together somehow. He obviously doesn't want any-body to know; but if I happen to have found out, you can be sure that other people have too. So he gets my nomination, on points, over Bootle. Agreed?"

"Yes," said Henry. "Yes, I'm sure you're right."

"Well," said Trapp, "there's no point in hanging around here anymore. You've seen all the people who matter. Want to take a look inside?"

The interior of PIFL's headquarters lived up to the Ed-wardian promise of the exterior. Trapp ushered Henry into a filigree wrought-iron elevator, which moved upward with agonizing slowness, finally heaving itself with every sign of exhaustion to the level of the fourth floor. Henry stepped out into the wide corridor.

The first thing that met his eye was the upright, uncom-promising figure of Baroness Bootle. She was sitting on a straight-backed chair, unbending as a statue in her magenta coat and shiny black straw hat; on the floor beside her was a large chintz bag from which emerged a length of navy-blue wool, which the Baroness was knitting with effortless speed into an unidentifiable garment. Every so often the busy clicking of the needles would stop for a moment as she counted stitches or slipped a temporarily unwanted group of them onto a big safety pin. Immediately beyond her chair was a door marked CONFERENCE ROOM. NO ADMITTANCE.

Trapp glanced at Henry, grinned, and said, "This way." He led the way up the corridor to the right, away from the conference room, and opened another door, standing back to let Henry enter.

The modern office equipment looked somehow out of place in that old-world setting of heavily carved wood and ornately plastered ceiling and cornice. The room, which was enormous, had been divided into two by a flimsy hardboard partition. Through the open door in this partition came the expert clatter of a typewriter, but the office in which Henry stood was empty.

"Welcome to the executive suite," said Trapp. "Take a pew." He sat down at one of the two big desks and began examining some papers. "Pierre and I share this commodious accommodation. He's in the conference at the moment interpreting away—Sir Bertram is currently holding the floor, which gives me a welcome spell of relief. Anything special you'd like to see?"

"I'd like to find out more about the dispute," said Henry. "If you have any documents that aren't top secret . . ."

"Good heavens, yes. You can read the complete transcript of the public hearings in either English or French. So-called public," he added.

"What do you mean so-called?"

"Just that. As I told you the other evening, I've never known a member of the public to bother to attend. Yvonne makes a summary of each day's speeches and sends duplicated copies out to the press, but they go straight into the news editor's wastepaper basket. Occasionally, if they're short of a three-line filler paragraph, a newspaper may report one of PIFL's decisions. These, I should say at a rough guess, make the least compelling or newsworthy items ever printed in our national press. Ah, well. It all gives employment." Gordon Trapp leaned back in his chair and lit a cigarette.

"I'd still like to read up on the present case," Henry said.

"My dear chap, nothing could be easier." Trapp heaved himself out of his chair and went over to the door leading to the second office. "Yvonne, my angel?"

The clatter of the typewriter stopped, and a gentle, attractive feminine voice said, "Yes, Gordon? What is it?"

"Got a copy of the transcripts of the public hearings?"

"Of course."

"One you can spare?"

"I've got a stack of them. Mambesi *v.* Galunga hasn't exactly been a best seller. Half a tick. I'll bring you a copy."

A minute or so later Yvonne came into Trapp's office carrying a bulky, rough-bound volume of duplicated typescript. The impression of neat efficiency which Henry had gathered in the street received a slight jolt. Yvonne was, indeed, neat and efficient. She was also quite sensationally lovely, with blue eyes as deep and cool as a great river, a pale skin, and small, perfect features. It was very easy to understand why Monsieur Pierre Malvaux enjoyed her company at lunch. She paused on the threshold and looked at Henry with slightly raised eyebrows.

"This is Mr. Tibbett," said Gordon; and added, "He's the chief foreign correspondent of the South Wimbledon *Gazette.* He's doing a story on PIFL."

"A journalist?" Yvonne's voice was tinged with amusement and patent disbelief.

Henry said, "That's Gordon's idea of a joke. I'm simply a very nondescript friend of his."

"And you're interested in PIFL?"

"Yes, I am."

"How funny," said Yvonne. "Well—here are the transcripts. I hope you enjoy them." She laid the papers down on the desk and went back to her own office, closing the door behind her.

Henry looked at Trapp and they both smiled. "She is, isn't she?" said Gordon. "Funnily enough, she is also very nice and very bright, an astonishing combination. I think I shall probably marry her."

"Shall you, indeed? Have you mentioned it to her yet?"

"Dear me, no. My technique is to keep them guessing."

"And what about Monsieur Malvaux?"

"Oh, Pierre. Nothing to worry about there. I can assure you, my dear Tibbett, that if I decide to marry young Yvonne, you may as well start choosing the plated fish knife straight away. Now, is there anything else I can do for you?"

"I think not," said Henry. "Your commission members are incommunicado for the rest of the day, I presume. I'll get back to my office and do my homework." He patted the fat volume.

"As you wish. Oh—I've just had an idea. Are you busy at noon tomorrow?"

"No more than usual. Why?"

"Then bring Emmy along to PIFL's farewell cocktail party. Twelve sharp in the conference room here. Be my guests."

"Farewell party?"

"Yes. This is our last working day of the present session. We break up this evening for the Easter recess. It was the chairman's idea to have this booze-up tomorrow, which is Saturday, of course, for anybody still in London."

"You mean all the members of the commission will be leaving London?"

"That's right. Easter holidays. Our happy little family will disperse for three weeks, reassembling for a final meeting, the formal voting, and the announcement of the commission's decision. A bit silly, really, but there was no way of getting the vote taken before the recess."

"You might have told me this sooner," said Henry. "It makes everything much more difficult."

"Does it? I thought it might possibly make it easier. Anyhow, I'll expect you both tomorrow."

7

Back at Scotland Yard, Sergeant Reynolds greeted Henry gloomily. He had spent the day in the dreary task of exploring all avenues and leaving no stones unturned, with no result. Peterson's story seemed unshakable, and was corroborated—for what it was worth—by Weatherby and Madeleine La Rue. None of the other regulars of The Pink Parrot would admit having been there at the time of the shooting; and every lead on Byers himself had proved an excursion up a blind alley. Mrs. Torelli, Mr. Bingham, Mr. Wardle, Mr. Taylor—all Byers' known contacts had been questioned again with no result whatsoever.

"Your criminal doesn't have to be clever, so much," the Sergeant remarked sadly, "as just to know how to keep himself to himself. Most of them give themselves away because they can't resist the temptation to talk, to show off, or impress a girl, or such. Byers wasn't that sort. He was an educated man. He knew how to keep his mouth shut."

Henry reflected briefly on this summing-up of the uses of education and then said, "There's one more lead I'd like you to follow up, Sergeant."

"Yes, sir?" Reynolds brightened visibly, like a dog who has seen his master pick up a stick. "A lead on Byers?"

Henry said, "I want all the information you can get on a street accident which took place in Oxford Street in February."

"Grievous bodily harm by motor vehicle?" asked Reynolds eagerly. "They get away with that too often, if you ask me. Too difficult to prove, and they know it. You think that Byers . . . ?"

"This case," said Henry, "concerns a man called Pereira."

"One of the Spanish gang from Soho would that be, sir?"

"No, Sergeant. Señor Pereira was a distinguished lawyer, one-time legal adviser to the Brazilian government. He was eighty-seven years old, and he slipped on an icy pavement on"—Henry consulted his notebook—"on February twentieth last, just outside Bourne and Hollingsworths. He fell into the street and was run over by a Number-73 bus."

"Very good, sir." Sergeant Reynolds did not actually sigh deeply, but he made it clear that he would have liked to have done so. He had the same facility for conveying dumb disapproval as the inimitable Jeeves. "This wouldn't have anything to do with the Byers case then, sir?"

"I really don't know, Sergeant."

"There's nothing more you'd like me to do about Byers, sir?"

"Not for the moment."

"The—the press are taking quite an interest in the case, sir." Sergeant Reynolds laughed a little uneasily. "Did you see the *News* this morning? That bit about the police persecuting innocent motorists with breath-analyzers, while honest citizens are being shot to death in broad daylight . . ."

"I saw it," said Henry.

"The policeman's lot is not a happy one, sir. I will go and get the details of that street accident, sir." Sergeant Reynolds withdrew, his resemblance to Jeeves more marked than ever.

Henry opened the massive document from PIFL and began wading doggedly through its legal phraseology. As far as he could disentangle fact from the lawyers' jargon, Henry decided that Gordon Trapp had given a very fair summing-up of the situation. As he read, he could gather that both Mambesi and Galunga were states which were very poor and very large. An extra strip of useless land would be a positive embarrassment to either of them. For the sake of prestige, however, each side claimed the territory. Mambesi rested her case on the famous treaty of 1876, while Galunga pleaded general usage, natural justice, ethnic considerations, and—most important—the fact that she was not bound by a treaty entered into on her behalf by France. It was agreed by both sides that the number of inhabitants involved was minimal: Mambesi estimated fifty persons, while Galunga, with a show of indignation, claimed that at least fifty-six people would be affected by the commission's decision. From every page, the moldering boredom of the whole dispute rose to the nostrils like ancient dust in a deserted attic. It was almost inconceivable that men should have been murdered, that violence should have erupted in an ugly spurt of dark energy as a result of this anemically academic dispute. And yet, Pereira was dead and so was Mr. Justice Findelhander, and gunshots had ripped the afternoon quiet of The Pink Parrot, leaving "Flutter" Byers bleeding to death on the lavatory floor.

Sergeant Reynolds returned before Henry had finished with the proceedings of PIFL. He laid a neat dossier on Henry's desk. "I think you'll find it all there, sir," he said.

Henry looked up sharply.

The Sergeant's face was carefully composed into a mask of no emotion.

"You're on to something, Sergeant Reynolds," Henry said. "Come on. Out with it."

"It may be just a coincidence, sir."

"I doubt it," said Henry. "Be a good fellow and put me out of my misery."

Reynolds almost smiled. "It's all there in the file, sir. A straightforward street accident, like you said, all recorded in the inquest report. The old gentleman was a Brazilian, working in London for some international office—something to do with the United Nations, I think. Anyhow, he was doing some late shopping, it being a Thursday. There had been rain, and then it froze—you remember that cold spell at the end of February, sir? The curb was icy and Mr. Pereira's eyesight was poor. The bus driver—a Mr. Simpson from Balham —he gave evidence that he was proceeding down Oxford Street at no more than twenty-five miles an hour. He applied his brakes at once, he said, but what with the road being so slippery and the poor gentleman falling so suddenly, with no warning—well—it had been too late. The coroner made a special point of saying that Mr. Simpson should not blame himself in any way. He said, the coroner, that it was a most unfortunate accident, which underlined the dangers of elderly and infirm people going out alone after dark in wintry weather. He sent his sympathy to Señor Pereira's family in Brazil. The verdict was accidental death, of course."

Sergeant Reynolds paused, and Henry said, "Come on then, Reynolds. Out with it."

"Just this, sir. The witnesses."

"What about the witnesses?"

"Well, apart from the bus driver, there were several passersby who gave evidence, but most of them couldn't help much. It happened at half-past seven in the evening, you see, when it was already dark, and all the people were busy with their own shopping. Most of them didn't even notice the old gentleman until after he had fallen. There was one witness, though, who came forward and said definitely that he had seen Mr. Pereira slip. He'd tried to save him from falling, he said, but had been just too late. The coroner thanked the witness and said he had given his evidence clearly and concisely, enabling the jury to get a good picture of what had happened. It had assisted them in coming to their verdict."

"And this witness was . . . ?"

"Major George Weatherby, sir. That's all. Just Major George Weatherby, described as the licensee of The Pink Parrot public house in Maize Street."

"That's very interesting, Sergeant."

"That's what I thought, sir. I might have known you wouldn't have gotten me to look up a simple traffic accident for nothing. But what on earth did Señor Pereira have to do with 'Flutter' Byers?"

"You're asking the wrong question, Sergeant. You should be asking what 'Flutter' Byers had to do with Señor Pereira, or with Mr. Justice Findelhander." Sergeant Reynolds' honest face puckered in bewilderment, and Henry grinned. "Sorry, Sergeant. That wasn't fair. I have inside information, you see."

"Oh yes, sir?"

"Which I can't tell you for the moment. Until I get it all sewn up, I daren't tell anyone, for fear of being laughed out of court. This new evidence has helped a lot and I'm very grateful. Meanwhile, I think I should have another word with the Major, don't you? Would you call him and ask him to pay us a visit?"

Reynolds smiled slowly. "He won't relish that, sir. Not twice in one day."

"That's what I'm counting on," said Henry.

If Henry had imagined that Major George Weatherby would arrive in a cowed or apprehensive frame of mind, he was quickly proved wrong. Weatherby strode into Scotland Yard's elegant gray-and-white marble foyer like an enraged bull, bellowed at the receptionist, and finally turned up in Henry's office snorting with indignation.

"What's the meaning of this, Superintendent?" he demanded, thumping Henry's desk with a gold-topped cane.

"Please sit down, Major Weatherby."

"Damned if I'll sit down until I get a reasonable explanation. Am I to be persecuted endlessly? First of all, your chaps come tramping all over my pub. Then you turn up, and I think you'll admit that I was completely frank and honest with you, sir. Nevertheless, this morning . . ."

"Don't bother to recite the catalog, Major. I know just how many times you've been interviewed."

"Then perhaps you'll explain just what you're about, sir. Good God, it's nearly opening time. Am I to be deprived of my livelihood just for the benefit of . . ." The Major suddenly stopped in midsentence. He had raised his hand again with the clear intention of making another demonstration with the gold-handled cane, when his eye had fallen on the PIFL report, which still lay on Henry's desk. Weatherby cleared his throat loudly and then said, "Well, let's get it over, sir. What may I do for you?"

"As a matter of fact, Major Weatherby," said Henry, "this has nothing to do with the Byers case."

"It hasn't? Then what . . . ?"

"I do wish you'd sit down."

The Major sat down. Henry was interested to notice that he had suddenly become nervous.

"In February you gave evidence at a coroner's court about a street accident."

"Perfectly correct." The Major's smooth red face was now the color of an overripe tomato. "A most unfortunate accident. Poor old sod—gentleman—accidental death, of course. But that was months ago."

"Yes. indeed," said Henry. "I understand that you were very helpful. The coroner thanked you."

The Major simpered, but his bloodshot eyes remained suspicious. "He was good enough to make a few kind remarks. Not that I deserved any special—that is to say, anybody would have done the same . . ."

"I don't think so," said Henry.

"Eh? What? What d'you mean by that?"

"Nobody else was in a position to do the same. Nobody else saw Señor Pereira slip and fall."

"Ah, well. That was just a matter of luck."

"Was it?"

"Or bad luck, from the poor old—gentleman's point of view."

"Singularly bad luck," said Henry dryly. There was a moment of silence, and then Henry said, "How much did they pay you?"

"I—I beg your pardon?"

Henry repeated the question.

"I have no idea what you mean, sir. None whatsoever. If you are implying . . ."

"I'm not implying that you pushed Señor Pereira under the bus," said Henry easily. "Not at this stage, at any rate. I am implying that you were paid a considerable sum of money to be at a certain place at a certain time and to give certain evidence at the inquest."

The Major appeared about to explode. "I have never

heard such poppycock in my life. I demand to see my solicitor . . ."

"What were you doing in Oxford Street at seven in the evening anyhow?"

"Shopping, of course. It was a late-shopping evening."

"To the neglect of your pub and the detriment of your livelihood? Come off it, Weatherby. You weren't shopping."

"I happen to have a maiden aunt in Cheltenham of whom I am very fond," said Weatherby belligerently. "Her birthday is on February 28th. I had been buying a box of handkerchiefs for her at Bourne and Hollingsworths." He glared at Henry, daring him to disprove this statement.

"You deny that you were anything more than an innocent bystander?"

"Of course I do."

"Then there is no more to be said for the moment," said Henry. He stood up. "Good-bye, Major Weatherby. You needn't think you have heard the last of this matter. If you take my advice, you'll go home and think things over—and then you'll come back and tell me the whole story. After all, as you pointed out, you have your livelihood to think of."

"What do you mean by that, sir?"

"You've never been in trouble with the police, have you? Not personally. What your friends do is their own affair. It would be foolish of you to risk the future of The Pink Parrot by trying to shield . . ."

"You are talking arrant rubbish, sir."

"Think it over, Major," said Henry. "Believe me, I'm not after you. There are bigger fish to fry, and we'd like your help. If you're determined to be obstructive, however . . ." He shrugged and turned back to his desk, picking up the PIFL report.

"Good evening to you, sir," barked the Major.

Henry saw that his eyes were on the document. He opened it very deliberately and began to read, as the Major stumped out of the room.

It was only a few minutes later that Henry rang through to

Sergeant Reynolds. "I'm off home now, Sergeant," he said. "You've got a man tailing the Major?"

"Two, sir."

"Call me at home when you get any news."

"Yes, sir. Er—how did you get on, sir?"

"I think I rattled him," said Henry. "I hope so. And I hope he didn't have as good an education as Byers did. If he sits tight and sticks to his various stories, there's mighty little we can do to shake him."

When Henry arrived home, he was greeted by a delicious smell of shrimp marengo wafting down the hallway. Before he had closed the front door behind him, Emmy came out of the kitchen carrying a tray loaded with glasses, a bottle of white wine, ice cubes, and a flask of black-currant liqueur.

"What on earth is all this in aid of?" Henry demanded.

"Why should it be in aid of anything? Why shouldn't we ever have nice things just for us?"

"First because we can't afford it, and second because there are three glasses on the tray."

"Well, as a matter of fact," said Emmy, "Gordon Trapp is coming to dinner."

"Are you out of your mind? He came to lunch."

"I know he came to lunch," said Emmy, "but it just so happens that he is also coming to dinner. I thought we might have our *vin blanc cassis* in the garden. It's such a lovely evening." She disappeared with the tray into the living room.

Henry followed her. "You might explain," he said, but she had already gone out through the open French windows and into the small, high-walled square of grass and paving that passed for a garden. She put the tray down on a white-painted iron table and said, "Bring out another chair, would you, Henry? And switch on the outside light. He'll be here in a minute."

Henry had just carried the chair into the garden when the front doorbell rang. Emmy whipped off her apron. "That'll be him. I'll go and let him in."

Henry deposited the chair and sat down in it. He then

poured himself a glass of white wine with a dash of *cassis* and awaited developments. It was wonderfully warm in the April twilight. A minute later Emmy and Gordon Trapp came out through the French windows.

"So we meet again, Superintendent," said Trapp. He grinned broadly. "The original bad penny."

"I'm delighted to see you, of course," said Henry, trying to sound sincere, "but I don't quite . . ."

"It's very simple. The plot has thickened."

"It has?" Henry was interested at once. "Koetsveen hasn't . . . ?"

"No, no. Nothing to do with him."

"Do sit down, Mr. Trapp, and have a drink."

"Gordon, please, Mrs. Tibbett. We're old friends now."

Emmy laughed. "Of course we are. And you must call me Emmy. And, incidentally, do stop addressing Henry as Superintendent. It makes me nervous."

"Nervous? Why? Have you a guilty conscience?"

"Of course I have. Haven't you?" Emmy was laughing, but Trapp suddenly looked serious.

"You believe that everyone has a guilty secret, do you, Emmy?" he said.

"That's putting it a bit high," said Emmy. She poured out a glass of wine and paused, with the cool stem between her fingers. "Let's say rather there are very few people who wouldn't feel a tremor if they were told that there was a policeman at the door asking to see them. Especially a Superintendent of the c.i.d. And superintendents' wives aren't immune from that feeling, I can assure you."

"How fascinating," said Trapp. "Thanks. Cheers." He took the glass, raised it, and drank. "Which of your crimes would leap to your guilty mind if the doorbell rang?"

"Oh—nothing terrible. Parking in the wrong place and exceeding the speed limit—things like that."

"Hardly worth the time and talents of a superintendent, I'd have thought."

"No, thank goodness."

"And what about you?" Trapp had turned to Henry.

"Me?"

"Have you a guilty conscience too, or are policemen exempt?"

Henry was aware of a growing feeling of irritation, which, because it was irrational, annoyed him even more than it should have. He said, "Policemen are not exempt from anything. On the contrary, they have to maintain a much higher standard than ordinary people." It sounded pompous even as he said it; he was also conscious that he had not addressed Trapp directly, because after Emmy's remark he did not feel that he could say "Mr. Trapp" and yet he could not bring himself to call the man "Gordon."

Emmy said quickly, "Gordon called me about half an hour ago, darling. He'd been trying to get you, but you'd already left the office." To Trapp, she added, "Henry has only just gotten home this minute, and I haven't had time to explain things. I'm so sorry."

"My dear Emmy," said Trapp, "I can think of no possible reason why you should be sorry about anything. You are the nearest thing to an angel which most of us are likely to encounter in this wicked world."

Henry's surge of anger was not damped by the fact that Emmy went pink and said, "Oh, don't be idiotic, Gordon," with obvious pleasure. There was an awkward little pause, and then she went on, "Well, anyhow, Gordon said he had something important to tell you, darling, so I asked him to dinner. And now I must get back to the kitchen or there won't be any."

The pause after Emmy had gone was even longer and more awkward. Then Henry said, "Well? What was it you wanted to tell me?"

Instead of answering Trapp said, "Did you find time to read the PIFL report?"

"Not in detail. I glanced through it."

"Come to any conclusion?"

"Not really," said Henry. "Only this. If I hadn't some—

90

some independent evidence that your theory might be correct, I'd have no hesitation in saying that we were both quite insane to take it seriously for a moment."

"Cryptic," said Trapp. He drained his glass and put it down on the table.

"Not cryptic at all," said Henry. "I'm taking this thing seriously because I have other evidence. I cannot believe that you would take it seriously unless you too had other evidence. Something that you haven't yet told me."

"That's what I came to see you about, in a way," said Trapp. "I wonder if I might have another drink?"

"Of course. I'm sorry." Henry knew very well that he had ignored the empty glass deliberately. He refilled it. "Well?"

Trapp leaned back in his chair, stretching his long legs. "When I was in Mambesi," he said, "I had quite a few friends out there. You get an odd lot of Europeans in those backwater places. Drifters, ne'er-do-wells, idealists, failures . . ."

"You make the place sound like a Maugham novel of the twenties," said Henry.

"Well, I'm afraid that it really is very much like that. There are also the more practical white people, the mercenaries, the merchants, the adventurers. The one common denominator is individualism, dislike of authority."

Henry laughed. "I should have thought that the present Mambesian government was more authoritarian than . . ."

"Ah," said Trapp, "but the authority is flexible, bendable. Or so these chaps assume. Sometimes they run their noses into a wall of steel. It always makes them look so surprised. You can see it in their faces—just before they die."

"I wish you'd cut out the melodrama and get to the point," said Henry.

Trapp ignored him. "Mike Honeyman," he said, "was a pal of mine in Mambesi. He's a pilot. He believes in free-enterprise airlines. He started up a concern called Mambesi-Galunga Airlines, which consisted of himself, another dead-beat pilot, an alcoholic navigator, and a few native mechanics. His fleet comprised three clapped-out Dakotas which would never have gotten air-worthiness certificates in any civilized country. He flew from anywhere to anywhere else, so long as he was paid, and thought he had a fifty-fifty chance of getting there alive. He wasn't fussy about his cargo—or anything else."

"You talk about him in the past tense," said Henry. "Is he dead?"

There was a tiny pause. Then Trapp said, "Surprisingly, no. Far from it. In fact, he turned up in my office half an hour after you had left it this afternoon."

"What did he want?"

"To be strictly accurate, he wanted to borrow money," said Trapp. "He's on his beam ends. He's been thrown out of Mambesi and all his aircraft, equipment, and assets have been confiscated. When I say 'thrown out'—the rest of his unfortunate associates have been arrested. Mike would have been too, but he's as slippery as an eel, and he has a sort of instinct about danger. He scented what was happening and beat it over the border to Galunga in a single-seater light aircraft which he borrowed from a trade rival. If 'borrowed' is the right word, which I doubt. In any case, by the time Mambesi realized he was missing and asked Galunga to extradite him, Mike had moved on to South Africa. He spent his last cent on a ticket back to England, and here he is, thoroughly broke. What's more natural than that he should look up his old friend Gordon Trapp, who, his spies inform him, has a steady job in London with PIFL and is therefore good at least for the price of a meal and a night's lodging?"

"I don't remember reading about any of this in the papers," Henry said.

"My dear Henry, of course you don't. That's not the way things are done. You should know that. However, there's no doubt that Mambesi is interested in my friend Mike."

"What has he done? Why was his property confiscated and his colleagues arrested?"

Trapp smiled indulgently. "That is a silly question," he said, "to which you can only expect a silly answer. The official reason was that he had spoken disparagingly of the prime minister and the regime and had attempted to bribe officials. The real reason, probably, was that the Mambesi government thought they could find a use themselves for a couple of Dakotas. But none of that is important." Trapp looked at Henry and laughed. "Really, Superintendent, you look like a small child who has just been told a tale by the Brothers Grimm. You've lived in England for too long, old man. You take law and order for granted. You think that the community can be neatly divided into law-abiding citizens and the criminal classes."

"That's not true," said Henry.

"Nevertheless, you are profoundly shocked at the idea of an entire government department being corrupt and lawless. Aren't you?"

"Of course I'm not," said Henry. "Everybody knows that such things happen." But an inner voice told him that Trapp was at least partly right. This whole affair was leading him into regions where the standards of a lifetime no longer applied. Then he thought of Lady Bootle and her knitting bag, and the overlapping of the two worlds seemed so ludicrous that he laughed aloud.

Trapp misunderstood this. "You may think it funny," he said, "but it may be far from amusing for Mike—and for Koetsveen."

"I'm sorry," said Henry. "I was laughing at something quite different. At myself, in fact. Go on."

Trapp said, "When Mike got away from Mambesi in that tiny aircraft, he was too canny to follow the usual airlane to Lungaville. He just headed for the nearest possible point on the frontier, which involved crossing the Blue Smoke mountains."

"In a small single-seater plane?"

"Apparently there's a pass through which you can fly in a small plane—if you know the way, which Mike did. As you know, if you've read the PIFL report, the stretch of country between the mountains and the river on the Galunga side is quite barren and uninhabited, apart from a few nomadic herdsmen. That's why Mike was so surprised when he spotted the encampment."

"Encampment?"

"In the foothills of the mountains on the Galunga side, slap in the middle of the disputed territory. Mike says that it wouldn't have been visible at all from the ground, but from the air he could see that a good track had been made, almost a road, he said, over the pass from the Mambesi side, ending up in this camp. And it wasn't just a camp either. There was equipment, mining equipment."

"So you deduce that Mambesi is sinking experimental mine shafts into the foothills of the Blue Smoke mountains in the disputed area?"

"It certainly sounds like it. And if they've found something valuable . . ."

"All right, all right. You don't have to spell it out." Henry put down his glass. "Did they see him?"

"See him?" Trapp laughed. "My dear old scout, they not only saw him, they tried to shoot him down."

"They were armed, then?"

"Only with army rifles. Which accounts for Mike's escape; but he says he had some nasty moments. It was only a tiny biplane, and he couldn't get her higher than a couple of hundred feet."

"I think," said Henry, "that I should speak to this man Honeyman. In fact, I think that several people should speak to him, people senior to me and in other departments—as soon as possible. Where is he now?"

"I left him in my flat," said Trapp. "I provided him with a bottle of whisky and a can of baked beans and told him to feed himself and then bed down on the sofa."

"Then let's telephone right away and get him around here," said Henry. "The dinner will certainly stretch to feed another mouth, and it may even be better than a can of baked beans."

But there was no reply from Gordon Trapp's apartment.

The telephone rang monotonously and persistently for the regulation span of time and then switched back automatically to the dial tone.

"Try it again," said Henry. "Sometimes it's a wrong number ringing."

They tried it three times, always with the same result.

"That's very odd," said Trapp. "Where can he be?"

"At the local having a pint, I expect," said Henry.

"What, with free whisky in the house?"

"Oh, I don't know," said Henry. "Draft bitter is draft bitter, and the average Englishman on his first evening home from foreign parts will make for the nearest pub like a homing pigeon. Let's have our dinner and I'll go home with you afterward. He'll surely be back by then."

8

The shrimp marengo was delicious, and so were the fresh fruit salad and the coffee, but, Henry noted with interest, Gordon Trapp was in no mood to linger over his meal. Several times he looked at his watch and at last he said, "Perhaps we should be off now, old man. It's nine o'clock."

Henry lit a cigarette with deliberate slowness. In fact, he was in no mood for procrastination, but it was worth a few moments' delay to observe Trapp's reaction to his apparent lack of any sense of urgency. "There's no rush," he said. "Give the chap until closing time. Have some more coffee."

"I thought you were in a hurry to see him."

"I am. But I can't see him if he's not there, and I don't intend to start searching all the pubs in South London."

"He'll surely be in by now." Trapp was like a cat on hot bricks.

"Why don't you try calling him again?" Emmy suggested. "Then if he is there, you can go around right away."

Gordon Trapp was out in the hall in a matter of moments, and Henry heard the gentle whirring of the dial as he tried the number. Then silence. A moment later Trapp was back in the room.

"Okay," he said, "let's go. He's there."

"You spoke to him?" Henry was intrigued.

"No, I didn't."

"Then how . . . ?"

"I got the busy signal," said Trapp. "That means that he's using the phone, so he must be there."

"Unless somebody else is trying to call your number," Henry pointed out. "That would also give you the busy signal."

"Oh, for heaven's sake, if you're not satisfied, go and try the number again for yourself."

"I think I will," said Henry.

The number was still busy.

"You see?" Trapp was already putting on his coat. "It couldn't be another caller or they'd have given up by now. Mike must be making a call, so let's get there. Good-bye, Emmy. Thanks for a marvelous meal—and don't let that guilty conscience trouble you unduly. We all suffer in the same way, you know."

Effingham Court was a vast, impersonal block of service apartments which had been built not far from Victoria Station in the thirties. As a microcosm of the world outside, it was equipped like a village, with its own complex of shops, its slightly shabby restaurant, its definitely shabby cocktail bar, its row of telephone booths, its basement swimming pool and squash courts. On the upper floors, corridors—like parodies of lanes, with their well-worn green carpet and peeling beechwood-veneer walls—stretched away in all directions; and along the length of this complicated network stood anonymous doors with near-astronomic metal numbers screwed to them. These doors guarded the sad privacy of hundreds of lonely people, for Effingham Court contained no homes, no families. Its residents were birds of passage, lone wolves, people with no roots in the city. All the apartments were single, all were furnished, and all were rented by the week.

It was half past nine when Henry and Gordon took one of the elevators to the tenth floor and followed the green corridor around several hundred yards of convolutions until they came to a door marked 1087. Trapp fished a key out of his pocket and opened the door. The tiny hall was dark, but a light was burning in the living room beyond.

"Mike?" Trapp pushed open the living-room door and walked in. "Hey, Mike, I've brought . . ."

Suddenly he stopped speaking and stood still. Henry, following him, could see at once that the room was empty.

"Mike!" Trapp called louder. The little room was very silent.

Trapp said, "He must be in the bathroom." But Henry could see through the open bathroom door that it too was empty. The minuscule kitchen was also deserted, but a can of baked beans stood unopened beside the electric stove. There was no sign of a bottle of whisky.

"It would appear," said Henry, "that your friend is still out."

"He can't be. The phone was busy."

"Or rather," Henry amended, "he must have come in, made a telephone call, and gone out again."

"Why in hell would he have done that? Anyhow, he had no money."

"You didn't lend him any, as he asked you to?"

"I couldn't. I had practically no cash on me and the banks were closed. I told him I'd let him have some tomorrow when PIFL pays me."

"Perhaps," said Henry, "he made a telephone call to another friend who was able to advance him enough for a decent meal in a restaurant. He doesn't appear to have eaten the beans, so . . ."

"He told me he didn't know another soul in London," said Trapp. "And anyhow—here, just a minute. His knapsack's gone, too."

"Knapsack?"

"It was all the luggage he had, a battered old khaki knapsack with a few clothes and a toothbrush in it. He wouldn't have taken that with him just to go out for a meal. Blast the man. He's simply pushed off, and not as much as left a note . . ."

Henry gave Trapp a long, serious look. Then he said, "You're not by any chance a very elaborate practical joker, are you, Mr. Trapp?"

"What do you mean by that?"

"Just that I haven't a vestige of proof that Honeyman was

ever here—or that he exists at all, for that matter. In fact, it's possible . . ." Henry broke off. He had walked over to the small table by the sofa, where the chipped off-white telephone was. He took a clean handkerchief from his pocket, wrapped it around his hand, and gingerly lifted the receiver. A small piece of folded cardboard fell on the floor.

"What . . . ?" Trapp began.

"There's the explanation of the busy signal," said Henry. He sounded a little grim. "I thought I heard a faint buzzing noise as we came in. The telephone was wedged so that it was, to all intents and purposes, left off the hook."

"But, that doesn't make sense. We were getting no reply earlier."

"That fact," said Henry, "had not escaped me. You gave Honeyman a key to this apartment, did you?"

"Yes. My spare."

"Does anybody else have one?"

Trapp hesitated fractionally before he said, "No. There are only the two keys."

"Well," said Henry, "it seems I have no alternative but to take the situation seriously."

"He's bound to show up tomorrow," said Trapp. "You don't know old Mike . . ."

"I said 'seriously,' " said Henry. "If the story you've told me is true, Honeyman is a vital witness and he is in extreme danger. If I start a full-scale hunt for him right now, there's a small chance of saving his life, but I wouldn't like to bet on it. If the whole thing is a hoax, I shall probably break your neck."

"I say, old man . . ."

"Is your passport in order?"

"Yes, of course. Why?"

"Bring it with you," said Henry. "You won't be coming back to this apartment again for some time."

"What on earth do you mean?" Trapp demanded.

"Don't be an idiot," said Henry shortly. "If Honeyman is

99

in danger, so are you. They probably hoped to get you both together. You will now go into cold storage for your own protection, and no arguments, please."

Henry's next move was to call Scotland Yard and arrange for a car to collect Trapp and himself from Effingham Court. He then replaced the cardboard wedge in the telephone, and the two men went down in the elevator. An ordinary car driven by a nondescript-looking man in a raincoat pulled up outside the main door of Effingham Court as they came out. They got into the car and were soon heading for nearby Scotland Yard. As far as Henry could tell, nobody unauthorized had been aware of their visit to Effingham Court.

Back in his fifth-floor office, Henry's first job was to arrange for a description of Honeyman to be circulated to every police car in the metropolitan area and to forces all over the country, a service carried out with impressive speed and efficiency by the Criminal Records Office. The hardest part was to obtain an accurate description of Honeyman. For this, Henry had to rely entirely on Gordon Trapp, who displayed the usual human inability to recall the color of the eyes, hair, complexion, and clothing of a man in whose company he had recently spent several hours. In the end, however, he decided that Honeyman was aged between forty-five and fifty, was over six feet in height, sturdily built, with fair hair going slightly gray, and a tanned complexion. His eyes were either blue or gray. He was wearing, as far as Trapp could remember, a pair of elderly cavalry-twill trousers, a blue shirt, beige pullover, and sheepskin jacket. He might well be carrying an ancient army-type knapsack.

This done, Henry sent Trapp off to the canteen for coffee and began to consider the reports which had been handed in by the plainclothes officers who had been detailed to shadow Major Weatherby. These were not very rewarding.

It appeared that Weatherby had taken a taxi from Scotland Yard after his interview with Henry and had returned directly to The Pink Parrot and his usual post behind the private bar. The detective who had been bold enough to remain in that sanctum for an evening's drinking reported that he had left the bar on one occasion only, to make a telephone call at 7:18 P.M. There had been no mystery about this call. It had been made at the request of Miss La Rue, who was also in the bar. She had asked her uncle to ring the local taxi stand and order a cab to pick her up immediately outside the pub. As soon as the Major reported that the taxi was on its way, Miss La Rue had left the bar, and Weatherby had resumed his duties as barman.

The detective reported that the other occupants of the bar consisted of the usual clientele of shady characters. He had hoped to be unrecognized, but felt sure that everybody had known who and what he was, for the good reason that the conversation had been, without exception, on a level of naïve innocence which could seldom have been achieved before in the private bar of The Pink Parrot. The officer had had the distinct impression that he was being mocked. Nevertheless, he had remained doggedly at his post until closing time, as had the Major.

The second officer had had the less enviable task of keeping watch in the street outside. His report consisted for the most part of a dreary and detailed list of arrivals and departures. As was to be expected, some of the patrons were known to him by sight and were mentioned by name. Otherwise, descriptions were terse. "Arrived, 8:14 P.M., one man, approx. 26, dark hair, blue suit, small mustache, abt 5′9″. Dep. 8:24 P.M., 2 men, 1 dark, 1 fair, raincoats, Trilby hats. Drove off in white Ford Cortina, No. . . ." and so on. An entry for 7:20 P.M. recounted that Miss Madeleine La Rue had come out of the building wearing a mink coat over a beige costume. A moment later a cab—number duly noted—had drawn up to the curb. Miss La Rue had gotten into it, and it had driven off in a southerly direction. She had, it seemed, returned to The Pink Parrot alone and in a taxi at 9:34 P.M. On her return she had been carrying a small suitcase as well as her handbag. At closing time the pub had emptied and Weatherby had locked up. From then until 11:00 P.M., when the report was phoned through, no other person had entered or left the premises.

Henry called the duty sergeant. "This man—what's his name?—Parsons, the chap who was on duty outside The Pink Parrot this evening. Is he still there?"

The sergeant consulted his records. "No, sir. He knocked off at eleven, after he'd put in his report. He's been replaced by Detective Constable Franklin. Parsons will be at home and in bed by now."

"Then get him up again," said Henry. "I want to speak to him. Yes, the telephone will do."

A sleepy Detective Constable Parsons answered Henry with some surprise. Yes, he said, as a matter of fact, he had been close enough to get an idea of what Miss La Rue had said to the taxi driver. He hadn't put it in his report, because he hadn't been sure that he had caught it right. He was very sorry. He had been told to report on Weatherby, and he hadn't realized . . .

"All right, all right," said Henry, "just get on with it. Where did she go in that taxi?"

"Well, sir, it sounded to me like the Domino, you know, the club in Soho. That's what it sounded like."

"Could it have been Dominic's?" Henry asked.

Parsons hesitated. "Yes, I suppose it could have been, sir. That would be more likely, really, wouldn't it? I mean, for a smart young lady like that. Dominic's Hotel being very exclusive and expensive . . ."

"I know all about Dominic's Hotel," said Henry. "Now, what about the number of the cab that brought her home at 9:34. It's not in your report."

"I know, sir. I did jot it down, but I'm afraid I didn't think . . ."

"You should try sometime," said Henry. He was very tired and knew he was being irritable.

"I'm really very sorry, sir." Parsons sounded as though he might burst into tears.

Henry, making a deliberate effort at warmth, said, "Never mind, Constable. You did well to note it. Let's have it."

Parsons, sounding chipper, said that he would just get his notebook, and a moment later reeled off the cab's number. Then he said, "If you're so interested in Miss La Rue, sir, there's another thing."

"Something else that didn't go into your report?"

"The report was on Weatherby, sir, and this seemed such a little thing, only it struck me as a bit funny."

"Well, what was it?"

"Well, sir—you'll see in the report that when Miss La Rue came back to the pub she had a suitcase with her. And as she got out of the taxi she was—well, sir—she was sort of twirling it around, only holding it with one finger. And I thought to myself, 'It's empty, that suitcase. I wonder why she's got an empty suitcase with her?' That's all, sir."

The first really interesting news came through at 2:00 A.M., when Henry was conferring with a sleepy but interested member of the Foreign Office who had been roused from his bed and brought, protesting, to Scotland Yard. The news came in the form of a phone call from Sergeant Reynolds. He had just interviewed the taxi driver who had driven Miss La Rue home, and he thought that Henry should hear about it at once. The man from the foreign office departed and the Sergeant took his place.

The driver, said Reynolds, was a jolly, likable man in his fifties called Jack Wotherspoon. He remembered clearly taking Miss La Rue to The Pink Parrot. He had thought it a bit strange at the time, he said, because he had seen the lady getting out of another cab in Kensington High Street, near Pontings, and paying it off. She had been carrying a small suitcase. As soon as the other taxi had driven away, she had hailed Wotherspoon and asked him to take her to The Pink Parrot. Outside the pub, she had jumped out of the cab as if in a hurry, pressed the fare plus a generous tip into his hand, and gone quickly indoors, letting herself in with her own key.

It was about an hour later, Wotherspoon said, when another fare had drawn his attention to the fact that a canvas knapsack had been left in the back of his cab. Wotherspoon couldn't be sure which of his fares had left it there, because it had been folded up and pushed down behind one of the tip-up seats in an obvious attempt at concealment. It might have been there all evening. Wotherspoon had completed his stint of duty, which ended at 1:00 A.M., and had then gone home, taking the knapsack with him. He had intended to turn it in to the lost property office in the morning. The knapsack now lay on Henry's desk. It was old and travel-stained and empty; but on the flap, in indelible ink, were the initials M.H.

Henry gave some urgent instructions to Reynolds, made several telephone calls, and then sent for Gordon Trapp, who was, to say the least of it, disgruntled. He shambled into the office like a sleepy bear, having been rudely awakened from the bench in the canteen where he had been snatching forty uncomfortable winks.

"For God's sake, Tibbett," he began before Henry could open his mouth, "this is beyond a joke. Keeping me here all night, as if I were a ruddy suspect. I can't see why . . ." He stopped dead and rubbed his eyes. Then he said, "That's Mike's knapsack."

"Thank you," said Henry. "Sorry about waking you up, but I hoped you'd be able to identify it."

Trapp sat down heavily in the chair vacated by the foreign-office man. He said, "Where did you find it?"

"It was left in the back of a taxi around half past nine last night."

"And Mike?"

"Heaven knows."

"You haven't found him yet?"

"No, not yet."

"But, my God . . ."

"We're doing all we can. We can be reasonably sure now that his disappearance wasn't voluntary. He's been abducted, and pains have been taken to make it appear that he never existed at all. If the kidnapers hadn't made an elementary mistake . . ."

"What was that?" Trapp sounded interested.

"Leaving the wedge of cardboard in your telephone," said Henry. "If it hadn't been for that, I might easily have refused to believe in Honeyman's existence . . ."

"But you had my word for it . . ."

"It may interest you to know," said Henry, "that both Mambesi and Galunga deny they have ever heard of the man."

"That's not surprising . . ."

"You accused me earlier this evening of being naïve," said Henry. "I think we can now call it quits. You were extremely lucky to have your unlikely story believed; and if I'd refused to listen to you, it would have been too bad for Honeyman. His knapsack would have been handed in to the lost property office, where it would have moldered for months. Its contents have almost certainly been burned. Honeyman would have disappeared permanently, with no questions asked."

"But I would have . . ."

"Exactly. Only you knew that Honeyman was in England. So you, too, would have been disposed of." Henry tapped his desk with a pencil. "Now, what we have to remember is that, as far as we know, the kidnapers think they have succeeded. Their next step will be to eliminate you."

Trapp was looking wide awake and distinctly uncomfortable. "I see what you mean, old scout," he said.

"I'm glad that you are taking your own position a bit seriously at last," said Henry. "Now, we have to proceed on the assumption that our friends are unaware of your visit to Effingham Court after dinner and of your presence here. So this is the way we are going to play it. You went out early this evening to dine with friends in Chelsea, leaving Honeyman in your apartment. Your dinner ended up as quite a party, in fact, you all went on to a night club. Your friends then persuaded you to come back and spend the rest of the night at their house. Now, I understand that, as far as PIFL is concerned, you are on vacation as of tomorrow."

"Yes, except for the cocktail party."

"You will miss that, I'm afraid," said Henry. "You have suddenly made up your mind to take a trip to the Continent."

"Have I? When do I leave?"

"Tomorrow morning, or rather, today. You will fly to Paris on the early plane."

"But I've no money . . ."

"That will be provided. Fortunately, you have your passport. From Paris you will go to the Gare de Lyon and get on a train heading south. At the first available stop you will quietly leave the train and make your way by the most inconvenient possible route to Amsterdam. There you will have a rendezvous on the terrace outside the American Hotel at twelve noon on Sunday. Or in the large bar, if wet."

Trapp was looking slightly dazed. "A rendezvous with whom?"

"With me," said Henry, "and with Emmy. We have decided to take a short holiday in Holland."

Trapp shrugged his shoulders and laughed. "I begin to see what happens," he said, "when you decide to take something seriously. Meanwhile . . ."

"Meanwhile," said Henry, "Emmy is waiting for you."

"Emmy is? Where?"

"At Dorabella's."

"Dorabella's?"

"Don't you know it? The discothéque in Bean Street, Mayfair. Emmy and Sergeant Reynolds are currently whooping it up. You will join them there; you will all leave when the place closes at four thirty; and you will go home to Chelsea with Emmy. She will offer you our spare bed for the night."

"I am speechless," said Gordon Trapp.

Henry smiled. "That's something, isn't it?" he said pleasantly. "Now, you'd better be getting along or Dorabella will be putting up the shutters before you get there. Here's some money. I'll give you some more and your plane ticket at home."

As Trapp was leaving the office, Henry picked up his telephone. He said, "Get me Parsons again, will you, the chap who reported on Miss La Rue . . ."

At the door Trapp stopped dead and then wheeled around to face Henry again. "What's that about Miss La Rue?" he demanded.

Henry put the phone down. "I beg your pardon?"

"I said, 'What's that about Miss La Rue'—in case you didn't hear the first time. You'll bloody well leave her out of this."

Henry was puzzled. "You know her?"

"Well, of course I do. And I refuse to have her dragged into . . ."

"Wait a minute," said Henry. "I must get this straight. You are a friend of Madeleine La Rue . . ."

"Madeleine? Who's Madeleine?"

"Miss La Rue, of course."

Trapp relaxed. "Oh, I get it. Sorry, old man. Case of mistaken identity. But it's a fairly unusual name."

"You know a Miss La Rue?"

"Certainly old man. And so do you. The beautiful secretary to whom I introduced you this afternoon, Yvonne La Rue. Well, so long. I'll be getting on to Dorabella's."

Emmy and Sergeant Reynolds were enjoying themselves. Emmy had long ago ceased to be surprised at anything Henry might ask her to do, and when he had telephoned her at 2:00 A.M. and told her to put on her glad rags and expect an escort in a taxi to pick her up and take her dancing, she had merely said, "Oh, very well. I wasn't actually asleep."

Sergeant Reynolds had had distinct misgivings about squiring his superior officer's wife to a smart night spot in such a way as to suggest a merry evening out on the town with a girl friend; but Emmy's natural good humor and unabashed enjoyment of the discothéque had soon broken down his reserve. He discovered that she was a good dancer as well as an amusing companion, and by the time Gordon Trapp arrived, anyone might well have been deceived into thinking that this was a gay tête-à-tête and that neither party was particularly pleased to be interrupted, even by an old friend.

However, they ordered another bottle of wine, and then Dorabella regretfully announced that she was closing for the evening, or, rather, the morning. So a taxi was called, which drove all three revelers back to Chelsea. There it dropped Emmy and Trapp before taking Reynolds on to his home in Battersea. The incident was watched with interest by a very cold, bored individual who had been surveying the house for several hours. He was very glad to be able to phone in his report and head for his bed.

Inside the house Emmy said, "What on earth is all this about?"

Gordon Trapp raised his eyebrows, "Don't you know?"

Emmy grinned. "With Henry," she said, "I've learned over the years to obey orders first and ask questions afterward."

"Is he always so melodramatic in his methods?"

"No," said Emmy, frowning slightly. "Actually, Henry isn't melodramatic at all. He must be taking this very seriously —whatever it is."

"His very words," said Trapp. "Well, I gather you are going to offer me your spare bed, which I accept with pleasure. And you'd better get your beauty sleep. You'll need to start packing tomorrow."

"Packing? What on earth for?"

"For your holiday in Holland."

"Oh, don't be silly," said Emmy. She yawned. "The spare bed is made up. See you in the morning. Or the afternoon, if you like. I won't wake you."

"If only," said Trapp, "your husband were more like you."

"What does that mean?"

"Only that he's booked me on an early plane to Paris, blast his eyes. I suppose he'll be along to kick me out of bed about seven."

But the fact was even worse. It was at six o'clock—little more than an hour after Trapp had collapsed into a deep and dreamless sleep—that he was awakened by an urgent shaking of his shoulder. He opened a bleary eye to see Henry standing by his bed, fully dressed, and holding a cup of tea.

"What in hell . . . ?"

"I'm sorry," said Henry. "It's six o'clock. We've so little time. Must talk to you. Have some tea." He sounded as tired as he looked.

Trapp grunted. Then reluctantly he heaved himself into a sitting position, accepted the tea, and swallowed it in one gulp.

Henry sat down on the bed and said, "I must know all about Miss La Rue."

"Yvonne? You'd better not start getting any unpleasant ideas about Yvonne or you'll have me to deal with. She's the . . ."

"If you're so sure about her," said Henry, "you certainly won't object to answering a few simple, innocent questions."

"Let's hear the questions first. Then I'll tell you if I consider them simple and innocent."

"Who is she? How long have you known her? How long has she been at PIFL? Where does she . . ."

"Here, have a heart, old man. One thing at a time." Trapp shook his head, as if to free it from a swarm of bees. "Who is she? You know who she is, PIFL's senior secretary. That's to say, she's permanent, as it were, and she hires minions to do extra typing and stenography when the commission is in session. I've known her for about six months. Since she took the job, in fact."

"You mean you've worked at PIFL for longer than she has?"

"That's right."

"So she joined the commission when the Mambesi-Galunga case was well under way."

"That's not a crime, is it?"

"It might be," said Henry grimly.

"I've never heard such a load of tripe." Gordon Trapp was wide awake now. "Why the hell shouldn't she take the job? We were in a hell of a hole, as a matter of fact, with Horseface pushing off like that . . ."

"Who doing what?"

"Yvonne's predecessor. Face like a horse, hence the nickname. Not a bad soul, and super-efficient. Been there for years. And then one day, out of the blue, she simply announced she was leaving. Handed back a month's salary in lieu of notice. Apparently she'd been offered some fabulous job overseas at a princely salary, provided she could start right away. So, of course, she upped and went. It was in the middle of the public hearings, and we were fairly lost until Yvonne turned up asking for a job. It seemed too good to be true—I mean, that any bird who looked like that could be a secretary as well. But it was a case of any port in a storm and she was signed up. The astonishing thing is that she's turned out to be even more efficient than Horseface."

"Very interesting," said Henry. "What is this Horseface woman's name, and where was the job she went to?"

"Philips. Joan Philips. The job was in America, I think."

"We'll find out," said Henry. "Now, who knows which way the members of the commission are going to vote?"

"What?"

"These private meetings where they air their views. Would Yvonne La Rue have access to minutes, or . . ."

"No, no. We don't take minutes."

"So apart from the commission members, only you and your fellow interpreter know what goes on. Curious that Miss La Rue should be so friendly with both of you."

"I don't think I care for your tone, old man. If you are implying . . ."

"Please don't waste time," said Henry. "Did Yvonne get you to tell her how the various members were going to vote?"

Trapp was looking worried. He said, "I didn't tell her anything. Those meetings are strictly private. I've told nobody except you."

"But she tried to pump you?"

"Well—no, you couldn't call it that. Naturally, we discussed the case sometimes . . ."

"And so, when she couldn't get all the information she wanted from you, she switched her attention to Monsieur Malvaux?"

"Look here, Tibbett, I've told you I don't like . . ."

"Where does Yvonne live?"

"In Kensington, 26 Beechwood Gardens, top floor."

"She lives alone?"

"Yes."

"No family?"

"Not that I know of."

"Not a sister, for example?"

"Not as far as I . . ." Trapp suddenly put down his teacup. "Here, wait a minute. Madeleine, you said."

"That's right."

"I've just remembered. A few weeks ago I was at Yvonne's place one evening. I was taking her out to dinner and we were having a drink at Beechwood Gardens first, when the phone rang. Yvonne went into the bedroom to answer it, and I heard her say, 'Hello, Mady, darling.' Then she shut the bedroom door, so that I couldn't hear any more, and she talked on that blasted blower for bloody hours. I was very fed up, because I'd reserved a table and we were late already, and I told her so in no uncertain manner when she finally emerged. And she said she was terribly sorry, that it had been a question of family business to settle. She'd been talking to her sister, she said."

9

Shortly after seven o'clock Sergeant Reynolds drove a still-yawning Gordon Trapp to London Airport to catch the plane for Paris. At Henry's insistence, Trapp had left the house not by the front door but by the small gate in the wall of the back garden, which gave onto a narrow mews. Henry had borne with good humor Trapp's heavily ironic comments on this cloak-and-dagger procedure. He had not mentioned—for there was no sense in alarming the man unnecessarily—that the detective watching the front of the Tibbett house had reported that he was not the only person apparently interested in the building. Nor did Henry think it advisable to confide in Trapp that one of his fellow passengers on the Paris flight would be a plainclothes policeman.

As soon as Reynolds and Trapp were safely on their way Henry went back to Scotland Yard. He arrived soon after half past seven and was informed that both the Misses La Rue were already there, having been hauled from their respective beds by the long arm of the law. In accordance with Henry's instructions, they were waiting in separate rooms, and neither knew of the other's presence. Yvonne, said the duty sergeant, seemed shaken and scared; Madeleine was merely angry. Henry sent for Madeleine and prepared himself for a stormy session.

As it turned out, however, she was deceptively docile. She walked quietly into the office, beautifully groomed as ever in spite of the early hour, and asked in a voice of pure honey how she could help the Superintendent. Had the police solved the mystery of poor "Flutter's" black-bearded murderer? Or could she help them to do so? It was terrible, wasn't it, to think of a man like that being at large, armed, and probably preparing to strike again? So anything that she could . . .

Henry said brusquely, "How did you spend yesterday evening, Miss La Rue?"

Madeleine's violet eyes opened wider than ever. "Yesterday evening? But why?"

"Just answer the question, please."

"But of course, Superintendent. Let me see. I went to my hairdresser in the afternoon, Pierre of Mayfair in Bond Street. I left there just after five, and took a taxi back to—to my uncle's place. He wasn't in. The barman told me that he had been asked to come here for another little chat with you." Madeleine favored Henry with a ravishing smile. "I went to my room. Soon afterward, my uncle came back. We had a drink together in his private sitting room, and then he went to take over the bar. I changed my dress and went into the bar myself soon after seven. I asked my uncle to telephone for a cab for me. I was going out, you see."

"Where to?"

"How inquisitive you are, Superintendent. I had arranged to meet a friend at Dominic's Hotel."

"And who was this friend?"

This time there was distinct mischief in Madeleine's smile. "I'm sorry to disappoint you, Superintendent. It was a girl friend."

"I would like to know her name," said Henry.

Madeleine's face clouded. "Oh, must I tell you?"

"Yes, I'm afraid you must."

"I was hoping I wouldn't have to . . ."

"Very chivalrous of you," said Henry, "but I must know."

"Well—then I shall have to own up. I told you a small white lie, Superintendent. It wasn't a girl friend I went to meet."

"I see. So it was a man."

"Oh, no. Certainly not. It was"—a tiny hesitation—"it was my sister, my sister, Yvonne."

Henry said nothing.

Madeleine went on. "We—we're not very close, Superintendent. Not like some sisters. I travel a great deal, and—let's face it—I'm a frivolous sort of person. Yvonne is quite different. A real career girl. We don't often meet, even when we are both in London. However, she telephoned me yesterday evening after I got in from the hairdresser's and suggested we should dine together, as there was some family business to discuss."

"So you dined at Dominic's with your sister?"

"Well—actually, no. When I got there I found a message from Yvonne at the reception desk saying that she wasn't feeling very well and asking me to go straight to her apartment —she lives in Beechwood Gardens—and have a light supper there. So I took a cab and went there. We had our meal, talked over our family business, and then I took a taxi home. At about half past nine." Madeleine paused for a moment and added, "I can see that you're going to ask me what the family business was. Well, I don't want to tell you, but obviously I must. It was about our mother. Father died some time ago, and mother is—well—to be frank, Superintendent, she's senile, poor darling. She's in a nursing home at Worthing. Yvonne and I between us pay for her keep. The matron had written to Yvonne to say that the fees were going up, so naturally we had to meet to discuss it." Madeleine's violet eyes were as open and innocent as a kitten's, and Henry reflected that it was bad luck for her that he had previously encountered her in a different mood. Otherwise, he might well have been taken in.

He said, "So you spent the entire evening with your sister in her apartment?"

"Yes. Oh—we went out once, to the liquor store on the corner to buy a bottle of wine. Yvonne had nothing to drink in the house. Otherwise, we were there the whole evening."

"Any other visitors?"

"No. Nobody."

"And you arrived at The Pink Parrot at about half past nine carrying a suitcase which you had not had with you when you went out."

Madeleine laughed ripplingly. "I can't think why you

bother to ask me what I did last night," she said. "It can have no possible bearing on 'Flutter's' death, for one thing, and for another, you seem to know as well as I do. I suppose you've got a man watching The Pink Parrot. Yes, you're absolutely right. I arrived home with a suitcase which I had borrowed from Yvonne, because I'm hoping to go abroad again soon. There was nothing sinister in the suitcase, Superintendent, I can assure you. In fact, it was empty."

"And why did you change taxis in Kensington on the way back?"

Again the amused laugh. "You know everything, don't you? It's very simple. The first cabby I found was on his way home and refused to take me farther than Pontings. Cabs are few and far between in Beechwood Gardens, so I agreed, assuming that I would pick up another quite easily in the High Street. And so I did."

Further than this Henry could not get. It was one thing not to believe a word of the story, and quite another to break it, and Madeleine knew that as well as Henry did. Also, he was hampered by not being able to mention Mike Honeyman; but he knew that his only hope was to prevent "them" from realizing that he knew anything about Honeyman. It must appear that all his inquiries had to do with the murder of Byers. He dismissed Madeleine but asked her to wait. He then began to check.

Miss Minster at Dominic's Hotel was helpfulness itself. Yes, she knew Miss La Rue well by sight; she often came into the hotel. Last evening, just before half past seven, a pageboy had brought an envelope to the reception desk. A message for Miss La Rue, who would be arriving shortly, he had said. Sure enough, a few minutes later Miss La Rue came in. Miss Minster had handed her the envelope. Miss La Rue had opened it and then said to Miss Minster that she wouldn't be dining at the hotel after all, as her sister wasn't well. She had asked the bell captain to get her a taxi.

The bell captain remembered that Miss La Rue had given the cabby an address in Beechwood Gardens. The proprietor of the liquor store remembered that Miss Yvonne La Rue, one of his regular customers, had come in around eight o'clock with another very attractive young lady, whom she had introduced as her sister. They had bought a bottle of Volnay. The nursing home in Worthing, whose name Madeleine had willingly divulged, confirmed that they had an elderly patient named Mrs. La Rue in their care.

Henry sighed. The story was as smooth and uncrackable as a marble egg. He told the duty sergeant that Madeleine might be allowed to go home and asked him to send Yvonne into the office.

There could hardly have been a greater contrast between the two sisters. Now that he knew their relationship, Henry could see that there was a family likeness; but this marked the beginning and end of any resemblance. Madeleine was honey-blond, seductive, and gay; Yvonne was dark, neat, and grave. While Madeleine played with fire as if it were a trinket for her amusement, Yvonne was white-faced, earnest, and afraid.

She gave a little gasp when she saw Henry. "Mr. Tibbett! Gordon Trapp's friend . . ."

Henry smiled, shook hands, and admitted his identity.

"But, Superintendent, there hasn't been any trouble at PIFL, has there? I mean . . ."

"No, no, no. My visit there was purely friendly. I had been lunching with Gordon and he offered to show me around." Henry cleared his throat. "Now, Miss La Rue, to get to official business. Your sister must have told you that she has been helping us with this shooting case in The Pink Parrot?"

"Well, yes, she did just mention it. We don't see much of each other actually . . ."

"But you saw her last night?"

"Yes."

"Please tell me about it."

Yvonne's story confirmed Madeleine's in every detail—the senile mother, the increased nursing home fees, the arrangement to dine at Dominic's. "But then, Superintendent, I developed a really terrible headache. I get them sometimes. I just couldn't face going out. So I telephoned Dominic's and left a message that Mady should come to my apartment. We had a very simple dinner—spaghetti and eggs—yes, we went out to the liquor store for a bottle of wine. Mady always likes to have a drink. No, I'm not teetotal, but I drink very little, only on social occasions. There wasn't a drop of alcohol in the house, so we went and bought a bottle of wine. I always use that liquor store if I'm having visitors; it's so convenient."

Madeleine, said Yvonne, had been most generous in offering extra financial help for their mother. Mady was a sweet, open, warm-hearted person, really; but—well—Henry could see how different they were, couldn't he? And then Mady was always on the move. "I expect she told you; she's off to the Continent again. I lent her my little blue suitcase. It's such a useful size."

"I'm interested to hear that your sister was able to offer more money for her mother," said Henry. "Has she a private income?"

Yvonne blushed. "Well, not exactly. That is, Mady has so many good friends. People are generous to her."

"Like her uncle?" said Henry ingenuously.

Yvonne was taken off guard. "Uncle?" She looked scared stiff.

"Hers and yours, of course," said Henry. "I presume that your mother was a Miss Weatherby."

"Oh." Yvonne recovered and smiled. "You mean Major Weatherby. He's not really our uncle. That's just a courtesy title. He's—he's an old friend of the family. Yes, he has always been especially kind to Mady."

Once again Henry was up against a blank wall. Once again the marble egg remained inviolate. Frustrated, Henry abandoned any idea of confronting the two sisters with each other. Their story had been too carefully worked out for any slip-up to occur. And, at the back of his mind, he was beginning to develop a nagging doubt. Of all the marble eggs he knew, the most uncrackable was the truth. There was, after all, no

117

proof that it was Madeleine La Rue who had left Honeyman's knapsack in that taxi. It would seem like a fantastic coincidence if it had been hidden there by another passenger, but truth can be stranger than fiction, and coincidences do happen. Henry thanked Yvonne and told her she could go.

He was just making arrangements to have Jack Wotherspoon questioned again, with a view to checking up on his other fares, when Sergeant Reynolds called to report Gordon Trapp's safe departure for Paris. There had been nothing suspicious at the airport, nothing to suggest that "they"—whoever "they" might be—knew of Trapp's departure. Detective Constable Arkwright had traveled on the same airplane.

Sergeant Reynolds had reached the end of his account and announced his intention of going up to the canteen for some breakfast when he suddenly said, "Hold on a minute, sir. Something's just coming in. I'm speaking from the Criminal Records Office, right near the teleprinter, and there's a report from Essex—Brittlesea—I'll check up on it and be right along, sir . . ."

A quarter of an hour later Sergeant Reynolds was in Henry's office in a state of high excitement. "I think we've got a line on Honeyman at last, sir."

"Good work, Sergeant. What is it?"

"This report from Brittlesea, sir."

"You mean, he's been seen . . . ?"

"No, sir, I'm afraid not. Not actually seen. But the secretary of the Brittlesea Flying Club has called the local police to report that a light airplane is missing from the club's hangar. It must have been stolen during the night."

"Stolen?" repeated Henry. "How on earth would anyone steal an airplane?"

"It seems it wouldn't have been too difficult in this case, sir, not for an experienced pilot," Reynolds added with a wealth of emphasis. "You see, the club airfield is out on the marshes, eight miles from Brittlesea. There's nobody there at night, no houses nearby, nothing. The lock on the hangar door had been broken, which wouldn't have been difficult to

118

do, the secretary says. I mean to say, it's not the sort of thing you expect, is it? Having airplanes pinched, I mean."

"And how would anybody have reached this airfield in the middle of the night?" Henry asked.

"Well, sir, the obvious way would be to have an accomplice drive one out there. But Honeyman could have done it on his own from London."

"How?"

"There's a good train service to Brittlesea, and the Friday-evening trains are always crowded with weekenders from London. The last train gets into Brittlesea just before midnight. And the police did find an old bicycle abandoned on the airfield. There's been the usual crop of bikes reported stolen in Brittlesea last night, and this could have been one of them . . ."

"I don't want to pour cold water on your lovely theory, Sergeant," said Henry, "but it does occur to me to wonder how in the name of glory Honeyman would have known anything at all about Brittlesea Flying Club. He only arrived in England yesterday, after ten years or more in Africa. He told Mr. Trapp he knew nobody in London . . ."

Henry stopped. Reynolds was looking at him with the expression of a cat who has stumbled on a bowl of cream.

"That occurred to me too, sir," said the Sergeant, rolling the words around his tongue. "And so I had the secretary go back over the membership records. It may interest you to know that Mr. Honeyman learned to fly there, just before the war, when he was a youngster. It seems the family lived up Brittlesea way, and Honeyman's father was a founder member of the club, so it would be only natural, wouldn't it . . . ?"

"It certainly makes a very neat, rounded picture, Sergeant," said Henry. "But I wonder why he didn't take his knapsack with him?"

"His knapsack, sir?"

"The one that was found in the taxi. And in any case, why should Honeyman disappear voluntarily? He had no money.

He had spent his last penny getting to England. He had told his story to Trapp and was eager to tell it in more influential quarters. If Honeyman decided to vanish of his own free will, I'll fricassee my bowler and eat it with tomato sauce."

Reynolds was looking decidedly crestfallen. "But, sir, it seemed so logical, his having been a member of the club and everything . . ."

"Exactly," said Henry. "You say he qualified as a pilot there. In that case, it's very likely that there's a mention of Brittle-sea on his pilot's license, which he would certainly have with him. If you ask me, this little stunt has been arranged very neatly to give the impression that Honeyman has run off. But I'd like to remind you that it wouldn't be the first time that a weighted body has been dropped into the North Sea from a light airplane. A very efficient method of corpse disposal."

Reynolds said nothing. His expression was now that of a cat whose saucer of cream has turned out to be soap suds after all.

Henry said, "Dammit, Sergeant, we're either the victims of a not very funny hoax, springing from Trapp's overheated imagination, or else we are up against a very big, rich, and powerful organization."

"Major Weatherby . . ." Reynolds began.

"Small fry," said Henry. "Weatherby, Byers—all small fry."

"And the Misses La Rue, sir?"

"I wish to hell I knew," said Henry. "I just don't. There's no reason why the brains behind all this shouldn't be a woman."

"Yvonne La Rue . . ."

"I shouldn't think so," said Henry. "She's been working in the field, as it were. An executive officer, but not the com-mander-in-chief. But Madeleine . . . By the way, Sergeant, she's not to be allowed to leave the country. Get me the Home Office. Her passport . . ."

It was, the Home Office pointed out, a delicate situation. Miss La Rue was not being accused of any crime, was she? Not at this stage, Henry said. She was, however, required as a witness. A witness in what case, against whom? Well—the investigations into the murder of Byers. Hm, said the Home Office. Yes. She could certainly be *requested* not to leave the country. As to impounding her passport, there were legal difficulties, as Henry must know. In the circumstances, a firmly worded request would seem to be the most satisfactory answer. Of course, if the Superintendent had solid grounds for suspecting Miss La Rue of a specific crime . . .

Feeling distinctly frustrated, Henry decided to handle the matter himself, which enabled him to get out of the somewhat oppressive atmosphere of the office. He drove to The Pink Parrot.

He got there at a quarter to ten. The building was apparently bolted and barred and showed no sign of life. However, in response to repeated peals on the doorbell, Henry at last heard a shuffle of feet inside the house, followed by the sound of bolts being shot and keys turning. Then the door opened, and Henry found himself gazing at the unappetizing sight of Major George Weatherby dressed in a loudly checked dressing gown. He was tousled, red-eyed, and predictably angry.

"Ye gods," he remarked, "you again! Second time this morning. Can't get a wink of sleep in this house. Policeman dragging my niece out of her bed at crack of dawn—just got off to sleep again—now this . . ."

"I'm sorry, Major Weatherby," said Henry politely. "You must remember that a murder has been committed on your premises. We're bound to take a close interest."

The Major made an unprintable remark about close interest and grudgingly allowed Henry to enter the bleak bar.

"As a matter of fact," said Henry, "it's your niece I want to see."

"Again?"

"Again. So if you don't mind calling her . . ."

"I certainly do mind," retorted the Major with spirit, "but as it happens, what I mind or don't mind doesn't come into it. She's not here."

"Not here? But she left the Yard . . ."

"Oh, yes. She got back here—waking me up again, I may say—soon after eight. And she stayed precisely long enough to do her packing. She's gone."

"Gone where?"

The Major shrugged elaborately. "Search me, Superintendent. She comes and goes, you know. I think she mentioned Amsterdam the other day, but she may well have changed her mind . . ."

It was, of course, too late. Miss Madeleine La Rue, subsequent inquiries showed, had arrived at London Airport at a quarter to nine. She had approached the KLM desk and asked the time of the next flight to Amsterdam. On being told that it left at twenty-five minutes past nine, she had purchased a ticket on the spot, paying in cash, and had boarded the airplane. By the time Henry and his legal machinery caught up with her, she had already disembarked at Schiphol airport a few miles outside Amsterdam and might now be almost anywhere.

And all the time, at the back of Henry's mind, was the picture of that uncrackable egg, the truth. Madeleine had been perfectly frank. She had not concealed from Henry her intention of going to Amsterdam. She had borrowed a suitcase from her sister for the purpose. Could there be no more to it than that? Henry swore mentally and went on to Beechwood Gardens.

Yvonne La Rue was at home. She had put a brightly printed cotton apron over her street clothes and was engaged prettily and domestically in running the vacuum cleaner over her apartment when Henry arrived. She welcomed him like an old friend and seemed much more relaxed than at their previous interview; after all, nobody likes being dragged to Scotland Yard at seven o'clock in the morning. She invited Henry in and apologized for the untidiness. She had not yet, she explained, washed up after last night.

The apartment consisted of the fourth floor of a narrow, ugly house in a nineteenth-century backwater. It had origi-

122

nally been the servants' quarters, and all the ceilings had sloping angles to them, which made them rather more interesting architecturally than the tall, square boxes of rooms on the more expensive floors below. There were three rooms—a reasonably sized living room, a small bedroom, and an overgrown cupboard which had been pressed into service as a dining room. A fourth room had been fitted with an *ad hoc* hardboard partition, which divided it into a minuscule kitchen and bathroom. Remembering what Trapp had said, Henry noted that the telephone was in the bedroom and that—since the living room was at the far end of the landing—it was unlikely that a telephone conversation could have been overheard from the living room if the intervening doors were closed.

There were dirty dishes in the kitchen sink and an empty bottle which had contained Volnay stood on the table.

Henry followed Yvonne into the living room, where she had been busy with the vacuum cleaner.

He said, "I'm very sorry to trouble you again, Miss La Rue, but I think you may be able to help me."

"Of course, if I can."

"I've just been at The Pink Parrot. By the way, does your sister always stay there when she comes to London?"

"She has a lot of friends, Superintendent. Sometimes she stays with them, at their houses—or in hotels. But when she comes here on her own, she generally stays with Uncle George."

"Who is not her uncle."

"Well, I explained. An old family friend. Surely one finds the same honorary uncles and aunts in every family."

Henry hesitated. Yvonne's "Uncle George," applied to Major Weatherby, sounded phony and almost obscene. And yet Henry could not deny that he himself was called "Uncle" by the daughters of an old school friend of Emmy's.

He said, "At all events I was unlucky."

"Unlucky?"

"I missed Madeleine."

"Oh—well—yes, you would have, wouldn't you?"

"What do you mean by that?"

"Well, she told me last night that she was off to Amsterdam this morning. That's why I lent her my suitcase."

"You never told me she was going so soon."

Yvonne smiled again, with a little touch of bewilderment that was very attractive. "You didn't ask me, Superintendent."

Henry had to concede that this was true. He said, "Well, be that as it may, can you give me any idea where she usually stays in Amsterdam?"

"I'm afraid I can't, Superintendent. As I told you, we saw so little of each other."

"You've no idea at all?"

"None. Oh, I am sorry. You've come all the way here and climbed my eighty-one stairs for nothing. At least let me give you a cup of tea. I was just going to make one for myself."

"No, thank you," said Henry. "It's very kind of you, but I seldom drink tea . . ."

"Oh, dear," said Yvonne. "I am a shocking hostess. Of course, you want a proper drink, and I can't offer you one. I never keep any in the house, and Madeleine and I killed the bottle of wine last night . . ."

Henry protested that he wanted nothing to drink, alcoholic or otherwise. His thirst was for information, and clearly he was going to get none.

It was entirely by chance that as he was leaving he happened to trip over the electric cord of the vacuum cleaner. Had he not been so clumsy, he would not have knocked the cleaner away from the place where Yvonne had left it, in front of the bookcase in the living room; and had he not knocked the vacuum cleaner to one side he would not have noticed the bottle of Highland Dream whisky, three-quarters full, which was standing behind a row of books on the lowest shelf of the bookcase. As it was, Henry did not remark on this interesting sight; he merely stored it up in his memory for future reference.

10

Gordon Trapp was having an uneventful journey. The plane to Paris was by no means full, and Trapp had been one of the first passengers to board it. With an expertise born of long years of short-haul air travel, he had stationed himself in the airport lounge at just the right spot to pass through the check-out door first, without any appearance of pushing; and, once aboard, he had made a beeline for the particular seat which he knew from experience was the most desirable on that make of plane for an economy-class passenger. This was the window side of the first pair of seats. Ahead was the partition giving onto the first-class compartment, and Gordon Trapp knew very well that his long legs would have room to stretch themselves in a way impossible for the serried ranks behind him.

For a while he thought that he was going to enjoy the supreme luxury of having the pair of seats to himself; but, at the last moment, another tall man came and sat down in the place beside him. The journey started with a customary, correct, and very British silence between the two men, but by the time breakfast had been served, Trapp and his companion were on cordial terms. They agreed on the martyrdom to which tall men were subjected on any form of public transportation. "All designed for dwarfs," said Trapp feelingly. His companion concurred.

This led naturally to a discussion as to the most tolerable means of traveling available to those over six feet in height.

"Cars are no use these days, unless one can afford a Rolls," remarked Trapp's companion. "If they're not Mini by name, they're mini by nature. And trains are just as bad, don't you agree?"

"Terrible," said Trapp. "Mobile sardine cans."

"With one honorable exception, of course, the T-E-E. Let us give honor where it is due."

"Ah, yes, the Trans-Europe expresses. Wonderful trains."

"But then, of course, quite apart from the extra expense, you can't always by any means get a T-E-E going where you want and when you want it." The tall man lit a cigarette and then hastily offered his silver case to Gordon Trapp. "So sorry, old man. Do you smoke?"

"Not for the moment, thanks."

The tall man drew deeply on his cigarette. "Well, at least Paris isn't too far." He glanced at his watch. "Another ten minutes, and our agony will be over. Or are you traveling farther on?"

"I am, as a matter of fact."

"You have my sympathy. Air or rail?"

"Rail."

"T-E-E, I trust."

"I fear not. Just an ordinary train."

"You're not heading southward, then?"

Trapp looked surprised. "Why do you say that? As a matter of fact, I am. I'm heading for a few days in Antibes and some sun, with any luck."

"Then, my dear fellow, why aren't you taking the Mistral?"

"The what?"

"The one-o'clock T-E-E to Nice. You must be out of your mind."

"But my train leaves at twenty past nine. It's a slightly dicey connection with this plane."

"My dear fellow," said the tall man, "I know that train. Stopping all the way and a change at Lyon—*if* you catch it, which you may not if the Paris traffic is bad. And it only gets to Nice an hour or so before the Mistral."

"Really?"

"I suppose you were booked on it by some wretched travel agent. Ought to be shot, the lot of them. Incompetent. They just look up the train that leaves first, without dreaming of using their common sense to check whether there may not be an express a little later. I'd change your reservation, my dear chap. I really would."

"I say, do you really think I could change trains?" Trapp sounded genuinely enthusiastic.

"Of course, old man. You have to pay the supplement, of course. But if there's a seat vacant, which there should be at this time of year . . ."

"And you say it arrives only an hour after the nine-twenty-one?"

"It does. So you can have a leisurely morning in Paris and travel in comfort."

"Well, I must say, it was a stroke of luck meeting you. I'll most certainly do that. How do I set about it, do you think?"

"Just go to the booking office at the Gare de Lyon with your ticket, old man. Simplicity itself."

"You must travel a great deal yourself to be so knowledgeable about French railways," said Trapp with a touch of envy.

"Oh, a fair amount, you know. Business rather than pleasure, alas." The tall man smiled attractively. "Am I to understand that you don't?"

"Very seldom, I'm afraid. Just the odd holiday, if I'm lucky. I wouldn't be here now, only the organization I work for is having an extra-long Easter break. I really am extremely grateful to you, Mr. er . . ."

"Pierce. Herbert Pierce. Let me give you my card." The tall man produced a pigskin wallet from his breast pocket and pulled out an engraved visiting card. It was inscribed: *Herbert G. Pierce. Export Manager. Amalgamated British Chemicals.*

Mr. Pierce smiled again, a little diffidently this time, and added, "And, if I may ask, whom have I had the pleasure of . . ."

At that moment a wasplike buzzing filled the cabin and a female voice crackled over the loudspeaker. "Ladies and gentlemen, may I have your attention please? In a few moments we shall be landing at Orly Airport, Paris. Please extinguish all cigarettes and cigars, and fasten your seat belts. Kindly

127

remain seated until the airplane has completely stopped. Thank you. *Mesdames et Messieurs, dans quelques instants . . .*"

The engine noise roared up as the pilot put the nose down to land.

Trapp shouted above it, "My name's Trapp, Gordon Trapp . . ." The tall man seemed very busy with his seat belt, and Trapp could not be sure whether he had heard.

When the great airplane had finally rolled to a full stop on the tarmac, the tall man leaped to his feet with great agility. He had ignored the hostess' injunction and had, in fact, undone his seat belt, put on his raincoat, and assembled his briefcase and Trilby hat while the plane was still taxiing.

"Well, old man," said Pierce, "I'll bid you *au revoir,* and *bon voyage.*"

"You're not traveling on yourself?" Trapp felt at a disadvantage, still imprisoned in his seat and fiddling with the metal flap of his canvas belt.

"No, no. I have an appointment in Paris—for which I shall be late if I don't hurry. Good-bye now."

With practiced deftness Pierce made off down the aisle toward the door at the rear, seeming to slide between the other passengers, who were still collecting their packages and struggling to get their coats down from the overhead rack. He was, in fact, the third person to leave the plane. Gordon Trapp was the last. By the time Trapp had passed through customs and immigration there was no sign whatsoever of Pierce, nor was he on the airline bus which carried the passengers from Orly into Paris.

At the terminal Trapp ordered a taxi to the Gare de Lyon. There, he went at once to the booking office and asked whether it would be possible to cancel his reservation to Nice on the 9:21 train and reserve instead a seat on the Mistral express at 1:10. He was only too willing, he said, to pay the necessary supplement. The clerk was most obliging. There was a seat vacant. Tickets were prepared and money changed hands. The transaction was completed.

Leaving the office, Trapp was almost—but not quite—sure that the small, slightly built man in the shabby raincoat who was buying *Le Monde* at the nearby newsstand had been on the plane from London. This fact, however, did not worry him unduly. He looked at his watch—a quarter past nine. There was quite a lot of time to kill. He walked into the station buffet, sat down at a small table, and ordered a *café complet*. He was perfectly happy to wait.

The secretary of the Brittlesea Flying Club was a jovial, portly, middle-aged man who was introduced to Henry as Squadron Leader Mandevell.

"Bad show, what? Never thought we'd have a kite half-inched out of the hangar. D'you know who did it then?"

"I've a pretty good idea," said Henry. "Do you remember a man called Honeyman?"

"Of course I do. Old Tubby Honeyman, one of our founder members. Flew with the R.F.C. in the first war and helped to found the club in the twenties. Great character. Dead now, of course."

"I think his son is the man I'm after," said Henry. "Mike Honeyman."

"Oh, yes. Your sergeant chappie said something about him. Yes, indeed. Mike joined us as a youngster shortly before the last little lot. Instructed him myself, as a matter of fact. Must be—what—thirty years ago. Good Lord. *Anno Domini* and all that. I thought young Mike was in Africa or India or somewhere."

"He was," said Henry, "but he came back to England yesterday. He would have been capable of flying this missing plane, would he?"

"Oh, surely. Not the same type that he trained on before the war, of course, but I understand he's specialized in light airplanes since then. Yes, Mike would have no trouble with her. But . . ."

"And how far could he have flown without refueling?"

"Oh, a considerable distance. As I pointed out to your chappies, this particular kite had been refueled on Friday afternoon, all ready for the Saturday morning pupils. She'd have a range of two hundred miles at least."

"Enough," said Henry, "to get to Holland, for instance?"

"Holland? Easily, old boy. Holland and back in time for tea. But why in heaven's name should young Mike Honeyman come sneaking along in the middle of the night and pinch a kite to go to Holland?"

"I don't know," said Henry. "It may well not have been him. Have you noticed any strangers hanging around the airfield recently?"

Mandevell looked at Henry pityingly. "My dear old policeman," he said, "flying clubs attract strangers like jam attracts wasps. People are always hanging around the perimeter, especially on fine Sunday afternoons, just to watch the pilots doing their circuits and bumps. There's a notice up about not parking cars, but . . ."

"I didn't mean outside," said Henry.

"Well, nobody's allowed inside except members and their guests. Girl friends, mostly. The lads like to show off a bit. Yes, we get quite a load of talent in the clubhouse of a weekend."

"But during this past week . . ."

"Nobody but our regular members, so far as I know, and not many of them. Weekends are our busy time, you see." Mandevell frowned and tugged at his enormous gray mustache. "What beats me is why young Honeyman should steal a kite? Goodness me, his father was one of my closest friends. He'd only to come and ask and I'd have let him have one, and welcome."

"That," said Henry, "has been bothering me, too."

By lunchtime Squadron Leader Mandevell was on his way back to Brittlesea, and Henry was snatching a quick meal in Scotland Yard's new canteen. It was half past one, and he was just embarking on his fruit salad when Sergeant Reynolds came in, a worried expression on his face and a paper in his hand.

"This has just come through, sir. I thought you ought to see it right away."

"What is it?"

"Detective Constable Arkwright's report from Paris, sir."

"Right, Sergeant. I'll get back to my office and take a look at it right away."

The report made cheerless reading, and the redness of the constable's face glowed through the regulation prose.

Trapp boarded the airplane at 0733 hours, taking the port-hand front seat in the economy class. I chose a seat further back, from which I could observe him. His seat neighbor was a fair man, about 6ft. 2in., unknown to me. During the flight Trapp chatted with this man, but as far as I could ascertain it was a casual conversation. Shortly before landing, the man handed Trapp a visiting card which he took from his wallet.

Trapp alighted from the aircraft at Orly at 0816 hours. He took a long time to undo his seat belt and assemble his hand luggage, so that I was forced to leave the airplane before him. I traveled with him on the airport bus, however, and at the Paris terminal I secured a taxi immediately behind his, instructing the driver to follow the cab ahead. This drove as expected to the Gare de Lyon. Here Trapp entered the booking office, and I overheard him changing his reservation from the 0921 train to the 1310 express, contrary to instructions. While buying a paper at the newsstand, I observed Trapp entering the buffet, but when I followed a minute or so later, I found that he had gone, leaving a pot of coffee and a plate of rolls untasted. It was now 0918 hrs., and I imagined that Trapp had been laying an elaborate false trail and intended after all to board the 0921 train as ordered. I made my way to the appropriate platform but can state positively that

Trapp was not among the travelers on the 0921. A further search of the Gare de Lyon revealed nothing, and I must now report that he did not, either, board the 1310 TEE train. Please confirm that Interpol should circulate Trapp's description . . .

Henry read the report twice, the first time with irritation and the second with a familiar and welcome sensation, a sort of prickling of intuition, which he sometimes referred to as his "nose." He rang for Sergeant Reynolds.

Reynolds was puzzled at Henry's request. "Peterson, sir? But he's made a full statement. It's here in the file . . ."

"I know," said Henry. "I've read it. It confirms Weatherby's story in every detail except the hearing of the shots, and you say that you believe Peterson."

"I do, sir. He's a good lad at heart, sir, and really trying to go straight. That's why he came forward to help us. He'd have nothing to gain by . . ."

"All right, Sergeant." Henry grinned. One of Sergeant Reynolds' most endearing characteristics was his readiness to champion any lost sheep who genuinely wished to rejoin the fold. "All the same, I'd like to see the young man. And quick. Can you get him in here right away?"

Bob Peterson was a dark-haired, sharp-faced young man with intelligent eyes. Henry liked him at once. Peterson's dossier showed the too-familiar, saddening story: the clever boy unable to take advantage of further education because of poverty at home, and so putting his brains to work to outsmart society; becoming involved with older men, less intelligent but more unscrupulous, and finally, inevitably, being left by them to pay the price in the form of a stiff prison sentence. But, it seemed, he was bright enough to realize that twenty-four is not too great an age at which to make a new start; bright enough to grasp that brains honestly applied can outsmart society even more profitably than those of the criminal—criminals being, as a rule, rather stupid, and the penalties of unsuccessful crime being singularly unpleasant.

Henry said, "I'd just like to run over this statement once more with you, Mr. Peterson."

"Oh, yes, sir?" Peterson sounded eager and helpful.

"You describe the gunman in these words . . ." Henry ruffled through the file, found the place, and began to read aloud. " 'He was wearing a dark overcoat, blue I think, rather long, and I think his trousers was dark gray, what you could see of them. He had a gray Trilby hat on. He was wearing big dark glasses, with sort of tortoise-shell rims, like; and this great big black beard that anybody could see wasn't real. You could see the elastic going behind his ears, and all. He was sort of ordinary otherwise, apart from his foreign accent. Not much tall or short, thin or fat, if you know what I mean. Just ordinary.' "

Peterson smiled confidently. "That's right, sir. I don't express myself as well as what I'd like, but . . ."

Henry said, "You didn't leave anything out?"

"Anything out, sir?" Peterson was all innocence. "What do you mean, sir?"

Henry repeated. "Not much tall or short, thin or fat. Do you stand by that?"

"Well, of course I do, sir."

Henry rapped out, "You told Sergeant Reynolds on the telephone that the man was tall." Peterson said nothing. "How much did Weatherby pay you?"

"I—I don't understand, sir . . ."

"Oh yes you do. Weatherby either bribed or threatened you into changing one small fact. I'm prepared to believe that you didn't think you were doing any harm, and doubtless you need the money." Henry was very stern now. "This is your last chance, Peterson. Do you want to amend that statement?"

Peterson looked as if he were about to burst into tears. "I didn't see no harm, sir . . ."

"I know you didn't, you young idiot," said Henry angrily.

"If you tell me the truth now, I won't hold it against you. Now, will you amend that statement?"

"Well, sir, he—well—he *was* a tall man, sir, the murderer. The man with the black beard. He was tall."

The headquarters of PIFL were dark and shuttered and silent as the grave, apart from two charladies who were clearing up after the farewell cocktail party; but the Foreign Office, after a lot of prodding (for it was also Saturday afternoon at the Foreign Office), at last came through with the London address of His Excellency Mijnheer Jan Koetsveen.

As Trapp had told Henry, Koetsveen's London abode was a small service apartment in a quiet, expensive street in Mayfair; but it was empty and dead, with drawn curtains and lowered shutters. The porter, however, willingly informed the nice young man from the Gas Board (alias Sergeant Reynolds) that "Mr. Cootsfane" had left only that morning for his holiday. Holland, that's where he'd be. Being Dutch, you see. Well, it was only natural, wasn't it? "Mr. Cootsfane" had gone off early that morning to catch a plane back to Holland. Freeland, or some such place. "Mr. Cootsfane" often talked of it. He had a farmhouse there, and he took his granddaughter there in the summer. He (the porter) had a granddaughter of his own, so he could understand. Such a nice gentleman, "Mr. Cootsfane." However, the Gas Board need not despair. He'd be back in three weeks. Had to be, see, for his work. So you can read the meter then, son.

Sergeant Reynolds thanked the porter and reported back to Henry. Henry swore and put through a message to Interpol. Interpol, in a remarkably short time, replied that Mijnheer Koetsveen's country address was a farm called Rustig Hoek, which was situated just outside a village called Ijlp, near the ancient town of Sneek in the province of Friesland.

It was late in the afternoon when Sergeant Reynolds brought to Henry the latest information which he had been able to glean about the current movements and whereabouts of the various characters in the case.

Miss Yvonne La Rue had attended the PIFL party and gone out to lunch afterward with Monsieur Pierre Malvaux. The two of them were now in the Majestic Cinema, Leicester Square, watching a film entitled *I Was Dracula's Teen-Age Aunt*. Major Weatherby was at The Pink Parrot, as he had been all day. He had just opened up the private bar for the evening. Miss Madeleine La Rue—well, as Henry knew, she was somewhere on the continent of Europe, probably in Holland. There had been no more news of her.

Mrs. Torelli had re-let Byers' room to a gentleman who traveled with hairbrushes. Miss Minster was on duty at the reception desk at Dominic's and, according to her, Mr. Nightingale was spending the weekend in Surrey, playing golf at Sunningdale. Mr. Wardle was up to his ears arranging to staff the thirty-place banquet being given by the President of Mambesi, who was staying at the hotel. Mr. Wardle had, however, vouchsafed the information that Mr. Taylor, of the floating pool of kitchen staff, had floated on to some other establishment; had left them on Friday afternoon, after Henry's visit, without so much as a word of explanation—but they were used to that sort of thing, alas. Mr. Bingham, the bank manager, had gone home to Streatham for the weekend. He had a heavy program ahead of him of caring for the one-sixteenth of an acre which went with his mock-Tudor detached house.

Henry gave certain instructions to Sergeant Reynolds. Then he went back to Chelsea, where Emmy had already started packing. In his pocket were a folder of travelers' checks and two airline tickets for the Sunday-morning flight to Amsterdam. Incidentally, Henry had also learned that there was no trace whatsoever of Mike Honeyman, the missing light airplane, or Gordon Trapp. He found this information encouraging.

11

Sunday morning was fine, clear, and crisp. From the plane window Henry and Emmy watched the sandbanks off the east coast of England probing like inquisitive fingers into the blue-green, crawling North Sea far below them. Near the coast numbers of white and red sails could be seen, as small pleasure boats plied from coastal port to coastal port. Henry and Emmy got a childish thrill from picking out the estuary of the River Berry, the scene of an earlier adventure*; they even imagined, erroneously, that they could identify one of their friends' boats among the handful of tiny, toylike sails heading out to sea in the sunshine.

A cup of coffee and a piece of pastry filled in the time which it took to cross the bare expanse of the sea. Then, coastal trading and fishing vessels began to appear below; the sea changed color as the water grew shallower; and there, suddenly, was the coast of Holland. Unlike the English coast, which was sandy, wooded, and full of welcoming inlets and harbors, the Dutch coast is a continuous wall: a rampart, a man-made dike, protecting the low-lying hinterland against the menace of the sea. Outside this dike, to seaward, are bleak gray sands and frothing shallows. On the dike itself, a procession of cars and trucks sped along the motorway which topped it; and to landward blue lakes and lagoons, which had once been tidal estuaries, provided idyllic sailing grounds for local sportsmen. The only exit to the sea seemed to be at the Hook of Holland, which was clearly visible from the air, together with all the busy traffic of the New Maas waterway leading up to the great port of Rotterdam.

The landscape, seen from the air, was fascinating. Roads straighter than even the Romans could have visualized were

*See Down Among the Dead Men.

already buzzing with Sunday traffic. Flat green fields were crisscrossed by canals, until they looked like a checkerboard. Whole acres of glass houses glinted in the sun, busy helping to achieve Holland's economic miracle by the exercise of factory horticulture. Then, as the plane swung northward, Henry and Emmy caught their breaths as they got their first sight of the bulb fields. Like a brilliant patchwork quilt, acres-square fields of early tulips glowed and gleamed in the morning sun—red, yellow, white, and purple. The daffodils were still spreading their sheets of white and yellow over the landscape, and hyacinths made carpets of blue, cream, magenta, and pink. To seaward of the bulb fields were the pale yellow sand dunes, and beyond them, the sea. To landward were the lush green pastures of the Netherlands.

Lazily, like a great bird, the plane began to circle, and within a few minutes touched down near the huge, octopus-shaped complex which makes up the new Schiphol Airport.

At the open door of the plane, Henry and Emmy were surprised to find themselves stepping directly into a long, upward-sloping tunnel, for their plane had taxied into position at the end of one of the giant tentacles which radiate from the main airport building. At the end of the tunnel the passengers were ushered onto a continuously rolling conveyor belt, like a flat escalator, and this carried them and their hand luggage effortlessly into the customs hall. A few minutes later Henry and Emmy were out in the fresh, tingling spring sunshine, watching their baggage being loaded into a taxi under the vast, Vermeer-ish sweep of a rain-washed Dutch sky.

If you know Amsterdam, you will know the American Hotel. If you are visiting the city for the first time, it is one of the places to which your Dutch or expatriate friends are sure to take you. They say that you will find it amusing, and you generally do.

In spite of its name, the American is completely Dutch, or, to be more precise, completely Amsterdam-ish, for Amsterdam is as untypical of the Netherlands as New York is of the United States. The American is a big, exuberantly ugly building which

137

flanks one side of the Leidseplein with its network of tram-lines and traffic lights. Next door is the city's principal theater.

To the right of the terrace of the American are the green of public gardens, the vast red bulk of the Rijksmuseum, and beyond that a residential quarter of tree-lined streets. To the left are the narrow, crowded Leidsestraat, the Bond Street of Amsterdam, and the heart of a bustling city. At nighttime there is the dazzling flash of neon signs, as garish and gay as Piccadilly Circus or Times Square. At any time, all around, is a fair cross-section of the people who make Amsterdam swing —actors and artists, *provos* and students, professors and fashion models, businessmen and barflies, journalists and tourists —they all come to the American, to drink coffee or Dutch gin, to gossip or argue, to see or to be seen.

When the weather permits, the plastic-topped tables and cane chairs on the wide terrace are crowded; when wind and rain lash the city in wintertime, the action moves inside to the enormous, slightly dingy bar, with its high-backed settle seats and *art nouveau* decorations. At one time or another, everyone in Amsterdam visits either the bar or the terrace of the American Hotel. It is at once the most conspicuous and the most anonymous place in Holland, and it was for that reason that Henry had chosen it for his rendezvous with Gordon Trapp.

The Tibbetts settled in at a small hotel on the Herengracht, overlooking the dreamy, filthy, enchanting, tree-shaded canal, and then made their way to the American on foot. They arrived at half past eleven. There was no sign of Trapp. They sat down at a terrace table in the sunshine and ordered two Dutch gins.

Henry said, "I feel like that character in *Waiting for Godot,* the one who says, 'At least we kept our appointment.' "

Emmy gave him a quick, heartening smile. "I'm sure he'll turn up."

"I'm giving him until one o'clock," said Henry, "no longer."

Around them, Amsterdam swung and surged, talked and laughed, and displayed that particular tough, vital, funny, endearing outlook on life which has so much in common with cockney London. American tourists flopped into welcoming café chairs, ordered Cokes and Scotches, and told each other how they had done the Rijksmuseum in twenty minutes flat and about the darlingest little antique shop on the Rokin— not at all expensive. A group of students—the boys with shoulder-length hair and the girls with tiny skirts and white-painted clown's faces—discussed the political situation of the Netherlands in the passionate, aggrieved voices which are only to be heard in truly democratic nations. An extremely pretty, skeletal girl in faded blue jeans talked earnestly to a stout, florid-faced young man wearing a threadbare suit and a flowing bow tie. A solemn, middle-aged man in an impeccable dark suit sat by himself at what was clearly his usual table and read his usual newspaper.

For no very good reason Henry remembered that Amsterdam was the only city in Europe in which the ordinary workmen had had the effrontery to strike—to *strike,* if you please —under Nazi occupation in protest against the treatment of the Jews. He wondered if Londoners would have done the same, and hoped very much that they would. At that point in his random meditations a clock struck twelve noon. And at the same moment a taxi drew up alongside the terrace and Gordon Trapp got out of it.

He looked extremely relaxed. He strolled up to the terrace, looked around, found an empty table, and sat down at it. A waiter approached, and Trapp talked briefly to him; then, with an almost convincing start of surprise, he appeared to see Henry and Emmy for the first time. He came over to their table.

"Well, well, well, of all the coincidences! It is Henry Tibbett, isn't it?"

"It is," said Henry. "You'd better sit down and have a drink."

"With the greatest of pleasure. I am," said Trapp, "enjoying myself."

"I'm glad to hear it."

"And I have an address in Friesland which may interest you."

"So have I," said Henry. "Where did you get it?"

Trapp grinned. "Simple, dear fellow. I telephoned the office and asked."

"The office? You mean PIFL?"

"Where else? All the members have to leave addresses. I put a call through in the middle of the cocktail party yesterday."

"And spoke to Yvonne?"

"Certainly. Is that a crime?"

"No," said Henry. "It's just a bloody blunder, and it's my fault. Never mind, the harm's done now." He broke off as the waiter approached. "What are you having? A *jenever*?"

"Thanks."

"*Nog een Oude Bokma, alst U blieft,*" Henry said to the waiter, who nodded and trotted away.

Trapp remarked appreciatively, "Dutch, too. Very smooth. Never been able to get my tongue around it myself. How many languages do you speak, Superintendent?"

"Never mind about how many languages I speak. What were you playing at in Paris?"

"In Paris?"

"Don't look so innocent. You changed your train reservation, and . . ."

"Gave your flatfoot the slip." Trapp finished the sentence with relish. "You never told me you were having me tailed. If you had . . ."

"It would have done you no good," said Henry, irritated. "Now, why did you change your reservation?"

"I told you."

"To score off a flatfooted shadow? I don't believe you. What about the tall man?"

"Well . . ." Trapp grinned. "He did point out that the

140

T-E-E was much more comfortable and convenient. I thought it would please him if I took his advice. He seemed such a nice fellow."

"Had you ever seen him before?"

"Not to my knowledge. But then, one meets so many people."

The waiter arrived with a tiny glass of colorless fluid, which he placed on the table in front of Trapp.

Henry said, "And what, in fact, did you do?"

"Well, now—I avoided the slow nine twenty-one train in order to baffle your bluebottle. I avoided the lunchtime T-E-E in order to baffle the tall man. Actually, I took a couple of buses and then a train, and arrived in Rethel last night."

"Rethel?"

"Near the Belgian border. The Hotel Moderne, opposite the station, has one of the finest restaurants in Europe, believe it or not. I thought it was worth a detour."

"So you spent the night there?"

"Correct, Super—or should I say, Mr. Tibbett? Or even Henry?" Without waiting for a reply Trapp raised his glass to Emmy, smiled, and said, "To your bright eyes, Emmy darling."

To Henry's annoyance, Emmy responded with a warm grin and a raised glass. He said, "Go on, Trapp. What happened today?"

"Happened? My dear Henry, you make things sound so melodramatic. I told you that I spent the night in the station hotel in Rethel. What more natural than that I should take the train in the morning? Rethel to Brussels, Brussels to Amsterdam, and here I am, all present and correct."

"And where were you when you telephoned Yvonne?"

"Let's see. I was between buses—somewhere near Reims."

"And what did you tell her?"

"Tell her?"

"She must have been surprised to get a call from France."

"Oh, I see what you mean. Yes—I just said that I was on my way to a holiday in Amsterdam."

141

"You're mad," said Henry. "Now everyone knows exactly where you are."

"Yvonne can hardly be called everybody."

"You'd be surprised," said Henry. "Well, you can't stay here, that's obvious."

"Why on earth not?"

"I should have said, if you want to stay alive, you can't stay here. I suggest a long holiday in the south of France."

"You've suggested that once already, old man. The idea doesn't appeal. I happen to like Holland, and I shall be spending quite a few days here."

Henry said, "I was hoping that you'd be able to introduce me to Koetsveen unofficially. That's out of the question now. I can't get you to leave Amsterdam by force, but if you'll take my very serious advice . . ."

"I'm not entirely idiotic, my dear old bloodhound." Trapp drained his drink. "I shall disappear. I'm good at it. Ask your copper."

"You can do what you like," said Henry. "But before you disappear, you can tell me something."

"Anything within reason, old man."

"What brand of whisky was it that you left in your apartment with your friend Honeyman?"

Trapp's eyebrows went up. "What an intriguingly bizarre question. It was a full bottle of Highland Dream. Now you can tell me why you are interested."

Henry smiled. "One of the few advantages of being a policeman," he said, "is that one is entitled to ask questions without having to answer them. In fact, I've got another for you. What about the tall man."

"Mr. Herbert G. Pierce? What about him?"

"Everything."

Trapp considered for a moment and then gave Henry an almost word-perfect account of his conversation on the airplane.

"And you were suspicious?" asked Henry.

"I'm always suspicious, dear fellow. I take my cloaks and daggers seriously."

"I wonder," said Henry. "All right. Now, since you can't come with us, tell me what you know about Koetsveen and this farm of his."

"Which goes by the attractive name of Rusty Hook?"

"Dutch for 'Peaceful Corner,' " Henry pointed out.

"What a language! What do you want to know?"

"Anything that you can tell me."

Trapp considered. "First of all," he said, "there's something that I should make quite clear."

"What's that?"

"That I need another drink," said Trapp blandly.

He beckoned the waiter, insisted on paying for the first round, and pocketed the penciled receipt. When a fresh set of glasses had been brought, Trapp went on.

"I can't tell you much about the farm. I've never been there, of course, but Koetsveen has talked to me about it. Apparently it's very fashionable these days to buy up an old Friesian farmhouse and refurbish it as a weekend cottage. 'Farm' is a euphemism, of course. Koetsveen doesn't go in for agriculture or cows or anything like that. It's just an old thatched house beside a canal, with a private landing stage and a couple of boats and a coopful of hens in the back yard for fresh eggs. His married daughter and her family use the place in the summer, and old Koetsveen lets down his back hair and putters around. That's about all I know."

"These boats," said Henry. "Is he keen on sailing?"

Trapp shrugged. "He's a Dutchman," he said. "They're all born either on two wheels or with a tiller in their mouths, or both. And some of them . . ." Trapp's voice trailed off into silence as his eyes focused on a point somewhere behind Emmy's head. He put his half-finished drink down on the table. "I shall disappear now." His voice had a richly appreciative note. "Best of luck, old sleuth. See you again perhaps. Or perhaps not. Thanks for the cash. I may pay you back someday. Good-bye, Emmy, love. Be good."

He stood up and moved away quickly through the crowd of lunchtime drinkers. He was following somebody, and Henry soon saw who it was. A tall girl with thick, golden hair and honey-colored skin, who was moving with the grace of a princess between the tables. Her back was turned toward Henry, but he would have known Madeleine La Rue anywhere.

As Henry watched, she reached the pavement, hailed a waiting cab, and got into it. Gordon Trapp was only a couple of paces behind her. He beckoned to the next cab and Henry saw him giving instructions to the driver. The two vehicles moved off, one following the other, and were engulfed in the traffic of the city.

Emmy was looking at Henry. She said, "You look as though you'd seen a ghost."

"Not a ghost," said Henry, "just a very lovely girl."

Emmy raised her eyebrows. "You'd better go after her," she said.

"I only wish I could," said Henry and then laughed as he saw the flicker of uncertainty on Emmy's face. "Don't be a goose, darling. That was Madeleine La Rue."

"But . . ." Emmy was half out of her chair. "Henry, if she's here, we must . . ."

"We haven't a hope," said Henry. "In any case, she's being followed already."

"By Gordon?"

"As you say, by Gordon. Which is strange. I would have expected her to be following him. I hope to God he'll be careful."

"I get the impression," said Emmy, "that he is very self-reliant."

"There I agree with you," said Henry, "but I'm not sure whether or not it's a good thing. I'm not besotted about the man, but I don't want to see him murdered. I would also like to know just who he's working for."

"He's working for PIFL."

"That's just what I mean," Henry said.

* * *

Back at the hotel on the Herengracht, Henry sat on the bed grumbling.

Emmy said, "I'm sorry, darling, but I thought the lunch was delicious. I just don't know what you're in such a bad temper about."

"Everything," said Henry. "That bloody fool Trapp principally."

"But he only . . ."

"Oh hell," said Henry. "You can't win, can you?"

"What does that mean?"

"Either you take people into your confidence or you don't. If you do, and they are secretly working against you, then you've played into their hands. If you don't, and they are as innocent as the day is long, they go and bitch everything up without meaning to. If you don't confide in them, and they're working against you, and they bitch things up just the same, it presumably means that they are cleverer than you thought."

Emmy, who was brushing her hair in front of the mirror, turned to look at him. She said, "What on earth am I supposed to understand by that?"

Henry smiled. "I suppose it does sound a bit obscure," he said. "I meant Trapp. I still don't know for certain whether he's with us or . . ."

"But, Henry, it was he who came to you in the first place . . ."

"I know he did, and on the face of it that makes him innocent. It would also provide the best possible cover for him."

"But unless Gordon had come to you, nobody would ever have suspected . . ."

"Maybe you're right," said Henry. "Maybe not. Two—no, three—men had been killed already. Mike Honeyman had already escaped from Mambesi. You can't expect me to have complete confidence in Gordon Trapp."

"And yet you trusted him to . . ."

"I didn't trust him at all. I didn't let him out of my sight from the moment he told us about Honeyman until I got him

145

on a plane for Paris. I sent a plainclothes man to watch him, a chap who was supposed to follow him here and make sure he didn't communicate with England. Trapp gave my man the slip. Was that really just for fun, as he claims? And then Trapp telephones Yvonne La Rue quite openly, and tells me about it. Is that innocent or too damned clever? The Lord only knows. All I'm sure of now is that I can't use Trapp as an introduction to Koetsveen, as I'd hoped to do. I'm also sure that if Trapp is innocent, he's in great danger. And if he's guilty, then we're all in it, up to our necks."

Emmy sighed. "I'm quite bewildered," she said. "I don't know who is who or what is what. Who is this tall man you're so interested in?"

"I don't know, myself," said Henry, "but I suspect he is the same man who put on a black beard and shot Byers in The Pink Parrot."

"But . . ."

"Don't keep saying but. I'm trying to concentrate."

"On what?"

"On how we get to Ijlp." Henry had spread out on the bed a complicated brochure of instructions and timetables which had been prepared for him in London.

After a moment Emmy said, "I don't want to sound alarmist, but if Amsterdam is full of sinister characters, they'll surely be keeping an eye on us. Couldn't it be dangerous?"

Henry looked up at her and grinned. "Only slightly," he said. "I'm passably well known as a police officer, and I've come over here without any show of secrecy at all. Our friends wouldn't want to take the risk of murdering me openly, as it were, especially since you're with me, so it would mean murdering you too. That's one reason I brought you along."

"Thanks very much."

"They might try to arrange an accident, of course. But I'm hoping that they'll feel we are pretty harmless so long as we stay in Amsterdam."

"I thought we were going to Ijlp."

"We are, but I've gone to some pains to ensure that anybody watching us won't know about it. We reserved for a week at this hotel, you may have noticed . . ."

"And I was going to ask you," said Emmy, "how we could go to Ijlp when you have an appointment with Inspector van der Valk tomorrow morning."

"Don't worry," said Henry. "The Inspector knows we won't be there. The whole idea was to make the appointment from a very public telephone line at the reception desk here and then to ask the hotel about tourist attractions in the city. If anybody was listening, I hope he'll have gotten the wrong idea. And if anybody is planning to follow us when we go sightseeing . . ." He paused, studying the papers in his hand. "Well, he won't be disappointed. We're off on a Rondvaart almost at once."

"On a what?"

"A round trip of Amsterdam by boat. An absolutely classic tourist attraction, so I understand. All around the old town and then out into the harbor, where you can see the big ships."

"It sounds fascinating," said Emmy.

"It is—and I'm sorry we shall miss it."

"But you just said . . ."

"Our particular Rondvaart," said Henry, "leaves from a quayside not far from here. It then stops briefly at the landing stage just outside the main railway station. We shall be leaving it there."

"But . . ."

"There you go again. Now, stop arguing and start packing."

"Packing? But . . ."

"Pajamas, a toothbrush, and some sailing clothes," said Henry with a smile. "Put them into your large shopping basket. Everything else stays here."

There was only a handful of passengers waiting at the quayside in the center of the old town, and they all boarded a tourist boat which was about to leave as Henry and Emmy arrived. Emmy started to run in order to catch the boat, but Henry restrained her. As soon as the first boat had left the

147

landing stage, a second glass-roofed craft moved up into position and a smart young man in blue uniform jumped ashore and set a gangplank. Henry and Emmy went aboard. They were the only passengers.

The young man hauled in the gangway and closed the door of the boat; at the controls, another man in blue moved a lever and the boat drew away from the quayside and started off down the canal. As the steward approached, he smiled broadly and said in excellent English, "With the compliments of Inspector van der Valk, madam. It all went very smoothly, I think."

"It did indeed," said Henry. "I'm very grateful."

"I'm afraid I'm not a professional guide, sir, but I'll do my best. On your right you can see the twin houses from the sixteenth century which are known as the Sisters. Near them are the Brothers, which are larger and not so beautiful, as is fitting. Ahead, on your left, we come to the famous Mint Tower, where all the money in the Netherlands used to be made. Up there, you can see the famous floating flower market . . ."

Under low bridges, beside barges laden with crimson and white blossoms, past churches and gabled houses, the Rondvaart followed the familiar route. On a quayside, in the dappled shade of the trees, a street organ threw its magical streamer of mechanical music into the crisp, sunny air, and Emmy exclaimed with delight. *"When it's spring again, I'll bring again, Tulips from Amsterdam . . ." ". . . Amsterdam, oh you lovely town . . ."* And then, in the same bright, cranked-out rhythm, a song from the war years, which Emmy had quite forgotten. And yet, with the tune, the words came back to her, as vivid as yesterday. *"My sister and I remember still . . . the tulip garden by the old Dutch mill . . . and the fun that we used to have, until . . . but we don't talk about that . . ."*

The young policeman, who could not have been more than a baby during the war, said, "Up there on the right, there is the Anne Frank house. It is now a center for youth activities of all sorts, and a—a sort of shrine, of course." He paused and then added, "Many young Germans come every year to pay their respects. That is good, isn't it?"

Emmy said, "I think that you Dutch must be very good people."

The young man smiled and shrugged. "We are just ordinary people," he said. "We have short tempers—no, that is not correct. You must forgive my English. I mean, we do not hold our anger for long." His eyes went again to the Anne Frank house. "But we have long memories . . ."

Near the Central Station a nestful of Rondvaart boats jostled each other at the landing stage, like fledglings competing for a worm. The boat with Henry and Emmy edged her way in at last; the doors were opened and the plank lowered; and Henry and Emmy jumped ashore into the anonymity of a crowd of prospective sightseers. As they climbed up the steps Henry said, "I hope that's given them the slip. I also hope they're not already in Ijlp."

A glance at the map of Holland will show that in spite of the new polders which have been reclaimed from the water, the name Hollow-land, or Land-with-a-hole-in-it, is well deserved. A century ago the Zuider Zee was a great tidal basin, around which the land clung, like a limpet on a rock. Now, tamed and cut off from the ocean by the modern miracle of the eighteen-mile-long Afsluitdijk—and rechristened the Ijsselmeer to show how reasonable and gentle it has become—the great lake still lies like soup in a plate, cutting the north of Holland into two halves. From Amsterdam, which lies at the southwestern corner of the soup plate, it is always a nice point to consider whether, in order to reach the northeastern corner, it is better to go around the lake by land or to cut across the water. Henry's advisers in London had been of the opinion that the water route was the better of the two.

Consequently, Henry and Emmy soon found themselves in a train headed for Enkhuizen on the western side of the Ijsselmeer, about halfway up, as Emmy put it. From there, they were assured, they could catch a ferryboat across the lake to Staveren. And from there, Ijlp was a stone's throw.

Enkhuizen was no more than a tantalizing glimpse from the station platform—of an ancient clock tower, rose-pink gabled houses, and a harbor full of black fishing boats and white yachts; for the ferryboat was waiting at the far side of the platform, which cleverly doubled as a dock. Henry and Emmy boarded the big ferry, and within minutes they were out of the railway harbor and headed across the Ijsselmeer toward Staveren.

It came as a surprise, illogically, when they realized that they could not see the far shore. A lake, after all, is only a lake, and Holland is a small country; but this was a sea, whipped up into steep little white-crested waves by the smart northeasterly breeze. And there was no land to be seen on the far horizon. They watched the tall clock tower of Enkhuizen fade into the distance astern, and still no sign of land appeared ahead. In fact, there was only a brief moment when they were completely out of sight of land, and then a dark line appeared on the horizon. Half an hour later the ferryboat was tied up alongside the dock staging of Staveren railway station. The train was waiting on the other side of the platform, and in another half hour it had deposited them in the lovely old town of Sneek. It was by then half past five.

Sneek is an inland town, but the province of Friesland is such a network of canals, rivers, and lakes, of bridges and barges and reedy banks and islands, that the feeling of water is everywhere, and the streets seem to be as full of boats as of cars, for waterways interlace the little town. And so it was that Henry did not head for an establishment which rented drive-it-yourself cars, although there were several in the town. Instead, he and Emmy made their way to a large, ramshackle building on a quayside which advertised *"Botjes te Huur."* It being Sunday in puritan Friesland, the establishment was bolted and barred; but arrangements had been made, and Henry rang a bell at a side door as instructed. The proprietor appeared, smart and neat in his best suit, and very soon the Tibbetts were the temporary tenants of a sturdy, workmanlike sailing sloop, equipped with a small but reliable engine, a mainsail and a jib, a bottled-gas stove, full fuel and water tanks, linen and cutlery as found, and a water map of the district. Her name was the *Vrouwe Beatrix*.

At eight o'clock they went ashore to a small, pleasant café, where they ate smoked eels and chicken salad, and by nine they were back on board the *Vrouwe Beatrix* and making up their beds, because they planned an early start in the morning.

12

The morning dawned fresh and sweet, with a rinsed blue sky and a gentle breeze. Sneek rose early, it seemed. By seven o'clock there was a merry rattle of traffic over the town's multitude of bridges; milk urns clattered on the cobbled streets; bicycle bells tinkled and barges hooted on the canals. Henry need not have bothered about an alarm clock.

By half past eight Henry and Emmy had been ashore, shopped for provisions, returned to the boat, and were sitting down to a large breakfast, during which they spread out on the table the waterway chart which showed their route to Ijlp. Ijlp was marked as a village situated on a canal which linked two small lakes, and calculations involving a small piece of string indicated that it was some fifteen kilometers from Sneek. Six opening bridges were marked between Sneek and Ijlp, and Henry took the precaution of looking them up in the *Water Almanack* to make sure that their opening was not restricted to certain hours of the day. Fortunately, all were listed as being ready and willing to open at any time on weekdays. So, as soon as the dishes had been washed and stowed away, Henry started the motor, Emmy cast off the mooring lines, and the *Vrouwe Beatrix* moved sedately through the town toward the first bridge. It looked very solid and very firmly shut, with a stream of rush-hour traffic moving over it.

Emmy said anxiously, "Are you sure it'll open for us?"

"The book says it will," said Henry. "Give it a hoot. Or rather, three hoots."

Nervously Emmy put the little brass trumpet to her lips and blew three times, while Henry throttled back the engine. There was a moment of anxiety as the road traffic plowed on and the *Vrouwe Beatrix* seemed to be moving at high speed toward the forbidding red lights; and then the lights turned to green, the red-and-white pole barriers came down to stop the traffic, and the mechanism moved slowly into action so that the bridge reared up to let the little boat pass through. Henry put her full-speed-ahead and acknowledged the friendly wave of the bridge keeper in his little glass house. The boat moved off down the canal, away from the shops and houses of Sneek and out into the green countryside.

One of the charms of Holland is that it is so completely itself—unique, unmistakable, changeless in spite of change, familiar when seen for the first time. The scenes that the Breughels and Potter and Vermeer and Ruisdael painted are still there, and over great stretches of countryside only the functional electric watermills alongside the ancient windmills indicate the change of century. In any Dutch landscape four-fifths of the canvas is filled with the wide, windy sky; the remaining fifth will show either red-brick, steeply gabled houses or fresh green fields, flat as paper, sprinkled with sleek black-and-white cows. There is certain to be water about, and very probably a boat or two. None of this has changed, and Emmy, who had not visited the Netherlands before, kept exclaiming delightedly on this sense of *déjà vu*, as each turn of the canal opened up a vista straight from an eighteenth-century canvas.

They soon became quite expert in the technique of negotiating bridges, judging to a nicety the exact moment to blow the hooter and the exact speed of approach. At one rustic bridge ("Straight out of Van Gogh," said Emmy) the keeper swung out a well-worn clog at the end of a ..shing line as the boat went through, and Henry dropped into it the toll money of twenty-five cents.

Five kilometers from Sneek, the *Vrouwe Beatrix* left the main waterway to turn left up a small side canal, which meandered peacefully among green meadows. In the larger canal there had been a brisk traffic of commercial barges, carrying loads of wood, milk, vegetables, gravel, and coal from town to town; but once off the main highway, as it were, *Vrouwe*

153

Beatrix had the place to herself. It was the Monday before Easter and early in the season for pleasure craft to be out. Even on the wide waters of the lake into which the canal led, there were only a couple of sails to be seen and a few small rowboats in which anglers sat, patiently tending their lines.

"Can we put the sails up now?" Emmy asked.

"I wish we could," said Henry, "but there's practically no wind and I want to get there as fast as I can. We'll go sailing when it's all over."

So the *Vrouwe Beatrix* chugged across the smooth surface of the lake at a steady four knots, and half an hour later was nosing her way into the canal on the far side, the canal that led to Ijlp.

"This," said Henry, "is where we keep our eyes open. I don't know which side of the village the farm is on, or even that it's on this canal—though I think it must be, since Koetsveen keeps boats. The other canals around here are too shallow for anything bigger than a rowboat. So keep a sharp lookout for a thatched farmhouse with a private landing stage."

By now they could see Ijlp—a huddle of red houses, a sharp steeple, a windmill. Between them and the village there seemed to be nothing but green meadows and piebald cows.

"Oh, well," said Henry, "we'll go through the village and have a look at the far side. If we still can't find it, we'll have to come back to the village and ask. But I'm not keen to do that. Better get the trumpet out. I can see the bridge."

Ijlp was a cozy little village; cottage gardens bright with tulips and hyacinths bordered the canal. Flanking the cobbled street, small stepped-gabled houses leaned at drunken angles, and outside the village stores bright yellow varnished clogs hung in strings, like Breton onions. The little wrought-iron weigh bridge swung up to let the *Vrouwe Beatrix* through, and a merry, apple-faced woman in traditional costume waved to Henry and Emmy as she waited on the road for the bridge barriers to be raised. It seemed incongruous and yet very typical of Holland that this attractive young lady—in her ankle-length black pleated skirt, her gay chintz laced bodice, and elaborate white starched headdress—should be at the wheel of a super-modern motorcycle.

It took only a couple of minutes to chug through the village and to emerge on the far side, where the meadows began again—meadow after green meadow, cow after dappled cow, and no sign of a farmhouse. Henry was on the point of turning back when he spotted a long, low metal rowboat moored to a stake at the side of the canal. In this boat three old men sat hunched over fishing lines, like grumpy parrots on a perch. Henry hailed them.

"Do you know a farm called Rustig Hoek?" he called in Dutch.

All three old men looked up at once, blinking.

Henry repeated his question, prefacing it with the polite, "Excuse me, gentlemen."

There was a long silence, while the three old men looked at each other. Then the one in the middle repeated slowly, with a thick Friesian accent, "Rustig Hoek?"

"That's right," said Henry. "Mijnheer Koetsveen."

"Koetsveen?" echoed the old man on the right.

They all looked at each other again.

"Farm, you said?" queried the old man on the left.

"Yes. Rustig Hoek farm."

They all looked at each other again. Then the one in the middle took his cigar out of his mouth and said, "Mijnheer Koetsveen hasn't got a farm. Never has had."

"But I was told . . ." Henry began.

"Not in these parts." The old man on the left spoke firmly.

"Mijnheer Koetsveen is a very important man," remarked the old man on the right. "Maybe he has a farm somewhere else. Zeeland, maybe. Or Holland." Silence descended again.

"This farm is just outside Ijlp," said Henry firmly. "It is called Rustig Hoek."

Three grizzled heads shook in unison. "Not here. Not in Ijlp. Not a farm."

"A house, then, a country house."

"A house?" The old man on the right looked inquiringly at his mates. "Maybe it's Rustig Hoek the gentleman means, eh, Nol?"

"Maybe he does," said the man in the middle, brightening.

"That's where Mijnheer Koetsveen stays when he comes here," agreed the old man on the left. "Could be that he means."

Once again silence fell.

Maneuvering the *Vrouwe Beatrix* in uneasy circles around the fishing dinghy, Henry said despairingly, "Of course I mean Rustig Hoek. Where is it?"

The old man in the middle had a long pull on his cigar, took it out of his mouth, regarded its glowing tip, replaced it between his lips, and said doubtfully, "*If* it's Rustig Hoek you want, which I doubt, myself, since you're looking for a farm . . ." He reeled his line in carefully and inspected the baited hook, while his companions nodded agreement at his masterly reasoning. "*If* it is, as I say, and if Mijnheer Koetsveen is there, which I doubt if he will be, so early in the year —well—as I was saying, *if* it's Rustig Hoek you want, it's just around that bend on your left."

Henry put the *Vrouwe Beatrix* into a tight turn and called, "Thank you, gentlemen."

The three old men beamed.

"Don't thank us, sir—a great pleasure—glad to be of assistance . . ."

They resumed their fishing, and the *Vrouwe Beatrix* proceeded down the canal. The bend referred to was about fifty yards ahead; and as soon as they rounded it, Emmy and Henry saw the house. It was set a few yards back from the waterside, separated from the canal by a beautifully kept lawn. From this lawn a wooden jetty marched out into the water, and on the jetty was fixed a name plate in rustic woodwork, which proclaimed in large letters RUSTIG HOEK, and in smaller ones underneath, "Private Property. Forbidden to Moor Here."

Henry said to Emmy "Well, we've arrived."

"So I see. What do we do now?"

"We tie up at the landing stage, go ashore, and play it by ear. You'd better take an empty water can so that we can always say we came to ask for water."

"But it's full."

"Then tip it over the side, unobtrusively. We'll go beyond the house, then turn and come back. Don't empty the can until we're out of sight around the next bend."

Five minutes later Emmy was jumping ashore onto the tarred wooden landing stage, as Henry maneuvered the *Vrouwe Beatrix* snugly up to the jetty. Emmy made the mooring line fast around an upright post, while Henry stepped ashore with the after mooring line. As the rattle of the motor died away, total silence drifted back over the serene landscape, lapping the house, the lawns, and the canal in its balm. Rustig Hoek seemed to be deserted. Henry went back on board, picked up the empty water can, and came ashore again. He took Emmy's arm and together they walked up the path to the house.

Rustig Hoek was a typical Dutch farmhouse dating from some two hundred years ago. It was a big, squat, square building, single-storied, with a steeply pitched, pyramidal thatched roof under whose eaves dormer windows peeped from the big attic. Originally only the front section of the house had been used as living quarters, while the back of the building had been an enormous barn. This arrangement, in which the barn is literally under the same roof as the domestic quarters, makes these farmhouses ideal for conversion into country cottages. Rustig Hoek had been repointed and rethatched, and freshly painted white woodwork sparkled against the warm red brickwork. The front door was made of handsome natural pinewood. As with all Dutch homes, a small metal plaque on the doorjamb proclaimed that J. KOETSVEEN lived here. Henry lifted the knocker, which was in the shape of a clenched fist, and beat a lively tattoo.

157

Nothing happened. Henry knocked again. The door remained closed and the house quiet. Then a small voice behind him said, *"Dag."*

Dag is the Dutch word for "day." It can mean "Hello," "Good-bye," "How are you?" or just "What the hell are you doing here?" Now it was spoken by a ltttle girl in faded blue jeans and a white T-shirt. She had rosy cheeks, china-blue eyes, and flaxen hair tied with two blue ribbons, and she looked about nine years old. She must have come from the back of the house, for she stood on the garden path behind Henry, regarding him unblinkingly.

"Dag mejuffrouw," said Henry. "Is Mr. Koetsveen at home?"

The child was carrying a small tin bucket, which she now inspected seriously, although it was empty. She said, "I'm Ineke de Jong. I'm eight and a half."

"I'm Henry Tibbett," said Henry. "I've come all the way from England to see Mr. Koetsveen."

"From England?" The blue eyes looked searchingly into Henry's. "Grandpapa Koetsveen lives in England. He only came back yesterday."

"I know," said Henry, "and I want to see him."

"Well, you can't," said Ineke with great finality.

"Why not?"

"Because he isn't here, that's why not." She added, "I've been feeding the chickens. There are six white ones and a red one called Little Annie. She's my favorite."

"I'd like to see Little Annie," said Henry.

"I'll take you and show you, if you like."

"That's very kind. And will you tell me where your grandpapa is?"

Ineke had lost interest in her grandfather. "Come on," she said in a voice which would have been bullying in anybody larger and less attractive. "If we hurry, we can see her finishing her dinner."

"What does she say?" Emmy asked in English.

"She's going to take us to see the chickens."

"What about Koetsveen?"

"He's out. She's his granddaughter. That's all I know so far."

"Come *on,*" said Ineke impatiently.

They went.

The hen coop was on the landward side of the house, near the backyard, and Henry and Emmy duly admired the six large white hens and the diminutive red Annie, who were all scratching busily in the dust and clucking importantly to themselves.

Suddenly Ineke lifted her blond head and said, "There's grandpapa now."

Henry and Emmy looked around, but there was no sign of anybody. The track that led from the back of the house up to the road was deserted.

Ineke, irritated at their stupidity, said, "His boat. Can't you hear it?"

Sure enough, Henry could now hear what the child's sharp ears had picked up several seconds sooner—the sound of an engine on the water. Ineke dropped her bucket and with a cry of *"Opa!"* went off at a trot around the corner of the house toward the canal. Henry and Emmy followed, in time to see a tubby little boat, of the kind known as a *Staverse jol,* nosing its way up to the jetty. The sails had been lowered and the small motor purred healthily. On the bow an attractive woman in her late thirties stood waiting to jump ashore with a mooring line, while at the helm stood the jolly, pear-shaped figure whom Henry had last seen hurrying up to the headquarters of PIFL in London.

Just at the moment, however, Mijnheer Koetsveen seemed far from jolly. He was grunting and swearing, with a good command of both Dutch and Friese, and it was plain that the object of his wrath was the *Vrouwe Beatrix*. Henry caught the words, "Bloody charter boat—private property—can't read plain Dutch—foreigners as like as not . . ." It did not strike him as being the ideal introduction to His Excellency, but it was better than nothing. Henry broke into a run, as he followed Ineke across the lawn and down to the jetty.

In fact, Koetsveen's protests had been occasioned by outraged principles and an overdeveloped sense of private property rather than by actual hardship, for there was ample room for both boats. By the time Henry arrived on the scene, the woman was ashore with the line, and the *jol*, whose name was *Koet*, was contentedly nuzzling the jetty behind the *Vrouwe Beatrix*.

Ineke was dancing in circles around the woman, whom she addressed as *"Mam,"* and telling a long story of which Little Annie, or Anneje, seemed to be the heroine.

Henry walked ahead of Emmy up the jetty and was waiting with outstretched hand as Mijnheer Koetsveen climbed clumsily ashore.

"Mijnheer Koetsveen?" he asked.

Koetsveen mopped his brow. "Is that your boat?" he demanded, indicating the *Vrouwe Beatrix*.

"Yes it is, sir, but . . ."

"This is a private landing stage, mijnheer."

"I know it is," said Henry. "I came to visit you."

"To visit me? I am not aware that I know you, sir." Koetsveen glared at Henry with rather engaging balefulness, such as the Laughing Cavalier might have displayed had he caught another gallant drinking from his tankard.

Henry smiled. "You don't know me, sir," he said. "My name is Tibbett, Superintendent Tibbett of Scotland Yard. May I present my wife?"

"Hm." Koetsveen grunted and mopped his brow again. "Scotland Yard, eh? English policeman. What's an English policeman doing in Ijlp, eh?"

"That's what I'd like to explain," said Henry, "if we could go indoors and have a talk."

"He's a nice man," said Ineke, suddenly losing interest in her mother. "He's called Henry and he's not going indoors with you; he's coming to see Little Annie with me."

"But I've seen her already, Ineke," said Henry.

"You can see her again. You can see her lots and lots of times. Come *on*."

Mijnheer Koetsveen beamed fondly, the Laughing Cavalier again. "I can see that you have met my granddaughter," he said. "Oh, forgive me. This is my daughter, Corry, Mevrouw de Jong."

Henry shook hands with Ineke's mother, who had finished mooring the *jol*.

"You speak very good Dutch," said Koetsveen with a slight note of suspicion.

"Yes, but I'm afraid my wife doesn't. So . . ."

"We will speak English," Koetsveen announced with an impeccable Oxford accent. "You, too," he added to Ineke.

"Does she really speak English?" Emmy asked.

"No, she doesn't," said Ineke loudly in Dutch.

"Come along, come along, come along," said Koetsveen. "Come, Ineke. Come, Corry. Let us go in and have a cup of coffee and see what it is that the good Superintendent wants of us." Like a genial vacuum cleaner, Koetsveen swept the whole party up the garden and in through the farmhouse door.

Inside, Henry and Emmy found themselves in a Dutch interior that could have stepped straight out of a Jan Steen painting—dark green painted beams, a tiled stove, painted furniture showing winter scenes of skating and pastoral summer landscapes, blue Delft plates ranged on the big dresser—it was all there.

Mrs. de Jong apologized quite unnecessarily for what she described as the chaotic state of the house, explaining that she had arrived only two days ago to open up the house for the summer.

"Ineke and I worked all day yesterday to get the place cleaned up," she said, "but it takes so long. I'm afraid I'm spoiled in Amsterdam, with my vacuum cleaner and my electric polisher. Here, everything has to be done with elbow grease, I fear. We have no electricity, you see, only gas. Everything is still in a great mess, but you are our first guests of the year, so I hope you will forgive us."

She then went off into the kitchen and returned with a steaming pot of sweet, milky coffee and a huge plate of de-

161

licious cookies. Koetsveen himself lit a big cigar, pressed one on Henry, gave Ineke a cookie, and eventually organized the whole party into a circle. They sat on upright, rush-seated chairs around a large table, which, Dutch fashion, was covered not by a cloth but by a dark red, richly patterned carpet.

"Now, my friend," he said to Henry, "what can I do for you, eh?"

"It's really more a question of what I can do for you, sir," Henry began.

"And what does that mean?"

"It means," said Henry, "that I am asking you to accept my protection, such as it is."

"Your . . . ? Are you out of your mind, sir?"

"No, I'm afraid not," said Henry. "I've brought a letter from—from someone in London whom you know. Perhaps you would read it." He took an envelope out of his pocket and put it on the table.

With a great deal of snorting and grunting and polishing of spectacles, Koetsveen read the letter. It was written by a senior member of Britain's foreign service, a wartime friend of Koetsveen's who was also friendly with the assistant commissioner of Scotland Yard. Koetsveen took a long time perusing this document. At last he looked up and snorted again.

"Rubbish," he announced. "Poppycock. I fear my old friend Archie must be suffering from senile decay at last."

"I think you are wrong, sir."

"Wrong? Wrong? Of course I'm not wrong." Koetsveen tapped the letter with a pudgy hand. "Talks about my life being in danger! My life! Here, in my own Friesland! Balderdash! And he doesn't even say what it's all about, just that I should listen to you."

"I'm afraid that Sir Archibald doesn't know all the facts, sir, and there was no time to explain to him. He very kindly wrote the letter as an introduction for me, that's all."

Koetsveen grunted again. Then he said, "Well, since Archie wants it, I'll hear you out, young man, but more than that I won't promise. Come on then. I'm waiting." He took a gulp of coffee, and then leaned back in his chair, pushed his spectacles up on his forehead, and closed his eyes.

It was no easy matter to put the story in a form which was at once concise, detailed, and convincing—especially as Koetsveen remained, to all intents and purposes, sound asleep. Henry did his best. When he had finished, there was a long silence. Then Koetsveen sighed, opened his eyes, and lit a fresh cigar, glaring at Henry all the while.

At last he said, "I'm not blaming you, young man. You've been sent here by your superiors and you can't be held responsible. But I can tell you one thing. You will go back to London and you will go at once, and cease to bother me. I am on vacation, and I regard this as an unwarranted intrusion on my privacy. Archie hasn't heard the last of this, I can tell you. As for your ridiculous tale—pure rubbish, as I said before. To start with—and to end up with, for that matter—nobody has the faintest idea how I am proposing to cast my vote in the Mambesi-Galunga case. *Nobody*."

"But an interpreter at your private meetings, sir . . ."

"I shall deal with Mr. Trapp when the appropriate time comes," said Koetsveen ominously. "It was a gross breach of discipline, privilege, and contract for him to divulge to any other person any details whatsoever of a private meeting of the commission. However, that is an internal matter, which concerns only PIFL." He puffed a little, and Henry noticed that he had gone very red in the face and was breathing heavily. It would be ironic, he reflected, if Mijnheer Koetsveen should now die of heart failure unaided by anybody.

Henry said, "Sir Bertram Clegg, the chairman, has agreed to reconvene the commission for Wednesday and to take an immediate vote. I think Sir Archibald explained that in his letter. It seems that it is impossible for some members to get back to London before Wednesday."

"Sheer nonsense. Archie doesn't know what he is talking about. We have a three-week recess. The idea of going back before Easter . . ."

"You will be getting a letter from Sir Bertram tomorrow, sir, I assure you."

"So you've persuaded Clegg to take your flights of fancy seriously, have you? The man's an idiot, always was and always will be. If he thinks he can get me back to London by Wednesday he's very much mistaken. The postal services in this part of Holland," said Koetsveen blandly, "are very bad indeed."

"Mr. Koetsveen," said Henry, "please listen to me. Once the vote has been taken and the decision announced, there is nothing anybody can gain by your death and you will be perfectly safe. But until then . . ."

"Fiddlesticks!"

"Until then," Henry persisted, "you are in very great danger. Today is Monday. All that I ask is that you accept my protection from now until Wednesday."

"Accept your protection? What does that mean, pray? Do as you tell me, I suppose?"

"Up to a certain point, yes."

"Barricade myself in my own house against some imaginary bogeyman? Rush back to London in the middle of my holiday! Bah!"

"Well, sir," said Henry, "you may not accept my protection, but you can't stop me from giving it."

"By God," replied the old man with spirit, "can't I? I can order you out of my house, young man. I can order you to take your boat off my private landing stage. I can forbid you to set foot on my property. And I do!" Koetsveen's color was rising dangerously with the volume of his voice. "And now, Mr. Superintendent, will you kindly get out? And stay out! Do you hear me? GET OUT!"

There was nothing to do. Henry and Emmy got out. As the door closed behind them, they heard Ineke say in a calm and authoritative voice, "You really shouldn't shout so loud, Grandpapa. Now Henry has gone away without saying goodbye to Little Annie."

13

Vrouwe Beatrix made her way back up the canal to Ijlp in a silence which was broken only by the purring of the motor. The three old fishermen waved a greeting as she went past. At last Emmy ventured to say, "What do we do now?"

Henry, who was at the helm, turned to her and grinned. "We tie up at a comfortable mooring in Ijlp. We make it very clear that we are English tourists taking an early vacation. We find out if there are any other strangers in the neighborhood. We go for walks ashore, because we are keen birdwatchers. I dare say some of our rambles may take us in the direction of Rustig Hoek farm. I must confess that I have a certain sympathy with Koetsveen, but he's going to be protected between now and Wednesday whether he likes it or not. I know the Dutch. They're as stubborn as hell. He'd never invite us back to help him, even if he was being threatened at gunpoint. So, we shall simply go back without being invited, or rather, I shall."

"If you go, I go," said Emmy.

"A charming and gallant sentiment," said her husband, "but we'll see how things work out. You might be more of a nuisance than a help."

"Thank you very much."

"Well, darling, be sensible. You'd be useless in a fight and you're not armed."

"Neither are you."

"I am, as a matter of fact. Inspector van der Valk was kind enough to provide me with a gun as carried by the Dutch police."

"Well, if I'm not going to be any use . . ."

"But you are. You will be our channel of communication."

"What do you mean?"

"My face is too well known," said Henry. "Yours isn't. Trapp knows you, of course, but for the moment we have to assume that he's on our side. Madeleine La Rue only saw the back of your head on a crowded terrace, and none of the other characters in this drama has ever met you. I shall lie low, while you do the chatting with the local shopkeepers and so on and establish yourself as a harmless vacationer. In fact, now that I come to think of it, I shall develop influenza."

"You'll do what?"

"I feel an attack coming on," said Henry. "I shall be confined to my bunk for a bit, which is why you will be shopping on your own and why we shall remain in Ijlp instead of going sailing. You can make a point of telling people in the village about my misfortune."

"In Dutch?" said Emmy. "Don't be silly."

"I think you'll find," said Henry, "that even up here there will be people who speak English."

A white motor cruiser, which they had noticed on their way through the village earlier, was still tied up to the main jetty at Ijlp. Henry took a good look at her on the way past, but all he learned was that her name was *Stormvogel* and her home port Sneek. There was no sign of life on board, and the blue canvas hood was firmly secured over the cockpit and doghouse. Nevertheless, having no desire for neighbors, Henry took the *Vrouwe Beatrix* on through the bridge and tied her up to a couple of wooden posts beside a grassy bank just outside the village.

As soon as the boat was safely moored Henry went below, while Emmy, armed with the shopping basket and a large pair of touristy sunglasses, went ashore and made her way to the main street of Ijlp.

She was back on board again within an hour, complete with a bulging basket, a lighter purse, and a fund of gossip.

"I struck it lucky almost at once," she said. "The woman in the general store speaks English—not very well, but enough to get by. And when the conversation got too complicated, she called her daughter, who had studied English at school and really speaks very well. I was absolutely insisting that I must have some grapefruit marmalade, you see . . ."

"You know I hate grapefruit marmalade," said Henry.

"That's not the point. I thought the best way to get chatting was to make a great point of asking for something that I could see they didn't have. By the time the daughter had understood what I wanted, and found that they didn't stock it, we were all tremendously chummy. I told them about my poor husband with influenza, and Mum said that there was a lot of it around. She said that the other English yachtsman from *Stormvogel* . . ."

"What's that?"

Emmy grinned. "Yes, indeed. Her very words—the other English yachtsman from *Stormvogel* had a very nasty cold. She had told him he should be in bed and call the doctor."

"What else did you find out about him? And where is he?"

"It's all a bit disappointing actually. Rather an anti-climax. The daughter said that he wasn't English but American. The mother said it came to the same thing, and there was quite a bit of discussion about that. Then the daughter said that anyhow he had gone back to Amsterdam, where he lived, on account of his cold. He arrived yesterday to start his vacation, she said, but had decided to postpone it; so he had shut up the boat and was leaving it in Ijlp until he got well again. Mother was eyeing daughter pretty suspiciously by then and demanded to know how she knew all this, whereupon daughter went pink and said she had happened to meet the American in the local café last night. He must have been making a bit of a pass at her. She's a very pretty girl."

"Oh, well," said Henry. "It sounds as though he's just a genuine tourist. Pity. Anything else?"

"Well, I changed the subject by asking if they had many visitors from England, and Mum said yes, in the summer season they did, but it was early yet. We were the first. Then came the interesting bit."

"Oh, do get on with it."

"Daughter said, 'What about the lady and gentleman in the

car yesterday, who stopped and asked the way to Rustig Hoek?' "

"What!" Henry sat up so abruptly that he bumped his head on the low cabin roof.

Emmy went on. "Mother said not to be silly; the gentleman had certainly been Dutch and the car was Dutch. Daughter said maybe so, but the lady was English, she was sure of it, even though she spoke Dutch. Mother agreed that the lady had had a foreign accent, but that didn't mean that they were visitors from England. In fact, she said, she knew they weren't, because the gentleman had told her that they were friends of Mijnheer de Jong's from Amsterdam, and she'd told them that Mijnheer wasn't at Rustig Hoek, only Mevrouw and the little girl. Then they lapsed into Dutch—the mother and daughter, I mean—and I couldn't understand any more."

"Mrs. de Jong said this morning that we were her first visitors of the year," said Henry.

"I know. Nevertheless, it does seem that two people, a Dutchman and a Dutch-speaking Englishwoman, arrived in Ijlp by car yesterday afternoon and asked for the farm. Presumably they didn't go there. Or else they did call, but Mrs. de Jong was out."

"She said that she and Ineke had spent all day cleaning the house," Henry pointed out. "Did you get a description of these people?"

"My dear Henry, how could I? It would have looked terribly suspicious if I'd started prying. No, I thought I'd done enough there, so I went on to the bakery. No good at all. There was a sweet old lady serving the bread, but I don't think she even spoke Dutch, just the local dialect. I had to point to the loaf I wanted and let her pick the right money out of my purse. The butcher was no better, because it's a tiny shop and it was crowded with local housewives. The two men were being run off their feet, and I just couldn't stay and chat. Then I had an inspiration."

"What was that?"

"The post office. I assumed I'd surely find somebody there who spoke English. So I went in and asked for stamps, and sure enough the young man answered me in the most BBC accent you ever heard."

"And did he tell you anything?"

"No, not about English tourists, that is. But I was able to find out about hotel accommodations in the village."

Henry beamed at her. "You are not," he said generously, "nearly as stupid as you look."

Emmy beamed back complacently. "I knew just how your mind would work," she said. "At least, I knew how I thought you would think that I ought to . . ."

"Let's take that as read," said Henry. "Just get on with it, will you?"

"Well, I said to myself, 'This couple in the car—if they really are friends of the De Jongs from Amsterdam, they'll simply have driven back home. But if they are dead set on connecting with Rustig Hoek farm, they'll have to stay in the neighborhood. They obviously aren't house guests at Rustig Hoek so, Q.E.D., they must be staying at a local hostelry.' So I asked the man in the post office."

"And he said . . . ?"

"That there's only one hotel in Ijlp, called something unpronounceable which apparently means the Golden Lion. It's not a hotel at all, really, just a café-bar with four bedrooms upstairs. Otherwise, the man said, most of the summer visitors come by boat or are campers. There's a big camping site near the canal, not far away. And some of the local people let rooms in the summer, but it's too early for that. So at the moment it's the Golden Lion or nothing."

"So you went there?"

"Of course. Right away. It's at the far end of the main shopping street opposite the church. I thought I was really rather clever."

"Did you now? In what way?"

"Well, obviously what I wanted was to get a look at the register without anybody spotting what I was doing. So I went

169

up to what passes for the reception desk, where there was a dear old lady busy knitting, and I asked her if my friend Mrs. van der Valk was staying in the hotel."

"Mrs. who?"

"Van der Valk. You know, Arlette, that charming French-woman we met in Amsterdam, the police inspector's wife. It was the only Dutch name I could think of on the spur of the moment."

"You asked this in Dutch?"

"Of course not. I kept on asking the same question in English, getting a few decibels louder each time. The poor old dear was completely flummoxed. In the end she did what I hoped she would. She put down her knitting and said, '*Engels*' in a hopeful sort of way, so I bellowed '*Ja Engels!*' And she said something about her son—at least, it sounded like 'son'—and bustled off. She came back with a rather nice-looking young man, and we established that Mrs. van der Valk wasn't staying at the hotel, and I left. But meanwhile I'd been able to sneak a look at the register."

"And what did you find?"

"Nothing very sensational. There *is* a couple staying there who may or may not be the couple in the car. They checked in yesterday, which would fit, but the name means nothing at all—an outlandish Dutch name, written in very sprawly hand-writing. I couldn't read it properly, but it looked something like Filamed."

"That doesn't sound like a Dutch name to me," said Henry. "Nor English either, for that matter. How was it spelled?"

"F-I-L-A-M-E-D—that's what it looked like anyhow. I told you the writing was bad."

"Any address?"

"Just Amsterdam."

"I don't . . ." Henry began and then suddenly stopped and said softly, "Of course. What an idiot I've been. Have you got a piece of paper and a pencil?"

"I think so—half a minute . . . Yes, here."

Henry took the pencil and wrote something. Then he showed it to Emmy and said, "Could it have been spelled like that?"

"I—well—yes, it could. D often looks like EL, and the A could have been—but does it help us?"

"I don't know about helping us," said Henry, "but it fits the jigsaw into place. Now at least we know who is who."

"What does that mean?"

"It means that we know who killed Byers and who is staying at the Golden Lion—or was last night—and who will almost certainly try to kill old Koetsveen before Wednesday."

"I suppose it's too much," said Emmy, "to ask you to explain."

"Not at all," said Henry. "It's a little complicated, but I'll do my best." And he did.

When Henry had finished, Emmy nodded thoughtfully. "Yes," she said. "Yes, of course. But who is the woman? Madeleine La Rue?"

"I expect so. Almost certainly." He paused. "There was no sign of either of them at the Golden Lion?"

"No sign at all. And no car in the yard outside."

Henry said, "Will you run another errand for me?"

"Of course. What?"

"Go to the post office and call this number . . ." He scribbled on the paper. "Ask for Inspector van der Valk. Ask him to try to find out about our friend's past history. If he's Dutch by origin he probably came to England during the war. Ask the Inspector to get Interpol to help. Tell him you'll ring again at four o'clock this afternoon to hear what he's been able to find out. Tell him where we are and that we don't need any help."

Emmy opened her brown eyes wide. "We don't?"

Henry grinned. "We do, of course, but the last thing I want is to alarm everyone—not least Koetsveen—by having swarms of gendarmes arriving in the village. Our best bet is to take the opposition by surprise, and I don't think they know we're here. If they're too clever for us—well—no amount of cops are going to be able to save the old man, which is the object of the exercise."

Emmy sighed. "You know best," she said. "Let's have that phone number."

It was at half past twelve, when all good Dutch citizens are firmly anchored to their dining-room tables, that the English couple from the *Vrouwe Beatrix* set off on a walk across the fields. The lady who ran the general store saw them go from her window and remarked to her daughter that the gentleman really should not be out if he had influenza; but her daughter, who spoke such excellent English, replied that he was well wrapped up, had a big scarf around his neck right up to his nose. Her mother also commented on the fact that he and his wife both carried binoculars, to which the daughter replied that Mevrouw had mentioned that they were keen bird watchers. Whereupon mother and daughter resumed their meal in silence.

It did not take Henry and Emmy long to discover that walking across the fields in Holland is a very different matter from doing the same thing in England. Apart from the fact that many fields are isolated by canals and therefore inaccessible, most of the lush green pastures of the Netherlands are little more than prettily disguised bogs. Even the sleek cattle sink up to their slender ankles while grazing, and human pedestrians are well advised to keep to the raised footpaths which run along the tops of dikes, if they wish to remain dry shod. If a Dutchman has to walk in the fields, he does so in clogs, which are miraculously waterproof and warm.

Between Ijlp and Rustig Hoek farm, dike-top paths were few and far between—and in any case, people walking on them are extremely conspicuous—so Henry and Emmy had to stick to the fields. As they squelched uncomfortably through the mud in their unsuitable shoes, they found themselves feeling rather less attracted to the Dutch landscape than they had been from the boat.

In spite of their slow and glutinous progress, however, they were in sight of the farm before two o'clock. The Koetsveen family was apparently at lunch, for there was no sign of life; and since the open green fields afforded very little cover anyway, there seemed no point in not getting as close to the house as possible. Finally Henry and Emmy established themselves on the bank of a narrow canal which ran down to the main waterway just beyond the hen run. From this vantage point at the side of the farm they had a good view in both directions. To landward they could see the backyard and the hen coop, where Little Annie and her white sisters were happily pecking grain. In the other direction they could see the landing stage and the front garden.

Emmy unrolled the two plastic raincoats which they had brought with them and laid them on the damp grass. Then the two of them stretched out prone, sheltered from view to some extent by the steep bank of the little canal, and trained their binoculars on the house.

There was nothing to see. The landing stage was empty and so was the backyard. In fact, the only thing that made the exercise tolerable was the fact that there actually were fascinating birds to watch. Henry, conscientiously, kept his glasses trained on the farmhouse, with its blind windows and closed doors; but Emmy let hers wander, and delightedly observed godwits, lapwings, oyster-catchers, a heron, and even, by great good fortune, a pair of ruffs. She was watching enthralled as the male bird displayed his enormous, unbelievable yellow ruff, which framed his sharp red face, making him look like an Elizabethan dandy, when Henry suddenly said, "Hello. Look at that."

"I can't," said Emmy. "Henry, you *must* watch this. I've never seen anything like it. It's fantastic."

"It certainly is," Henry replied, training his binoculars on the landing stage. "Bold as brass, right up to the front door."

"What's that?"

"Look, for heaven's sake. Our friends have arrived. The question now is—what the hell do we do?"

Emmy swung her glasses away from the courting birds with some reluctance and focused on the jetty. She saw a sturdy metal rowboat of the kind that can be hired in nearly every Dutch waterside village bobbing on the canal beside the landing stage. A tall man dressed in gray flannel trousers and a yellow sweater had jumped onto the jetty and was tying the boat's mooring line to a post. This done, he turned and held out a hand to help his companion scramble ashore.

"It is Madeleine La Rue," whispered Emmy.

"Yes. There's no need to whisper. They can't possibly hear you. More important to keep your head down. We don't want to be seen."

"And that's—him?"

"It is. Mr. Nightingale in person, alias Filomeel."

"But . . ."

"Ssh."

Madeleine, looking ravishing in slim, sky-blue denim pants and a beige shirt, was standing on the jetty now, laughing, her corn-colored hair thrown back from her tanned face. Nightingale laughed back, then leaned toward her and said something. She nodded, and they both walked up the lawn to the house.

Emmy said, "They make a handsome couple."

"Charming," said Henry dryly. "Blast it," he added as Nightingale and Madeleine disappeared from view. "Come on. We've got to get nearer the water so that we can see the front of the house."

"They'll see us."

"Not if we're careful."

Still sheltered by the canal bank, they wriggled along until they were in line with the front of the house. From here they watched Nightingale ringing the doorbell. The door was opened—impossible to see by whom—and a smiling, explanatory conversation took place. Then Nightingale and Madeleine went into the house.

Henry swore. Since the *jol* was not at the landing stage there was a good possibility that Koetsveen was out sailing, in which case Nightingale and Madeleine would be able to do no more than make some sort of plan to come back later on. On the other hand, Koetsveen might be at home, and Corry and Ineke out in the boat. In which case . . .

"Hello, Henry," said a piping voice behind Henry's left ear.

He rolled over and found himself looking up into Ineke's smiling face.

"What are you wearing that funny scarf for?" she demanded. She dropped down on the grass beside him.

"I've got a cold," said Henry.

"Oh, I see." Ineke considered. "I thought perhaps it was because you didn't want to be recognized, because Grandpapa was so cross this morning. I recognized you right away. I was over there"—she gestured toward a distant canal—"looking for frogs. Why did you hide behind the bank and watch our house through those telescope things?"

"Ineke," said Henry, "where is your grandpapa?"

"Don't worry," said Ineke, "he won't catch you. He's out in the boat. He said he wouldn't be in until suppertime."

"And when is that?"

"Oh, about seven."

Henry breathed a sigh of relief. He said, "Will you do something for me, Ineke?"

"It depends."

"It's a sort of game, you see."

"What is?"

"I can't tell you yet, or it would spoil it. I want you to go into the house now . . ."

"There's a lady and gentleman in there with Mummy," said Ineke. "They came up in a rowboat. You were watching them. Are they part of the game?"

"In a way," said Henry. "They—they're the other side. We're playing against them. I'd like you to be on our team."

"All right. What do I have to do?"

"Go into the house and sit very quietly and listen to what the lady and gentleman say to your mummy, and then come back here and tell us after they've gone."

Ineke considered. "What will you give me if I do?"

175

"Nothing," said Henry. "But if you don't, I'll never play with you again. And I'll never tell you what the game was about."

Ineke giggled. "All right," she said. "You wait here."

And she scampered off toward the back door.

Emmy said, "I'm frightened for the child, Henry. I don't think you should have done that. If she blurts out . . ."

"She won't," said Henry. "Ineke is a very competent young woman. In any case, how else could we find out . . . ?"

"I'll be happier when she gets back to us safe and sound," said Emmy. "Oh, well, I suppose all we can do is wait."

Some ten minutes later Nightingale and Madeleine emerged again from the front door. This time Mrs. de Jong was with them. She walked them down to the jetty and helped them into their rowboat. Then she cast off the mooring line for them, waved, and watched as Nightingale propelled the little craft back up the canal toward Ijlp. As she turned to go back into the house, the back door opened and Ineke came skipping out. A minute or two later she was squatting on the grass beside Henry.

"Well?" he asked.

"They wanted to see my daddy," she said, "but he's in Amsterdam. Mummy told them so."

"They didn't ask for your grandpapa?"

"Wait a minute. I'm coming to that," said Ineke importantly. "They said they were friends of Daddy's and that he had told them to call here if they were ever in Friesland. The lady spoke in a funny sort of voice, like a foreign person. Like you do. So that one can understand, but it's not really proper Dutch."

"And the gentleman?"

"Oh, he spoke just ordinarily, like anybody from Amsterdam."

"So what happened when they heard your daddy wasn't here?"

"They said, when would he be? And Mummy said not until Easter—that's at the end of the week. And they said what a pity, because they had to go to England then. So they got up to leave, and just as they were going the lady said she hoped Mummy wouldn't think her rude, but that she had seen Koetsveen—that's Grandpapa's name—written up by the front door, and surely it couldn't be His Excellency Jan Koetsveen? Well, it is, of course, and Mummy said yes, he was her father; and the lady said fancy that, Willem, to the gentleman, and he said"—Ineke paused long enough to take a deep breath—"he said, yes it was an extraordinary co—co—something. A long word. And then he said to Mummy that he must explain. His wife had been a little girl in Holland in the war, and my grandpapa had helped her to escape to England. My grandpapa was very brave in the war. I'm saying that myself; it's not what the gentleman said. But he was. My mummy has told me. He helped lots and lots of people to escape. So he must have been brave, mustn't he?"

"He certainly must," said Henry.

Ineke swept on. "Then the lady said what a pity Grandpapa wasn't here, because she had always wanted to meet him again one day. She couldn't really remember him at all from the war, she said, because she had been so little, not quite six, which is *very* young, you see," Ineke explained, from the superior height of her own eight and a half years. "So of course Mummy said that he *was* here, only out in the *jol*, and that he'd be in about seven this evening, and wouldn't they come and have some sherry; and they said they would, and then they went away. Is that what you wanted to know?"

"It's exactly what I wanted to know, Ineke," said Henry. "You've done very well indeed. I'm proud of you."

"Is that the end of the game?" Ineke sounded disappointed.

"Not quite," said Henry. "There's one more thing for you to do."

"What? Something when they come this evening? Shall I listen again and come and tell you?"

"No, not this time. What I want you to do is to let me know when they arrive."

"You'll see them."

"I may not. It gets dark quite early, and we shall be out on the canal in our boat."

"Will you? Can I come with you?"

"No, not today," said Henry.

"Oh, *why* not?"

"Because if you were in the boat with us, you couldn't be playing the game for our team in the house, could you?"

Ineke bowed to the logic of this. "Why are the lady and gentleman on the other side?" she demanded. "I thought they were nice."

"That's something I can't explain yet," said Henry. He put his hand into his pocket and brought out a small pocket flashlight. "Do you know what this is?"

"Of course I do. It's a flashlight."

"Not an ordinary flashlight," said Henry.

"Why isn't it?"

"Because it's extra strong so that it can be seen from far away."

"Show me."

Henry pressed the switch and the little flashlight blazed with a thin beam of light which was, indeed, much more powerful than its modest exterior suggested.

"Now," he said, "when the lady and gentleman arrive, I want you to light this flashlight and put it in the window beside the front door facing out over the canal so that I'll see it from my boat. Draw the curtain and put the flashlight behind it on the windowsill. And be sure nobody sees you do it. All right?"

"Is that all?"

"Yes, except to put the flashlight out again when they leave. And don't say anything to anybody, not even your mummy. It's a big secret."

"When I put the flashlight in the window, and you see it, will you come up in your boat?"

"I expect so, but I'm not sure."

"And I can listen to what they say as well, can't I?"

"If you like, but you don't have to."

"I do like. And if you don't come up to the house in your boat, I shall come out here to this very spot, and you must be here too, and I'll tell you all of what they say, like I did just now."

"I wouldn't do that," said Henry. "We won't be here."

"You must be here, if I say so," said Ineke imperiously. "I shall come and look anyway, when I come out to give Little Annie her supper."

"Ineke! Where are you?" Mevrouw de Jong was calling from the back door.

"That's Mummy," said Ineke. "I'd better go now." She slipped the flashlight into the pocket of her jeans and skipped off across the fields. Henry just heard the beginning of a complicated explanation involving frogs, before the back door closed behind mother and daughter.

Emmy said, "You'd better translate. I didn't understand a word of that."

Henry told her. When he had finished, she said, "My sister and I . . ."

"What do you mean? Whose sister?"

"That song from the war about the children who escaped from Holland. They were playing it on the barrel organ in Amsterdam."

"Well, what about it?"

"Yvonne and Madeleine La Rue. I wonder what their real name is?"

"You surely don't believe that Koetsveen really smuggled them out of Holland as children? That was just . . ."

"Well, why shouldn't it be true? How else would they know about what he did in the war?"

"I don't suppose his activities were kept secret, after the war, I mean. Plenty of people must know."

Emmy ignored the interruption. "And she speaks Dutch, which is quite unusual. I mean, it's not generally taught in English schools . . ."

179

"She has a strong foreign accent."

"Well, that's not surprising, if she's lived in England since she was five."

"Whereas," said Henry, "Nightingale speaks, according to Ineke, like anybody from Amsterdam—which I find interesting."

"So what do we do now?"

"We go back to the boat," said Henry, "and you telephone Van der Valk, as arranged."

"Perhaps we could find Mr. Koetsveen in his boat and warn him."

"Perhaps pigs could fly. Heaven knows where he is, and if we did find him, he's too bloody stubborn to listen to us. It's going to be harder saving Koetsveen from himself than from Nightingale. Come on."

14

Ijlp on a Monday afternoon in April could hardly be called a hive of activity. The village drowsed peacefully under the watery sun. A golden spaniel bitch, asleep in a patch of sunlight on the pavement outside the bakery, yawned and stretched and slept again. The pretty daughter in the general store listened to pop music and painted her fingernails and wondered when the handsome American would come back. The old lady in the Golden Lion knitted placidly behind the reception desk; she looked up briefly as a car engine revved up in the yard of the inn and saw that it was the lady and gentleman from Amsterdam, who had packed their bags and paid their bill and were now presumably on their way, leaving the little hotel to its usual out-of-season calm. As the noise of the powerful motor died away in the direction of Amsterdam, silence descended like a falling blossom on the cobbled street.

Half an hour later, at a quarter past three, an engine noise of a different sort brought the pretty girl to the door of the general store just in time to see *Stormvogel* leaving her mooring and making off down the canal. So he was back, and he had *promised* to take her out. He must have decided to go for an afternoon's spin in the boat, but he would surely come back this evening. The girl called to her mother to mind the shop and ran upstairs to wash her hair and iron her best dress.

Soon after this Henry and Emmy arrived back at the *Vrouwe Beatrix*, damp and footsore after their trek across the fields. Henry went below, and Emmy walked up to the post office to telephone, taking her shopping basket with her.

She came back to the boat bearing an unwanted package of

coffee, the price of the latest gossip gleaned from the general store. This was chiefly negative, consisting as it did of the two departures from the village—the couple from the Golden Lion and the American gentleman in *Stormvogel*.

"But *he* may be back this evening, according to Mrs. General Store," Emmy added. "She sounded a bit miffed about it. I dare say her daughter has a date with him and she doesn't approve. Otherwise, there's about as much going on in Ijlp as there is in a deserted rabbit hole."

"And what did Van der Valk say? Any line on Nightingale?"

"Well, now, interesting, but not conclusive. There's no record anywhere of anybody called Filomeel or even Philomel, and the only Nachtegaals known are blameless citizens of Amsterdam. As far as the Dutch police are concerned, our man is simply Mr. Nightingale of London, a British citizen visiting Holland. However, it's apparently a fact that during the German occupation in the 1940's there was a resistance worker—something of a hero and a great daredevil—who went by the pseudonym of Filomeel. He was an Amsterdammer, which would fit with Nightingale's accent, and he'd be about the right age. Filomeel's real name was Willem van Dam, which I gather is about the equivalent of John Smith over here."

"Ineke said that Madeleine called him Willem."

"I know. There's only one snag. Filomeel is dead."

"I wonder," said Henry. "Go on."

"Well, the Inspector says that Van Dam came from a good family and was a bright, high-spirited boy, so high-spirited that he'd been in trouble with the police by the time he was seventeen—joy-riding in cars that didn't belong to him. Of course, the adventure of the resistance movement would have been just the thing for a boy like that, and he became a sort of Robin Hood figure."

"Did he work with Koetsveen?"

"I asked that, and the Inspector said he couldn't be sure, but he didn't think so, although they certainly must have known of each other. Apparently Koetsveen masterminded a lot of escapes and was just as brave as Ineke says. Anyhow, by late 1942 things had gotten too hot in Holland for Filomeel. Not only were the Gestapo after him, but he had fallen out with a lot of his own people, for reasons which I'll explain. Anyhow, he did a flit, with some other refugees, in a small boat bound for England. The boat never arrived. It ran into a gale in the North Sea and apparently there were no survivors among the five people on board."

"Only apparently?"

"Well, the Inspector says that there *was* a rumor afterward that Filomeel had survived, been picked up by an English merchant ship and taken to England."

"But if that was so, why didn't he come forward after the war? Why make a secret of it?"

"Ah, that's just the point. When I said that he was a sort of Robin Hood, I meant it. Robbing the rich was one of his favorite hobbies. That is to say, he would arrange escapes for wealthy people for a price. The other members of his group didn't know at first that their precious nightingale was feathering his own nest out of the pockets of grateful clients, and when they did find out they were pretty angry, as you can imagine. Rumor has it that he left the country just in time to escape their wrath, *and* with a considerable fortune in his pocket in the form of jewelry. Actually, if he did manage to survive, the wrecking of the boat was extremely fortunate for him.

"As far as the Dutch are concerned, he's officially dead, but the Inspector thinks it is just possible that he survived and landed in England as a refugee. He'd have given a false name —Nachtegaal, probably, since it's quite a common Dutch name and the non-poetic equivalent of Filomeel. So that eventually he would have been naturalized as Mr. Nightingale, the English translation of his Dutch name. Very naturally, he hasn't declared his existence to the Dutch authorities. He knows that there are some of his old comrades who would still be prepared to settle their scores with him."

Henry laughed. "What a marvelous piece of cheek," he said. "It must be the same man."

"What's marvelous cheek?"

"That when he does come back, he registers at the hotel as Mr. Filomeel. A small country inn, to be sure, and only for one night; but there's a sheer, crusty impudence about it that appeals to me." He lit his pipe. "Well, I dare say we can check back in England, but there's no time for that now. And personally, I've no doubts, have you? Our Mr. Nightingale is the wartime Filomeel, alias Willem van Dam. Quite a formidable opponent."

There was a little silence, and then Emmy said, "I'm thinking about Ineke."

"So am I," said Henry. "But he's not after her, thank God."

"So, what do we do now?"

"We set out for an evening cruise in the direction of Rustig Hoek," said Henry. "We look for Ineke's light. After that, we play it by ear. Yvonne La Rue knew about Koetsveen's weak heart, so you may be sure that Nightingale knows it too. My guess is that there won't be any open violence. Poor Mr. Koetsveen will have a heart attack—if possible, after the charming Mr. and Mrs. Filomeel have left the farm. Not even Mrs. de Jong will suspect that it's anything but natural; she'll tell the doctor that he got overexcited talking about wartime exploits with old friends . . ."

"How will it be done?"

"A stimulant drug, I imagine, the same thing that finished off old Findelhander—in the last drink of the evening."

"So we mustn't allow this little party to develop?"

"We must not," said Henry. "Let's get going and try to break it up before it starts."

The canal was very quiet and still in the deepening dusk. There was no breath of wind, and the calls of the marsh birds sounded clearly and mournfully through the limpid air. In every direction the flat, misty horizon seemed very far away, and the afternoon warmth faded as the sun went down. Wisps of mist rose from the water and drifted like ghosts

184

over the fields. The *Vrouwe Beatrix,* her motor just ticking over, glided slowly up the canal and came to rest, with her nose in the reeds, just below Rustig Hoek farm. Henry threw out a bow anchor on the reedy bank, switched off the engine, and settled down in the cockpit to wait.

He had a clear view of the farmhouse door and of the window beside it. There was a light in the kitchen at the back of the house, but none in the hallway, and no flashlight beam from the window. Henry and Emmy waited, and the whole darkening landscape seemed to hold its breath.

The next thing that happened was the arrival of the car. The headlights—hardly necessary in the twilight—blazed out a moving trail of brightness across the distant fields, even before the noise of the engine ripped the quiet air. Henry could follow the progress of the car by its lights, as it came roaring down the Sneek road, turned off on a small secondary road beside a narrow canal, and finally, at a much slower pace, swung into the rutted track that led to Rustig Hoek farm.

The front door of the house, of course, faced the waterway, so that visiting vehicles were parked outside the kitchen door in the yard at the back, and their occupants had to walk around the house to the canal side if they wished to ring the doorbell in the orthodox way. The big black car pulled up outside the back door of the farm out of sight of the watchers on the water, but they could hear its engine being switched off and the banging of doors as the visitors got out. Simultaneously, the curtain was drawn across the little window beside the front door, as a light came on in the hall.

A moment later Nightingale and Madeleine, clearly recognizable in silhouette even in the twilight, came walking around the house and up the path to the front door. If they noticed the *Vrouwe Beatrix,* which was partially but not completely hidden in the reeds, they gave no sign of it. Nightingale rang the doorbell and a moment later Mrs. de Jong opened the door with a smile of welcome. The visitors stepped into the lighted hallway, and the door closed behind them. Less than a minute later a small hand stole around the edge

185

of the curtain on the windowsill and a beam of light stabbed into the dusk. Ineke was being as efficient as ever.

"He's not back yet," said Henry quietly. He looked at his watch. "It's only just seven. Our friends were impatient. Now they'll have to wait for him."

"And so what do we do?"

"I think in the circumstances," said Henry, "that we must intercept him and try to batter some sense into his stubborn Dutch head. With any luck we can arrange for a sensational anti-climax. If Koetsveen will only cooperate, we'll get him to take the boat back to Ijlp and telephone from there that his motor has broken down. There's no wind, so he can't sail home. It'll seem quite natural if he says he's decided to stay with the boat and have dinner at the Golden Lion. Nightingale can hardly stay at the farm all night drinking sherry. He'll have to come looking for the old man in Ijlp, and that will be much more difficult for him and easier for us."

"I wish we knew which direction *Koet* will be coming from," said Emmy. "We must try to intercept her before she gets to the jetty."

"I know. As far as I can see, there's nothing to do but to patrol the canal in both directions, and hope that nobody in the house gets suspicious."

So the anchor was disentangled from the reeds and the *Vrouwe Beatrix* began pounding her beat—half a mile up the canal toward Ijlp, turn around, back past Rustig Hoek landing stage, and half a mile beyond it in the other direction. Then turn around again. Each time they passed the farmhouse, Emmy and Henry saw the flashlight beam shining steadily from the hall window and light streaming from the uncurtained living-room window at the side of the house. There was no other sign of life.

On the third leg of this tedious patrol the monotony was suddenly broken by the high-pitched chatter of an outboard motor, which ripped the silence like an electric drill; but it turned out to be nothing more sensational than the flat fishing dinghy from which they had asked directions that morn-

186

ing. It was making its way noisily back to Ijlp with three bent figures crouching over their creels.

It was on the next run toward Ijlp that they saw the *jol, Koet*. She had passed through the bridge, which was now being lowered behind her, and was plowing a straight course down the canal toward home. Henry opened up the throttle and put on as much speed as the *Vrouwe Beatrix* could muster so as to intercept the *jol* before she reached the bend which hid Rustig Hoek from Ijlp. The farther away from the farm, the better. As Henry strained his eyes in the deepening dusk to watch the black shape of the tubby little boat, she suddenly stopped. As far as he could make out, she had pulled into the reeds beside the canal several hundred yards short of the bend.

Much intrigued, Henry slackened speed and allowed his boat to creep up through the dusk toward *Koet,* where she lay nuzzling the reeds; and then Emmy, who had gone up to the bow, said, "Oh, it's only the fishermen." She clambered back into the cockpit.

Henry said, "The three old men we spoke to this morning?"

"Yes. They've pulled up alongside Koetsveen's boat. I expect they're old friends of his, and . . ."

"Shut up," said Henry suddenly. He switched off the motor. Silently the *Vrouwe Beatrix* drifted toward the *jol,* carrying her way and assisted by a gentle evening breeze which had lately started to rustle the reeds.

"Look," Henry whispered.

On the face of it the scene represented the epitome of pastoral calm. The only light came from a small hurricane lantern on the bow of *Koet,* and the two boats rode gently side by side in the shelter of the reeds, outlined against a red-and-golden sunset. But a closer inspection showed signs of elements that were strangely at odds with this peaceful picture. In the small fishing boat the central figure sat slumped on the thwart, as if asleep. One of the others was in the act of jumping aboard the *jol,* in a manner altogether too youthful and

187

athletic for an aged fisherman. In his right hand he held something that Henry could not identify but which suggested the squat, sinister shape of a blackjack. The third man, who was standing up in the fishing boat, was shining a flashlight on the deck of the *jol*. None of them appeared to notice the silent presence of the *Vrouwe Beatrix,* or if they did, they had decided that it was not worthy of consideration.

Just then a portly figure, also carrying a flashlight, came up from the cabin of the *jol.* He had what looked like a bottle in his hand. Henry recognized the voice of His Excellency Jan Koetsveen.

"Dear me," he said in Dutch. "Poor old Nol. I've told him a hundred times he shouldn't stay out so late on the water at his age. Here, give him a drop of brandy. That'll make him . . ."

He got no further. The two agile fishermen were by now on board *Koet,* and there was a curious, muffled sound as all three figures disappeared into the cabin below. The man in the fishing boat remained motionless, his head nodding toward his knees.

"My God," said Henry. "I should have guessed . . ." He started the motor. "Keep the boat going slow and not too far away. I'm going on board Koetsveen's boat."

"Henry—you can't . . ."

"It's two to one, but I'm armed."

"I'm coming with you!"

"Don't be a bloody fool. Stay at the helm and stand by to pick me up—or do whatever I say. Take her, now!"

There was no time for argument. Emmy grabbed the helm of the *Vrouwe Beatrix* as Henry clambered up on her deck. He had brought her alongside the *jol,* separated from the tubby hull only by the fishing boat and its unconscious occupant. As the boats bumped together, Henry jumped into the *jol*'s cockpit.

There was no doubt that his arrival on board caused a sensation. The light in the cabin went out, and at the same moment a brawny head and a pair of shoulders appeared in the cockpit, cursing in English. "Who the hell . . . ?"

Henry had just time to reassure himself that the safety catch of the 9-mm. automatic was on; then he raised the gun as if to fire, but instead brought it down with all his force against the temple of the brawny man. The latter grunted and slumped down, half in and half out of the cabin, blocking the entrance.

As Henry tried desperately to drag him out into the cockpit, he could hear a medley of confused Dutch and French coming from the cabin. Koetsveen was shouting and demanding help, which at least showed that he was still alive. A robust French-speaking voice from the darkness indicated that its owner would take pleasure in settling conclusions with the interloper and that he was armed.

Henry paused for a moment, considering the dilemma. Framed against the sunset, he was uneasily aware that he made a splendid target for a gunman hidden in the darkness of the cabin. Henry himself dared not fire into the cabin for fear of hitting Koetsveen. On the other hand, as long as the inert body of the English-speaking thug blocked the cabin exit, the Frenchman would be unable to shoot Henry, protected as he was by the human sandbag in the cabin doorway.

So far as Henry and the armed Frenchman were concerned, this created a situation of stalemate. Still, the Frenchman had Koetsveen in the cabin with him. Henry guessed that his orders had not been to kill the old man outright but to fabricate an accident; however, in the changed circumstances, it was anybody's guess how a man with a gun would react, and the risk to Koetsveen was too great. Somehow or other the Frenchman must be lured out of the cabin.

Henry called in French, "Don't shoot! I am a friend. I have new orders from Filomeel!"

"Liar! You're an Englishman!"

"Come up into the cockpit and I'll explain . . ."

"I take my orders from Filomeel. Nobody else. And if you're a friend, why did you hit Charlie?"

189

"Because he attacked me. He's not hurt. Just come up . . ."

"I'll come up when I've finished the old man off, not sooner. And then it'll be your turn."

Henry laughed. "Do as you please, my friend. But wait until Filomeel hears about it."

"I have my orders . . ."

"To shoot Koetsveen?"

"No. But . . ."

"And I suppose you've been paid already?"

"You know very well we haven't. Only a retainer . . ."

Henry's heart rose. Two things were becoming clear—that this Frenchman was beginning to believe that Henry was, indeed, part of Filomeel's organization and that the very name of Filomeel inspired terror.

He said, "I've got the rest of the money here with new orders. If you choose to ignore them and kill the old man, go ahead. I'll go back and report to Filomeel."

"You're lying." But there was less conviction in the voice now. "Who are you?"

Who am I? Henry wondered desperately. At a venture he said, "My name's Weatherby. You've heard of me."

There was a pause. Then the voice said, "Get back to the after end of the cockpit, where I can see you. And put your gun down. I'll come up to talk, but I'm armed, and if there's any funny business, I shoot."

Henry dared not argue. The man's suspension of disbelief was hanging on a gossamer thread, and somehow he had to be lured out of that cabin away from Koetsveen.

He said, "Suspicious devil, aren't you? Okay. My gun." He threw it down onto the cockpit seat and then moved aft. "There. Do I make a satisfactory target?"

The Frenchman grunted. "I'll come up," he said. "No, don't move. I'll get Charlie out of the way . . ."

It was at that moment that Henry realized Emmy and the *Vrouwe Beatrix* had disappeared. He was alone and unarmed, with no line of retreat open to him, on a small boat with a couple of gunmen—one of them unconscious, certainly, but only temporarily, and the other climbing slowly but steadily out of the cabin, gun in hand, pushing aside the inert body of his colleague as he came. There was only one thing to be done. Henry took a deep breath and leaped down on his opponent, who was still only halfway out of the cabin, still hampered by the unconscious Charlie.

The gun went off wildly, with a shattering report, and Henry felt a sharp pain in his left arm. For a moment the three men were tangled in a confused melée of arms and legs in the cockpit well; then, as the Frenchman launched himself on Henry, the latter's arm sent out a stab of pain that brought a scream to his lips. At that moment the large Englishman began to stir. As pain surged through him, and he went crashing down on his back in the cockpit, Henry realized that it was all up. He'd failed. He'd been a bloody fool, trying to go it alone, and now he was going to pass out, and . . .

Suddenly there was a great deal of noise. The Frenchman stopped twisting his injured arm and there were a series of decisive thuds. Then Henry found himself lying on the cockpit floor in company with a comatose Frenchman and Charlie, whose return to the affairs of the world had been exceedingly brief. Squatting on the cockpit seat, grinning down at him and fondling the Dutch police automatic in a practiced manner, was a large, sturdy man with graying fair hair, a man whom Henry had never seen before.

"Superintendent Tibbett, I believe," said this apparition in a voice with a marked South African accent. "Pleased to meet you, pal. My name's Honeyman."

15

Henry sat up slowly. His arm was throbbing and stiffening fast, and he could feel the stickiness of blood on his sleeve. His head ached as though it would explode. No time to wonder now how the legendary Mike Honeyman should have materialized in the middle of a Dutch canal to save his life. He said, "Where's Emmy?"

"Where's who, chum?"

"My wife. Emmy. And the boat . . ."

Another voice, cheerful and apparently disembodied, said, "Not to worry, dear old soul. She's off on some harmless ploy of her own."

Henry put a hand to his brow. "Trapp! Where are you, for God's sake?"

Gordon's head popped over the side of the *jol* like a water sprite's. "Greetings, friend Tibbett. You've met Mike, have you? Jolly good. I'm in this very damp dinghy, ascertaining that this poor fellow is still alive. Which, mercifully, he is. I suppose they just slipped him some species of Mickey Finn."

Henry said, "Koetsveen is in the cabin. He may be hurt." He began to struggle to his feet.

Honeyman put a hand the size of a small ham on Henry's shoulder, pushing him down. "You stay right where you are, mate," he said. "You've had a nasty crack on the head and I just hope you're not left-handed, because that arm is going to be out of action for quite a while." He leaned over the side of the boat and addressed the invisible fishing dinghy. "Come aboard, Trapp, and get a line around our friends before they begin to wake up. I'll go see to Koetsveen."

Honeyman heaved his considerable bulk down into the cabin, where he lit the paraffin lamp. At the same time Gordon Trapp jumped nimbly over the gunwale of the *jol* and proceeded to truss up the two unconscious villains in a businesslike manner, using a hank of nylon line from the after locker.

Henry achieved an upright position, found his head spinning dizzily, and sat down again heavily on the cockpit seat. He said, "Where's Emmy?"

"I told you. Went off to see— That should do you, *mon ami*—" he added, giving an extra tug to the knot securing the Frenchman's wrists. "I last saw this character at the Gare de Lyon. He was in better shape then—yes, Emmy's gone off to see a girl friend—don't worry . . ."

"A girl friend?" Henry still felt dazed. "What girl friend?"

Honeyman stuck his head up from the cabin. "The old boy's okay," he said. "They'd bound and gagged him, but there doesn't seem to be any serious damage—except to his ego, of course . . ." A sort of rumbling growl came from the cabin behind him. Honeyman winked. "See what I mean? Back soon . . ." He retreated into the cabin again, saying, "Yes, well, what can I do for you, sir?" with all the false heartiness of a male mental nurse.

Henry said, "So Honeyman was the American in *Stormvogel?*"

"American? What do you mean, American?"

"Never mind. How did you know where to find him?"

Trapp put the finishing touches to Charlie's bonds. Then he said, "It's a long story actually. You see, old Mike and I have known each other a long time, and I remembered that he once said that if ever . . ."

Henry stood up shakily. "What girl friend?" he said.

"I beg your pardon?"

Henry was shaking. "Emmy," he said. "What girl friend? I must be mad. She hasn't any girl friends here. What . . . ?"

"Here. Take it easy." Trapp sounded alarmed.

"What girl friend?"

"I don't know, my dear fellow. She just called out from the boat as she passed *Stormvogel*. Told us to go and help you, and . . ."

Consciousness was retreating; giddiness washed over Henry in recurring waves. He said again, "What girl friend?"

"She said she was going to see Ineke . . ."

"Ineke . . ."

From inside the cabin came a bellow from Koetsveen. "What's that about Ineke?"

"Come down into the cabin," Henry said to Trapp. "Got to talk."

"We've got to get you to a doctor, old sport."

"No, no. No time. You don't understand . . ."

Again Koetsveen's voice rose angrily above Honeyman's soothing murmur. "What about Ineke? And what in hell's name is Trapp doing here? Will somebody kindly explain . . . ?"

"Oh, my God," said Henry. "Now he'll probably have a heart attack and save Nightingale the trouble of . . ."

Koetsveen's ears were sharp and his physique seemed to be in good form. He elbowed Honeyman out of the way—no mean feat for any man—and his head and shoulders emerged like a snail into the cockpit.

"Heart attack? And why should I have a heart attack, may I ask? What could possibly give anyone the idea that I might have a heart attack?"

"Well, sir . . ." Trapp began.

"What are you doing here, Tibbett?" Koetsveen demanded. *"And what about Ineke?"*

Henry sat down again. The giddiness was getting worse. "Trapp thought you had a weak heart, sir," he said.

"Me? And what gave you that notion, young man?"

Trapp was embarrassed. "That day in the lavatory . . ."

Koetsveen gave him a hard, affronted stare. "If you are referring to my temporary lack of breath, there is a very simple explanation. I had gone into the lavatory to take an indigestion pill, and I had the misfortune to swallow it the wrong way . . ." He glared, defying contradiction. Then he addressed Henry. "And as for you, I thought I told you to keep out of my way and off my property . . ."

He stopped, chiefly because of an attack from the rear. Honeyman was disputing the narrow companionway with Koetsveen, and Henry was reminded of a contest between the walrus and the buffalo for the privilege of leaving the ark first.

Honeyman was no respecter of persons. He smote Koetsveen mightily on his spacious trouser seat and said, "Here, you. Lay off Tibbett, will you? He only saved your life just now, that's all."

"Saved my life? But it was you, dear sir, who . . ."

"And got his arm badly wounded into the bargain; but you don't care, do you, you ungrateful old bastard?"

"Gentlemen," said Henry, "please. We must talk. Let's go below."

"And what about Ineke?"

"That's the point, sir, Ineke and my wife."

"Oh. Ah." Koetsveen had the grace to look abashed. "Very well. And take your hands off me," he added belligerently as he lowered his posterior into the cabin past Honeyman.

Trapp helped Henry, and a moment later the four men were sitting tight-packed around the table in the boat's tiny cabin.

"Now," said Koetsveen, "I want explanations. Fast." He glared resentfully at his rescuers.

Henry said, "I did warn you this would happen, sir."

Koetsveen brushed this aside. "All right, all right. Get on with it. So I was attacked."

"And luckily for you, Tibbett was on the spot to save you," said Honeyman. "More than you deserved, chum, and that's telling you straight."

"You are a very impertinent young man," said Koetsveen, but he looked a little sheepish. "Now, for the tenth time, what about Ineke?"

Henry made a great effort to muster his reeling senses. He said, "You must realize, sir, that the two rather comic villains in the cockpit are only small fry. The brains behind all this is Filomeel."

195

"Filomeel?" Koetsveen looked as though he had seen a ghost. There was a moment of dead silence. Then he said, "Filomeel's dead. He's been dead for twenty-five years."

"He's not," said Henry. "He's very much alive. In fact, he's in Rustig Hoek farmhouse at this very moment with your daughter and Ineke."

"By God!" Koetsveen jumped to his feet, hitting his head against the cabin roof. He subsided again, massaging his bald crown. "I'll kill him, the young devil!"

"You knew him during the war?" Henry asked.

"Certainly I did. Oh, I don't deny he was brave. Ingenious, too. But when we found he'd been fleecing those wretched people just to put money into his own pocket, I can tell you, when news got back to Holland that he'd drowned in the North Sea there were plenty of us who thought he'd gotten no more than he deserved. And now you tell me . . ."

"You worked in the resistance movement yourself, didn't you?" asked Henry. As he sat in the cabin, the giddiness was just controllable, but still troublesome.

"I did, like most people. Nothing to make a fuss about."

"You helped to organize a lot of escapes from Holland?"

"A certain number, yes."

"Do you remember two little girls? About four and six years old. Madeleine and Yvonne La Rue."

"La Rue? La Rue? Never heard of any such—oh, you mean the Van Dam children."

"What?"

"Madeleine and Yvonne. Dear little girls. But . . ." He was grim again. "What makes you mention them?"

"Van Dam, you said?"

"Yes. Commonest name in Holland. They were the daughters of Piet van Dam." He paused and cleared his throat. "Willem's brother."

Henry said softly, "Filomeel's brother. So they are his nieces."

"The Gestapo got Piet." Koetsveen was dreaming, reliving the past. "Piet, and Ineke too."

196

"Ineke?"

"His wife. A beautiful girl. My granddaughter is called after her—in her memory. The Gestapo got them and deported them, and they were never seen again. And it was then—then . . ." The old voice shook with bitterness. "It was then that this great and famous hero, this Filomeel, this gallant patriot, refused to save his brother's children because the money wasn't right. There was no money at all, of course. That was when I finally broke with the young scoundrel. I arranged myself to get the little girls to England. They were so pretty—like my little Ineke . . ." Koetsveen sat up again and changed vocal gears. "And, for the umpteenth time, what is all this about Ineke? Is she in danger? What . . . ?"

Quickly, and still battling with the mists of pain and dizziness which had renewed their assault, Henry described Ineke's part in the evening's events, and what Emmy had called to Trapp.

"I can only think," he said, "that the flashlight must have gone out—Ineke's way of telling us that Filomeel and Madeleine were leaving. And then, Ineke said something about looking for us in the fields if we didn't come to the house. I told her not to, but, as you know, she is a very stubborn young woman."

"Can't imagine where she gets it from," remarked Honeyman to nobody in particular.

"So," said Henry, "I dare say Emmy saw her signaling from the field with the flashlight and . . ."

Koetsveen began to say something explosive about people who involved innocent children in dangerous enterprises, and then he caught Honeyman's eye, changed his mind, and said, "Well, what are we sitting here for? Let's get back to the farm and find out what's happening, for God's sake. And what about poor old Nol, the fisherman?"

They made their plans quickly, and in what Henry realized was an unsatisfactory and makeshift way; but, weak with pain, he allowed the others to map the plan of campaign.

Trapp was to take *Stormvogel*, which was moored nearby in

the reeds, back to Ijlp with a bizarre cargo—the two trussed criminals, the unconscious Nol, and Henry. The first two were to be handed over to the police and the others to the doctor. Koetsveen and Honeyman were to take the *jol* back to the farmhouse. The Frenchman's gun would remain on board, in case it should be needed, and Trapp was to carry the Dutch police gun. When Trapp had disposed of his passengers, he was to bring *Stormvogel* back to Rustig Hoek, with or without Henry according to the doctor's verdict. Henry started to make an urgent protest—and passed out; only for a moment did he lose consciousness, but it weakened his position hopelessly. He was overruled and forced to agree to the plan.

Trapp jumped ashore, ran down to where *Stormvogel* was moored, started up the motor, and brought her up alongside *Koet*. Old Nol, who was beginning to stir and moan feebly, was carried on board, followed by Charlie and the Frenchman, both of whom had recovered consciousness and were complaining loudly. Henry followed reluctantly, refused to go below, and sat morosely in the cockpit gazing astern into the darkness, watching the *jol*'s lantern, a single pinprick of light, as it disappeared in the opposite direction, headed for the farm.

The village of Ijlp was hardly equipped to deal with such sensational goings-on. The local policeman, accustomed to dealing with nothing more drastic than a few Saturday-evening drunks or a summer tourist-season traffic jam, blanched when he heard Trapp's story, as interpreted by Henry. Very firmly he said that all he could do was to call his superiors in Sneek, who would provide a police wagon for the prisoners. He also consented to telephone Ijlp's only doctor—a blithe, busy little man called Visser, who turned up at the police station within minutes and bore Henry and Nol off to his office by car.

By now the old fisherman was fully awake, although still dazed, and full of indignation at the durned furriners who had hired his boat for the afternoon and, as he concluded, made him drunk on some filthy furrin muck that no good

Frisian could stomach. He became even more indignant when Dr. Visser insisted that he should go to the hospital in Sneek for observation, as a precaution.

"D'you think I've never had too much to drink before?" he demanded blearily. "Just a bit of a hangover, that's all. The wife'll fix me up. Hospital, indeed. Never heard such rubbish . . ." He was removed, grumbling healthily, by a couple of stalwart ambulance men.

Dr. Visser then turned his attention to Henry. The bullet from the Frenchman's gun had passed clean through his left forearm, happily missing the bone, but leaving an unpleasant flesh wound to be disinfected and dressed. For the rest, the doctor suspected concussion, and ordered an X-ray of Henry's skull as soon as possible, with complete rest in the meantime. Feeling remarkably like old Nol, Henry protested that this was out of the question. He had come merely to have his arm patched up. They were still arguing when a call came through from Trapp, who was still at the police station.

"Henry? How are you, old man?"

"I'm fine."

"Well, in that case I think we should get back to Rustig Hoek as soon as we can. Mrs. de Jong has just called the police station."

"Why? What's happened?"

"Nightingale and the girl left some time ago, it seems, but for some reason Koetsveen and Mike haven't arrived. And . . ." Trapp paused.

"Well, go on."

"It seems that little Ineke is missing. She went out to say good night to her pet hen at half past seven and it's now eight. Mrs. de Jong has searched everywhere . . ."

"What about Emmy?"

"She says she hasn't seen Emmy at all."

Henry said, "Get a car. Quickly."

"How the hell can I get a car in Ijlp at this hour?"

"The police must have a car."

"My dear chap, I don't think they've got a bicycle."

"Start calling car-rental firms in Sneek, then," said Henry. "I'll be right along."

"You're going nowhere but to bed," put in Dr. Visser, who understood English.

"And shut up, you," said Henry.

"I didn't say a word, old man," said Trapp.

"Get going on that car," said Henry and hung up. He turned to the doctor. "Where can I beg, borrow, or rent a car?"

"You can't," said Dr. Visser shortly. "And if you could, I wouldn't allow it. You're to go straight to bed."

"It so happens that I haven't a bed to go to," Henry said.

"What do you mean?"

"My bed," said Henry, "is on board a boat, which also contains my wife, and both are missing. I'm going to look for them."

Visser shrugged. "You're mad," he said. "I take no responsibility for . . ."

The telephone rang. The doctor spoke rapidly for a minute or so in Dutch, ending with, "Just wrap him up and keep him warm. I'll be along right away."

He hung up, grabbed his coat, and said, "I have to go out. Little Wim Dijkstra has pulled his mother's kettle off the stove and scalded himself. I've told that girl a hundred times . . ." He scribbled on a piece of paper. "Take this to the X-ray department at Sneek hospital tomorrow. And meanwhile, go to bed!"

"Where?"

"Oh, get a room at the Golden Lion. I warn you, it's extremely dangerous . . ."

They were both outside the house by then. The doctor, rumbling threats and exhortations and denials of responsibility if his orders were disobeyed, climbed into his car and roared off down the village street. Henry hitched his arm sling into a more comfortable position and walked back to the police station.

Bad blood had evidently developed between Trapp and the

policeman. The latter obviously resented having his telephone commandeered by a lunatic Englishman, who had already disrupted the evening quiet by arriving with a boatload of desperadoes and who could not even speak Dutch, let alone Frisian. When Henry got there, the police wagon from Sneek had just arrived, together with an efficient young sergeant. Henry was thankful that the good Inspector from Amsterdam had had the foresight to provide him with a letter of authentification, for the sergeant clearly bristled with reservations and suspected a practical joke. However, once Henry had been able to produce satisfactory credentials, he became helpful.

There was just one snag. The two villainous pseudo-fishermen, Charlie and the Frenchman, who were now sharing the village lock-up, knew enough about their rights to demand to be treated as innocent citizens against whom wicked, lying accusations were being made. To make their detention legal, the sergeant explained, Henry must depose a formal complaint; verbal statements must be taken, transcribed, read through, and signed.

In vain Henry pleaded the urgency of getting on the trail of Emmy and Ineke. It was half past eight already. The sight of Henry's wounded arm, as well as his impressive documentation, had indicated to the sergeant the seriousness of the complaint against the two prisoners; but the temporary absence of a middle-aged English lady on a boat and of a notoriously mischievous little girl who was undoubtedly playing truant, he considered as a couple of storms in teacups. As for Henry's request that he should obtain a description of Nightingale's car from the Golden Lion, with registration number if possible, and send out an urgent alert that it should be stopped and searched—well—that was out of the question.

At this point Trapp asked if he might be allowed to leave the police station for a few minutes to buy some cigarettes. His quest for a car had proved fruitless. The sergeant told him he could do what he liked, and Henry was gratified to see Trapp making off in the direction of the Golden Lion. He came back ten minutes later, just as Henry had an inspiration.

The person who should really be making the complaint against the two men, he pointed out to the sergeant, was Mijnheer Koetsveen. It was he who had been attacked. But the old gentleman had had a frightening experience, which had left him weak and exhausted. The sergeant accepted this monstrous untruth with grave acquiescence. Koetsveen was obviously a name to conjure with in Ijlp. Therefore, Henry continued, surely the two suspects could be left in the lock-up while the sergeant, Gordon Trapp, and Henry proceeded in the police car to Rustig Hoek to take a statement of complaint from His Excellency. Justice could then proceed on her stately course. There was a breathless moment of hesitation, and then the sergeant agreed. They finally set out at a quarter to nine.

The police wagon was not an elaborate affair like an English Black Maria, but an ordinary mini-bus, with bars on the back window, a stout lock on the door, and a partition between the driver and his passengers, which was pierced by a small, barred window through which the driver could keep an eye on his charges by glancing in the rearview mirror. Henry and Trapp climbed into the back and sat on the wooden benches provided. The sergeant apologized for the discomfort of the vehicle, made a little joke about not locking the door on them, and went around to the driver's seat. He started up the engine, switched on the powerful headlights, and set off on the winding road toward Rustig Hoek farm.

Trapp gave Henry a cigarette, took one himself and said, "A big black American car, 'like a wedding,' according to the old lady. That means a Chrysler or a Cadillac, I suppose. They use a lot of them for weddings and funerals over here."

"Registration number?"

"No luck, I'm afraid. The old woman thought it started with GM, but her son said no, it was GA. After that they went all to pieces. The whole discussion sank onto the 'I'm-sure-there-was-a-seven-in-it' level. Not much help. I suppose it's a rented car. In fact, now I come to think of it . . ." He stopped.

"When we get to Rustig Hoek," said Henry, "I shall telephone Amsterdam and get the police there to trace it. The sergeant will be busy with Koetsveen, with any luck. If only we had some damned transportation ourselves."

Trapp glanced up at the little barred window which separated the passengers from the driver. Through it, silhouetted against the white glare of the lights, the back of the sergeant's head looked uncompromising, set four-square on a solid neck. Trapp said, "I can drive one of these things."

Henry looked at him and grinned. He was feeling rather better. He said, "You are a man of many accomplishments, Mr. Trapp. You can also speak Dutch." Trapp grinned back. "I suppose you had some reason for concealing the fact. Ah, here we are."

The first thing that became apparent, as Henry climbed down from the back of the police wagon, was that Rustig Hoek farm was in darkness. He tried not to feel alarmed.

"The front door is on the canal side of the house," Henry said. "I expect they'll be around there."

The sergeant grunted suspiciously. He switched on a powerful electric flashlight and started out along the stone-paved path that led to the front door. From the hen coop Little Annie clucked softly in her sleep. Otherwise, all was quiet. The waterside frontage of the house was dark too, and the landing stage deserted; but a little way up the canal, among the reeds at the bank, Henry spotted the dark outline of a boat.

He said, "Sergeant, I think that's my boat in the reeds. I'm going to see."

The sergeant did not answer. He was busy ringing the front doorbell with the firm pressure of authority. Henry heard the shrilling of the bell in the dark, silent house. He also noticed that Gordon Trapp had disappeared. He set off across the dark lawn toward the mast which rocked gently among the reeds.

It was the *Vrouwe Beatrix,* and she was deserted. Her nose

203

had been rammed against the soft, muddy bank and the light anchor thrown ashore to hold her. The cabin door was open. Henry, only slightly hampered by his arm sling, jumped aboard and felt for the flashlight which he knew was on the shelf just inside the cabin. By its light he examined the interior of the boat. Everything was as he had last seen it—his spare sweater thrown carelessly on the bunk, the open box of crackers on top of the stove, the book Emmy had been reading open and face downward on the table. Even Emmy's handbag was there, tucked behind the cushion on her bunk. All the signs were that Emmy had left the boat voluntarily, but in a hurry.

Henry jumped ashore again. The sergeant was still standing at the front door and Trapp was now with him. Henry saw the two of them conferring, and then they went to the living-room window, where the sergeant appeared to be shining his light into the interior of the house. Henry ran across the garden, around the back of the hen coop, and out into the field near the canal where he and Emmy had kept their vigil earlier in the day.

By the feeble beam of his flashlight he began to search the dew-damp grass. There was no sign that anybody had been there before him, only darkness and a faint, chilly white mist rising from the beeline of the narrow canal. Henry gave up and started to make his way back to the house. It was as he passed the hen coop for the second time that he saw it: a small, fluttering piece of pale fabric caught in the wire netting of Little Annie's coop, near the ground. He went down on his knees and carefully extracted it. By the beam of his flashlight he saw that it was not white but pale blue, not cloth but ribbon—one of Ineke's hair ribbons. And more than that. In the light's gleam he saw that somebody had scrawled on it the letter E, apparently with a ballpoint pen. E for Emmy; the ribbon for Ineke. Emmy always carried a ballpoint in her pocket. Feeling very cold and unhappily aware of the pain in his useless arm, Henry stood up, put the ribbon in his pocket, and walked slowly toward the house.

The sergeant had made a decision. The living-room window was now open, and Henry was just in time to see the sturdy body of the Law disappearing cautiously through it. Gordon Trapp strolled up the garden path to Henry. It was too dark to see his face, but Henry could hear the amusement in his voice.

"Our conscientious friend is intrigued," said Trapp. "The house is obviously empty, and I have persuaded him that it is his duty to investigate more closely. By a fortunate chance the window was not locked, and we got it open quite easily."

"My boat is down there by the bank empty," said Henry. "And I've found a message from Emmy."

"A message?"

"One of the child's hair ribbons, with an E scribbled on it. Emmy and Ineke are somewhere in that black American car, or I'm a Dutchman."

"Which you are not." Trapp's voice came lightly through the darkness. "And where would you say Mike and Koetsveen are? Not to mention Mrs. de Jong?"

"Wherever the *jol* is," said Henry.

"Exactly," said Trapp. "So, do we play it legal and give chase in your boat? Or do we stretch the law a little and borrow that convenient police wagon?"

After a tiny pause Henry said, "We'll take the boat."

"Coward." Trapp was laughing.

"Not at all," said Henry. "I can hardly resist the idea of roaring around Holland in a stolen police vehicle, but the boat is more sensible."

"How do you work that out?"

"I'll tell you as we go. Meanwhile, I shall inform the sergeant of our plans."

"Are you crazy? He'll hold us as material witnesses or something . . ."

"He'll try," said Henry. "At least, I hope he will. I shall tell him we're off, and then we will both run like hares for the boat. I'll get the motor going while you cast her off."

"But why tell him, in heaven's name? He's perfectly happy prowling around inside the house. He'll never know until we're gone."

Henry said, "I want him to come after us with the biggest force of gendarmes he can muster. We may need them. Now, no need for you to hang around here. Get down to the boat and stand by to cast off."

Trapp gave a mock salute. "Sir," he said and disappeared into the darkness of the garden.

Henry stuck his head in through the open window. He could see the beam from the sergeant's flashlight probing the hall at the back. He called, "Sergeant!"

"What d'you want?" The answer came from the dark depths of the house.

"I'm off now, Sergeant," said Henry cheerfully. "With Mr. Trapp. We're taking my boat, the *Vrouwe Beatrix*, and going to look for my wife."

From inside the house came an angry bellow. "You'll stay here. There's something odd going on in this house. The kitchen door's locked, and I can smell . . ."

"Terribly sorry," said Henry. "I have to go."

There was a shattering, splintering noise from the dark interior, as the kitchen door yielded to the sergeant's shoulder. Then came another bellow—even louder than the first and full of alarm. "Mevrouw—Mrs. de Jong . . . What— Are you all right?" A moment of silence. Then heavy footsteps thundered toward the window.

"You, there—come back this minute . . . Mrs. de Jong is in there—knocked out, the gas oven on . . . Thank God it can't have been on for long, but . . ."

Before the sergeant could reach the window, Henry had slipped away into the protecting darkness. He ran quickly to the boat. Trapp was waiting, mooring line in hand.

Henry jumped aboard and said, "Give her a good shove off and get aboard."

Trapp gave the bow a push out into the stream and jumped on the foredeck. As Henry got the motor going, Gordon scrambled down into the cockpit. He said, "Is the sergeant giving chase?"

"I'm afraid not." He steered down the canal, away from the farm, away from Ijlp toward the second lake. "He has his job cut out for him, poor fellow."

"What d'you mean?"

"He's found Mrs. de Jong."

"Found her?"

"In the kitchen, unconscious, with the gas oven turned on. I have no doubt that the telephone will be mysteriously out of order. I don't think the sergeant will have time to bother about us, worse luck."

"Shouldn't we have stayed . . . ?"

"Mrs. de Jong seems perfectly all right," said Henry crisply. "She's been found in plenty of time, and she's in good hands. Also, it means that the scene of action, which is where we are heading, can't be far away."

"How do you make that out?"

"Use your head," said Henry. "Meanwhile, tell me how you found Honeyman. And take the helm. You've got two hands, you lucky devil. Light me a cigarette, will you?"

Trapp lit a cigarette and handed it to Henry. Then he took the helm. The boat chugged slowly through the darkness, her motor throttled back to make a minimum of sound.

"Where are we going?" Trapp asked.

"I've no idea. Keep going slowly in the center of the canal. And tell me about Honeyman."

"Oh, that's simple enough. I knew Mike very well in the old days, in Mambesi, and he used to tell me about Holland. He knew this country well, you see. He told me that if ever he wanted to lie low, nice and snug, he'd come to Sneek and hire a boat from his old friend Mr. de Neut, and slip off to somewhere like Ijlp. So when I realized that he must have left England, I . . . ."

In the darkness Henry smiled. As if he had seen the smile, Trapp stopped speaking.

Henry said, "It won't do, will it? How did you know he'd left England?"

"Well—I guessed . . ."

"You knew very well that he'd pinched an airplane from the Brittlesea Flying Club and made for Holland, and *then* you remembered what he had said about a boatyard at Sneek . . ."

"Well—all right. Of course, it was quite easy to track him down. I found him in Sneek . . ."

"You're a very bad liar," said Henry. "You found him in Amsterdam. He had hired the boat on Friday and brought it to Ijlp, but he then went back to Amsterdam. You found him there and came back to Ijlp with him."

"Well—I remembered that he had said that when he was in Amsterdam . . ."

"My dear Trapp," said Henry, "I do wish you'd stop trying to shield Yvonne."

"I don't understand."

"You understand perfectly. You telephoned Yvonne from Amsterdam. And she told you a lot of things, because she was scared. She told you how she and her sister had been instructed by Nightingale to go around to your apartment and get Honeyman out of it. How Madeleine had dropped into Dominic's to pick up an envelope full of ready cash from Nightingale, and how the two girls then went to your apartment as casual callers. They found Honeyman and took him off to a so-called party at Yvonne's apartment. Honeyman, with no money but a generous nature, brought his contribution to the festivities in the form of the bottle of whisky you had left him. That was unfortunate, for the girls. Yvonne probably told you that I spotted it in her apartment."

"How on earth do you know all this?"

"Never mind. Honeyman was more than a match for the two girls. He gave them the slip and departed, together with a sizable chunk of the money Nightingale had given to Madeleine. Nightingale was very foolish to entrust such a mission to a couple of scatterbrained females, but he had no choice."

"Who is this Nightingale everyone keeps talking about?" asked Trapp. "Yvonne always called him . . ." He stopped again.

"Oom Willem?" suggested Henry. And added, "You knew very well she was Dutch. That's why you pretended not to know the language. And she must have described Madeleine to you in detail, so that you recognized her outside the American Hotel."

"Yvonne was very worried about her."

"I bet. And, of course, the two little girls were as innocent as daylight, just doing a favor for Uncle William. Never mind. Did Madeleine lead you to Honeyman?"

"Of course she didn't. She took that cab to a car-rental firm in the Overtoom, one that specializes in weddings actually . . ."

"Where she joined Nightingale in the hired black American car. I wish to God you'd told me sooner. Never mind. What did you do then?"

"I went to meet Mike."

"To meet him? By appointment?"

"Not exactly."

"But you knew where he'd be. How?"

"You do go on so, old man," said Trapp in a pained voice as he moved the tiller slightly to keep the boat on course. "Not the best way to get information, you know. Avoid the clipped question and the brusque tone of voice. They create a bad impression."

"For God's sake, get on with it," said Henry. His arm was throbbing; his head was aching; and his patience was wearing very thin.

Trapp said, "What Mike actually *did* tell me was that if he ever had to make a getaway from England, he'd snaffle a kite from his old flying club and go to an aunt in Amsterdam. He and I both know that everybody in Amsterdam turns up at the American sooner or later, so I assumed that if he was in the city, he just might have left a message there for me. Didn't you see me asking the waiter when I first arrived, before I joined you and Emmy? When the fellow came back to our table with the bill, it had Mike's message written on the back of it. Just an address, to be given to me if I turned up and asked for it. Simple."

"Where was this address?"

"Oh, one of those staid streets behind the museum. His aunt is a delightful old lady, the widow of a Dutchman. Mike was there. He told me he'd hired the boat and gone to Ijlp, but there had seemed to be no action, so he'd come back to Amsterdam. I convinced him we should contact you, but you had inexplicably disappeared from your hotel. That gave us the idea that the action had really started in Ijlp, so we rejoined the *Stormvogel*, with the result that you . . ."

Henry said, "All right. Look. There, on the right." He leaned down and moved the throttle control so that the motor cut back to a gentle, idling purr. Just at the point where the canal opened out into the lake the unmistakable, rotund outline of the *jol* could be seen, rocking peacefully among the reeds. There were no lights on board, no sign of life.

"So this is the final rendezvous," said Henry softly. It sounded ridiculously melodramatic, but for once melodrama seemed justified. Things had not gone as he had planned. He cursed Nightingale for leaving Mrs. de Jong at the farm as a helpless decoy. All police activity would now be concentrated there. Instead of the comforting thought of posses of police roaring to the rescue, with screaming sirens and stabbing searchlights, there was nothing in sight—or in prospect—except the damp, dark, lonely, blanket-flat Dutch countryside. Henry had one arm out of action. Koetsveen and Honeyman were presumably in no position to attack, since Nightingale, it was supposed, held the two precious hostages, Emmy and Ineke. Gordon Trapp had a gun, it was true, but the opposition would also be armed.

Henry took the helm from Trapp and steered the *Vrouwe*

Beatrix toward the bank, some hundred yards away from the *jol*. He whispered, "Get up on the bow and jump ashore with the anchor. Then come back on board."

"What's the plan?" Trapp's whisper came through the darkness.

"Your guess," said Henry, "is as good as mine."

16

After Henry had left the *Vrouwe Beatrix* to board the *jol,*
Emmy continued her patrolling of the canal with very little
enthusiasm. It was getting darker by the moment, and Emmy
never relished being left in sole charge of a boat, even in happier circumstances. In her experience boats were compara-
tively easy to get started, and child's play to keep going, but
pure hell to stop. At any moment Henry was going to shout to
her urgently to stop the *Vrouwe Beatrix*—precisely *here*—or
else . . . Besides, she was sure that Henry was in danger.
There had been sounds of a scuffle as he boarded *Koet,* but
whatever was going on, it was happening in the deep well of
the cockpit out of Emmy's view. She found that her hand on
the tiller was sweating, although the evening was chilly.

She glanced back over her shoulder toward the *jol;* by now
it was too dark and too distant to make out any details. She
imagined she could see figures moving on board, but she could
not be sure. *Vrouwe Beatrix* was downstream from Rustig
Hoek, getting too far away to be of any use to Henry. Emmy
put the helm down and turned the boat in a tight U, heading
her back toward Ijlp. It was then that she noticed that the
light in the farmhouse window had gone out. She throttled
down the motor and let the boat drift, straining her eyes in
the fast-deepening dusk as she watched the house. Then she
heard the sound of a car engine starting up and the chatter
of voices.

As the *Vrouwe Beatrix* drifted to the other side of the farmhouse, Emmy found that by looking over her shoulder she
could see a good part of the yard at the back. The kitchen
door must have been open, for a splash of yellow gaslight
spilled out into the yard, illuminating the great black car

which was parked there. Nightingale was already in the driver's seat, revving up the engine. Madeleine had paused in the open door near the passenger seat to say good-bye to her hostess.

Emmy could hear Mrs. de Jong's voice, and Ineke's, from the kitchen doorway, and although she could not understand the rapid flow of Dutch, it was evident that cordial farewells were being said. Then Madeleine got into the car and shut the door. The headlights leaped into life and the car moved away up the track which led to the road.

Then came Ineke's voice. Once again Emmy could not understand, but she caught the words "Little Annie"; Mrs. de Jong replied, evidently in the affirmative. The kitchen door closed, cutting off the light; but a bright beam of a flashlight ran across the dark yard, past the hen coop, to emerge on the other side of the house. It hesitated and then moved out into the field by the narrow canal, where Henry and Emmy had met Ineke earlier in the day.

"The silly child," thought Emmy. "She'll catch her death of cold. I hope she doesn't stay out there looking for us . . ." And then, with cold fear, she realized something else: that she could no longer see the headlights of the car. On this flat landscape they should have been visible for miles. The only explanation was that they had been switched off and—yes, there it was—the faintest, gentlest purring sound, which would have been quite inaudible from inside the house; and down the track, toward the farm, a bulky black shadow moved. The Cadillac, its lights out and its motor barely idling, was creeping back toward Rustig Hoek; and Ineke was alone in the field, advertising her presence for all the world to see by flashing Henry's powerful little light.

Emmy felt panic rising in her throat. She must get to Ineke, send the child indoors, warn Mrs. de Jong. But how could she abandon Henry, who might be fighting for his life in the *jol?* It seemed like the answer to a prayer when she heard the throb of a motorboat coming up the canal behind her. At

213

least, here was another human being; if not exactly a friend, at least, she hoped, not an enemy. Somebody who could call the police, get help . . .

As the white motor cruiser came up alongside the *Vrouwe Beatrix*, Emmy could distinguish two men aboard. She called in English, "Please—stop . . . I need help . . ."

And it seemed like a miracle when Gordon Trapp's imperturbable voice answered, "My dear Emmy. What a delightful surprise."

It was at that moment that the gun went off in the *jol*. Desperately Emmy shouted, "Henry's on board that boat! You must help him."

Stormvogel was already nosing into the bank. "Okay, love," called Gordon. "Don't panic. Reinforcements are at hand. Will you join us?"

Emmy leaned on the tiller of the *Vrouwe Beatrix*, bringing her around in the direction of Rustig Hoek again. "Tell Henry I've gone to find Ineke . . ." It was all she had time to say before she opened up the throttle, drowning her own voice, and made for the bank beyond the house.

There was nothing moving in the lane now. The car must have been parked under the shadow of a tree. From the farm's kitchen window lamplight showed that Mrs. de Jong must be in there, preparing supper to the accompaniment of Beethoven's Choral Symphony, which poured out from a portable radio on the windowsill. And in the dark field beyond the hen coop, the flashlight traced crazy patterns in the air, as Ineke amused herself by swinging it in circles, making continuous rings of light.

Inexpertly but effectively Emmy drove the nose of the boat into the soft mud of the bank and switched off the engine. Then, snatching up the light anchor which was secured to the Samson post in the foredeck, she jumped ashore. She dug one fluke of the anchor into the yielding soil of the grassy canal verge and set off in the direction of the whirling light.

Ineke was hopping around the field in high spirits. She greeted Emmy joyfully. "There you are!" she cried in her perfect English. "You're late! I've been waiting ages! Where's Henry? Did you see my light signal? I switched it off when they left. They didn't say anything interesting. They just talked to Mummy about silly old things like the weather, and then they said they couldn't wait for Grandpapa any longer, and they went away. What was that bang just now? Was it a gun? Is it part of the game?"

"Ineke," said Emmy, "you must go back to the house at once. I'll come with you."

"I don't want to. I like it out here."

"You must."

"Where's Henry? And where's Grandpapa? He's late."

"Ineke, please."

"Suppose Henry comes looking for us and we've gone indoors? He won't know where we are and . . ."

Emmy grabbed the small hand. "You'll come at once when I tell you to," she said.

"Shan't!" yelled Ineke. "Shan't, shan't, shan't. So there!"

"It's dangerous to stay out here!"

"I like being dangerous."

"You're to go in this minute!"

"I won't!"

Emmy was near to tears of exasperation. The Koetsveen family, she decided, were the most awkward kind of people to do a good turn for that she had ever met. She said, "If we leave a message for Henry, will you come indoors?"

"How can we leave a message?"

"We—we can—I know. I've got a pen in my pocket."

"There's nothing to write on."

Emmy had an inspiration. "Take off one of your hair ribbons," she said, "and we'll write on that. We'll write a long ribbony letter to Henry."

"Oh, yes!" Ineke was all enthusiasm. She pulled off one of her pale blue ribbons and unknotted it carefully. "Now," she said importantly, "I'll shine the light on it, and you can write; but I'll tell you what to write. You must write 'Emmy and Ineke are in the kitchen with Mummy and . . .'"

215

Emmy laughed. "Here, not so fast. 'Emmy and Ineke . . .'"

She had gotten no further than the initial E when the attack came—from behind and quite silently. A pair of muscular arms was clamped around her like a vise; a large masculine hand covered her mouth and nose and nearly suffocated her. She had just time to realize that Ineke was being similarly dealt with by the girl called Madeleine, when she felt herself picked up and carted off unceremoniously across the field. Emmy fought and kicked and bit, but it was no good. All that she managed to do was to drop the hair ribbon, which had been clenched in her hand. Perhaps somebody would find it. For a moment she hoped wildly that Mrs. de Jong might hear something, as the captives and captors passed quite close to the kitchen window, but the relentless music had reached the climax of the last movement. To the glorious accompaniment of choir and orchestra, Emmy and Ineke were bundled into the back seat of the car and the door slammed and locked. The man and the girl, both of whom were wearing grotesque nylon-stocking masks, jumped into the front seat, and the Cadillac accelerated sharply away up the rutted track.

Emmy gathered her senses as rapidly as she could. Ineke was yelling with fright and anger, but—Emmy could hardly believe it—neither of them had been bound or gagged. The driver of a car is notoriously vulnerable to attack from the back seat, as many unwary motorists who have given lifts to hitchhikers know to their cost. But the kidnapers appeared quite unconcerned. Neither of them as much as glanced into the back of the car. They—that was strange—Emmy, still half dazed, shook her head and put her hands to her ears. Have I gone deaf? she thought. For although the couple in the front of the car were conversing earnestly, she could hear no words; and the engine was no more than a gentle purring. And then she stretched out her hand and understood. This was a car which had been intended to be chauffeur-driven. A solid panel of glass divided the rear compartment from the driver. She and Ineke were in a neat little prison cell, which

216

was traveling at seventy miles an hour through the deserted blackness of the Frisian countryside.

Emmy pulled off her sweater and wrapped it several times around her clenched right fist. If she could break the glass there might be a chance. She slammed viciously at the partition and only succeeded in jarring her shoulder. The thud made Madeleine glance back, but only for a moment; then she resumed her conversation with Nightingale. Emmy looked around desperately for any heavy implement with which to shatter the glass, but there was nothing. The ashtrays were embedded in the upholstery of the armrests; the door handles were made of plastic and were in any case immovable; the window handles—wait a minute. Windows could be opened. As far as Emmy knew, it was impossible to lock car windows from the inside. Impossible to jump or climb out at this speed, of course, but if she could throw something out . . .

Ineke, who had recovered from her initial shock, had stopped yelling and now said conversationally, "Is this part of the game?"

"Yes," said Emmy, "yes. You mustn't be frightened."

"I'm not. Well, I was a little at first. Why didn't you tell me it was going to happen?"

"Because I didn't know."

"Oh." Ineke pondered. "Is it the same lady and gentleman? I can't recognize them with those funny things on their faces."

"It's the same people," said Emmy.

"Does that mean that their side is winning?"

"Only for a bit," said Emmy, trying to sound more confident than she felt. "Our side will win in the end."

"D'you think Henry will find my hair ribbon?"

"I hope so."

"I dropped the flashlight, but it rolled into the canal. That lady hurt me," added Ineke, aggrieved. She put her tongue out at the back of Madeleine's head.

"Ineke," said Emmy, "will you give me your other hair ribbon?"

217

"Yes, if you like. Are you going to write another letter?"

"I can't. I lost my pen in the field. But if we drop it out of the car window, Henry will be able to tell where we've been."

"How will he find it?"

"Heaven knows. But we can try, can't we?"

"And even if we've been there, we're going so fast that we won't still be there when Henry finds the ribbon, will we? We'll be miles and miles and miles away."

"Trust you to look on the bright side," said Emmy gloomily. "Give it to me anyhow."

"Oh, all right." Ineke pulled the second blue ribbon off her fair hair and handed it over. At that moment the car began to slow down. Emmy wound the window down a couple of inches and let the strip of blue silk be whipped away in the slipstream, just as the black Cadillac made a sharp left turn and began bumping over the rutted surface of what must have been a cart track.

Nightingale switched off the lights, and the big car bumped along for a hundred yards or so in total darkness. Then, as Emmy's eyes became more accustomed to the gloom, she saw a huge, monstrous form taking shape ahead, an enormous, Dali-like apparition with great skeletal arms looming up out of the night.

Ineke said, "Look! It's a windmill! You never told me we were going to a windmill."

As the car stopped, Nightingale jumped out, and, with uncanny speed, opened the door on Ineke's side and dragged the child out. The interior light of the car had come on automatically as the door opened; in its glow his face looked obscene in its flattening mask.

He said in Dutch, "Don't move. I didn't realize there would be a nursemaid."

"I'm English," said Emmy. "I don't speak Dutch."

"Ah, I understand. *Au pair.* Well, if you do exactly as you are told, you will come to no harm. Otherwise . . ." He shrugged. "The lady will now tie your hands and feet. If you make the slightest resistance, I will kill the little girl."

His voice was as quiet and poised as if he had been showing Emmy into the restaurant at Dominic's Hotel. "Get out of the car, please, and stand with your hands behind your back."

"What a nasty man," said Ineke.

Nightingale slapped her viciously across the face. After a moment of incredulous silence, Ineke let out a bellow which Emmy felt sure must carry for kilometers through the still night. Nightingale smiled behind the mask.

"Yell as loud as you like, my dear," he said. "Nobody will hear you. This mill is deserted—for the time being. Nevertheless, I think a gag would be advisable."

Emmy, in furious helplessness, had to submit while Madeleine tied her hands behind her back and then hobbled her ankles together. The same treatment was then meted out to Ineke, who was now sobbing hopelessly. Finally, both of them were gagged and carried like sacks of potatoes inside the little white fence which marked the circular compound of the mill.

Nightingale did not attempt to take them inside the mill but threw them down on the damp grass. Gazing upward into the night sky, Emmy could see the huge blade of the mill arm poised high and motionless above her head, its canvas sail reefed on the wooden struts of the framework.

As Nightingale and Madeleine walked back to their car, they were talking in English. Emmy caught odd phrases. "Deal with the mother—more rope—have to come back . . ."

Then the car started with a roar; there was a quick dazzle of headlights as it turned. And then the sound of it died away, leaving only the silent night and Ineke's sobs.

Emmy wriggled close to the child, trying to give her what warmth and comfort her body could provide. But Ineke still wept. At last the game had ceased to be amusing.

17

Henry and Gordon Trapp had good reason to be thankful that the reeds grew tall and thick on this stretch of canal bank. Their progress on hands and knees through the slimy black mud of the canal's edge was far from comfortable, but at least they were hidden from view as they approached the *jol*. It was apparently deserted—not a light, not a sound.

Then both men froze to silent immobility. A car was traveling along the road which ran parallel to the canal at the far side of the fields. It came not from the direction of Rustig Hoek but toward Henry and Trapp. Watching the headlights, they saw it slow down and stop. Then two bright red rear lights indicated that the car was backing toward the canal, off the road, presumably into a farm gateway.

Trapp whispered, "They can't drive down across this field to the water. Too boggy. They'll have to leave the car and come on foot."

Henry nodded and took a firmer grip on the 9-mm. gun in his right hand. Sure enough, a minute or so later, two figures emerged from the darkness, walking across the muddy grass. At one point the girl stumbled, and the man took her arm to steady her. Then they were on the bank beside *Koet*.

Nightingale called softly, "Koetsveen!"

For a moment dead silence. Then, very slowly, the cabin door of the *jol* opened and the old man put his head out. In a voice full of weariness and disgust he said, "Filomeel. So it is you."

Nightingale said sharply, "The gun please."

"Here." Koetsveen threw something on the bank at Nightingale's feet.

"Light the lamp in the cabin. I want to make sure you are alone."

"You think I would risk Ineke's life by disobeying you?"
Koetsveen shook his gray head sadly. "Ah, I was forgetting.
You wouldn't understand. You were prepared to let your own
brother's girls be murdered because they couldn't pay . . ."

Madeleine gave a soft, inaudible exclamation.

Nightingale, who had picked up the gun, said, "Cut it out,
will you? Light that lamp."

Koetsveen retreated into the cabin and a moment later put
a match to the paraffin lamp. With the cabin door swinging
wide open, all the watchers on the bank could see clearly
that there was no other living soul aboard. In such a small
boat there was no possible hiding place.

Trapp breathed in Henry's ear, "Where the hell is Mike?"

"Right," said Nightingale. "We'll come aboard." He
jumped on the *jol*'s deck and held out his hand for Madeleine.
She ignored it, jumped inexpertly in her high-heeled shoes,
and landed on the deck swearing.

"What's the matter?"

"Twisted my bloody ankle . . ."

"Your own fault for wearing those damn fool shoes. Get
below."

Limping, Madeleine went into the cabin. Nightingale followed.

Koetsveen made as if to close the cabin doors, but Nightingale stopped him. "No, you don't. Leave them open. I don't
trust you in a confined space. Get up forward."

Henry crept closer. He was delighted to discover that he
would be able to overhear every word.

After a moment of silence Koetsveen said, "Well—what do
you want of me?"

"Can't you guess?"

"Pereira and Findelhander," Koetsveen said uncertainly.

"Exactly. You are quick on the uptake, Mijnheer Jan. You
always were."

"You want my vote for Mambesi? Is that it? If I swear to cast
my vote for Mambesi, you will let Ineke go?"

Nightingale laughed. "My dear Jan . . ."

221

"And don't call me Jan, you traitorous, lying, son of a . . ."

"My dear Koetsveen, I'm afraid you are not so quick on the uptake as I thought. It was always your trouble, of course, even in the old days . . ."

"What was?"

"This touching and impractical faith in honor—even among thieves. A gentleman's word is his bond. You're such a damned old fool that you might even keep your word to me, but you needn't think that I'm prepared to risk it. Once you get back to London . . ."

"But if you keep the child until the decision is announced . . ."

"And give you time to get every policeman in Holland on our trail?" Nightingale laughed again. "You haven't grasped the point, Koetsveen. You know who I am. You know about Pereira and Findelhander. Surely you see that I cannot possibly allow you to stay alive."

"Then why didn't you simply kill me, damn your eyes!" Koetsveen was shouting, with all his old fire. "Why did you drag Ineke into it?"

"My friend," said Nightingale, "we did our best. You must admit that. Oh, I agree that we made mistakes. We understood that you had a weak heart, and we didn't realize that you would keep a gun on board. My men were ordered not to use too much violence, you see. We were aiming at a convenient heart attack, assisted by . . ."

"Get on with it, damn you, Filomeel!"

"I suppose you handed Pierre and Charlie over to the police. You needn't think that will worry either them or me. They are common little crooks, but they have been carefully briefed and they will tell the right story. They will get light sentences for attempted robbery and will find nice, fat bank balances waiting for them when they come out. Almost anything is possible, you know," he added conversationally, "if one has almost unlimited funds to play with."

Koetsveen gave a roaring snort of disgust.

Nightingale went on. "Except, as I was about to say, in the

case of a really honest man, such as you. However, you have your Achilles' heel. You are a sentimentalist. So, we work through your one weak spot—Ineke. A charming child, even though she has inherited your quick temper."

Koetsveen said, "Once I am dead, Ineke is no more use to you. For God's sake, kill me and let her go."

"But I don't intend to kill you, Mijnheer His Excellency Jan Koetsveen, hero of the resistance, beloved national figure of the Netherlands." Nightingale spoke softly, like a snake.

"You don't intend to . . . ?"

"It would create an unpleasant national scandal. The whole nation would be up in arms and hunting the killer. It could be dangerous and disagreeable for me."

There was a silence. Then Koetsveen said, "So what are you suggesting?"

"I'm not suggesting, Koetsveen. I am telling you my price, the price of Ineke's life. It is very simple. You will commit suicide."

There was a moment of absolute silence.

Then Koetsveen said, "I think you are the devil himself, Filomeel."

Nightingale said quietly, "Please don't be melodramatic. If you follow my instructions to the letter, all will go smoothly. There will be no doubt about your suicide and no blame will attach to anybody. There will be general mourning and deep sympathy for your family."

"And what is supposed to drive me to suicide, if I may ask?"

"That will be made clear in the note which you will leave for your son-in-law."

"For my . . . ?"

"You will be driven to suicide by the tragic death of your daughter, Mevrouw de Jong, as a result of an accidental gas leak in her kitchen . . ."

"You . . . !"

Koetsveen must have jumped to his feet, for there were sounds of a scuffle.

Then all was quiet again, and Nightingale said, "That's better. Please sit quietly. There is nothing to be gained by a display of temper at this stage. Your daughter is already dead. I promise you that she didn't suffer. This tragedy will unhinge your mind. You will write a letter to your son-in-law and post it in Ijlp. You will then walk into the police station, produce your very efficient weapon, and shoot yourself under the very eyes of the duty constable."

Koetsveen was moaning. "Corry, my little Corry—dead . . ."

"Are you listening to me, Koetsveen?"

When the old man spoke again it was in a low voice with a power of hatred behind it that drove each word home, like a pile driver. "Did I say you were the devil, Filomeel? I should apologize to Beelzebub for classing him in your company. There is no hell low enough for you to rot in for all eternity, there is . . ."

"Oh, cut it out." Nightingale was impatient. "There's not time for this nonsense."

"By God, I'll take all the time I want!"

"Then you will be very foolish," said Nightingale softly, "because in—" he paused, consulting his wristwatch "—in just over half an hour, if you are not dead, Ineke will be."

"You're bluffing," said Koetsveen, but his voice was trembling. "Your two thugs are in prison. You haven't an unlimited number of accomplices in Friesland. You are on your own, you and this—this lady . . . And if you intend to kill Ineke, you'll have to do it yourself."

"Oh, no. We shall be far away at the time."

"So you have another accomplice . . ."

"Oh, no."

"Then how . . . ?"

"I have taken advantage of local conditions," said Nightingale.

"What is that supposed to mean?"

"Local conditions happen to provide a—how shall I put it —an effective instrument of execution, which will come into

224

operation at ten o'clock precisely. I'm afraid I told a white lie to Ineke and your *au pair* girl."

"My . . ." Koetsveen began, but blessedly checked himself.

"I'm sorry about her, but she was with Ineke, so she had to go along too. I told them that the windmill was deserted. So it is, but it is a working windmill and subject to the schedules of the Rijkswaterstaadt. It is due to come into operation for pumping purposes at ten o'clock. Ineke and the girl are immediately underneath one of the sails. These unfortunate accidents happen from time to time, as I am sure you know. A single blow from the arm of a windmill . . ."

"You're lying!"

"I'm not. In fact, I am prepared to take you to the mill and show you. It is not far away."

"And if I do as you say?"

"I shall be outside the police station. As soon as you are dead, I shall return to the mill and release Ineke and the girl. Neither of them will recognize us again, and in any case, we shall be far, far away. I am sure that Ineke will live happily with her father."

There was a long silence. Then, in a low voice, Koetsveen said, "Very well. Give me pen and paper and I'll write your letter." He raised his voice slightly. "You win, Filomeel. I can't do any more, nothing more at all . . ."

Henry grabbed Trapp's arm.

Gordon whispered, "What was all that about?"

Henry said, "Take the gun, get aboard, and tackle Nightingale as best you can. And tell Koetsveen his daughter is okay. Get him to make a fight for it. I've got to go and find a windmill . . ."

"A what?"

"A windmill. And I've so little time . . ."

It was then that they saw a dark head in the water, an arm creeping up over the side of the *jol*, a bulky body heaving itself, dripping, out of the canal and into the cockpit like an ungainly water monster. There was a shout from the cabin, and a shot.

225

Trapp yelled exultantly, "So *that's* where Mike was! Look out, chaps! Here come the marines!"

He flung himself into the pandemonium that had already broken out in the *jol*. Henry, panting, ran back to the *Vrouwe Beatrix* and fumbled in the helmsman's drawer. At last he found a small knife. He put it in his pocket and started to run across the fields toward Nightingale's car. He felt sick with anxiety. He had a useless arm and no transportation, unless he could get the Cadillac going. And he had to locate an unknown windmill in the dark. He had just half an hour.

As he ran across the field, Henry marshaled his wits as best he could. First and foremost, the windmill could not be very far away. Apart from what Nightingale had said about taking Koetsveen there, if one worked things out . . .

Nightingale and Madeleine must have staged a departure from Rustig Hoek and then returned clandestinely. Having presumably left a note for Koetsveen at the landing stage—because he had not returned to the house—they had then kidnaped Emmy and Ineke. Why Emmy? Filomeel had said that she was with Ineke. Emmy had told Trapp she was going to Ineke. Only one explanation—Ineke had gone out into the field, as she had threatened to do; Emmy had gone ashore to her and fallen into the same trap. And there was the evidence of the ribbon.

Now, think clearly. Mrs. de Jong must have been fit and well at that stage, because it was after eight when she had telephoned the police at Ijlp to say that Ineke was missing. Sometime later, when Emmy and Ineke had already been taken to the windmill, Nightingale must have returned to Rustig Hoek to deal with Mrs. de Jong. By nine, when Henry, Trapp, and the sergeant had arrived at the farm, Nightingale had left again, to keep his rendezvous with Koetsveen. But— The dizziness was coming back. Henry fought to keep his brain clear.

If Nightingale had gone straight from Rustig Hoek to the rendezvous with Koetsveen, he would have arrived well ahead of Henry and Trapp in the *Vrouwe Beatrix*. But he hadn't. He had arrived several minutes later, at about ten past nine. Normally the journey by car from Rustig Hoek to the rendezvous would have taken about five minutes. The sergeant had said that the gas had not been on in the kitchen long enough to affect Mrs. de Jong. That meant that Madeleine and Nightingale must have left the farm only just before the sergeant's arrival—say, at five to nine. So they had taken a quarter of an hour to drive a journey which should have taken five minutes. And the car had arrived at the rendezvous from the other direction. A ten-minute detour—where could it have been except to check on the kidnap victims?

Henry had reached the car. The front doors were unlocked, presumably to facilitate a quick getaway; and—thank God—it was as he had hoped. Like many modern cars, the ignition key turned a ring on which three positions were marked—Lock, Garage, and On. The On position started the engine; the Lock position not only switched it off but also locked the steering wheel—an effective anti-thief device —but the Garage position was intended for switching off the engine when the owner left the car for small repairs or in a big parking garage where it might have to be moved around. In this position the engine could be switched on by inserting any small coin into a groove and turning it; but all gear positions except first and reverse were blocked, making it useless for a thief to try to drive the car away.

Henry knew from experience that it could take several seconds of fiddling with the ignition key to release the control from the Lock position, and so it must have been with the idea of a quick departure that Nightingale had left the switch in the Garage position. Henry found a twenty-five-cent piece in his pocket, inserted it in the ignition switch, and turned it. The engine leaped into life. Henry switched on the headlights and moved off in first gear at a noisy crawl.

As Henry had seen from the bank, the car had been reversed off the road into a gateway, so that it was pointing in the right direction, another potential time saver. Rustig Hoek farm lay down the road to the right, but the car had approached from the left, so Henry turned left, retracing the route. One blessing of this marshy countryside, he reflected, was that there were not many roads to choose from. Nightingale *must* have come this way, because there was no other way.

If only the night had been a little less dark—outside the brilliant lane of the headlights, all was Stygian black. There might be a dozen windmills, but he couldn't see them. Henry switched down to side lights, trying to accustom his eyes to the darkness, crawling at five miles an hour. Still he saw no windmill, no side turning, nothing but the straight road and the blackboard landscape. Henry looked at his watch. Twenty minutes to go.

Five minutes later he came to the crossroads. In a star formation, not four but five roads converged, giving him a choice of four different routes. He switched on the headlights again. An octopus-armed signpost mocked him. SNEEK—IJLP—BOLSWARD—OOSTEREND. It might be any of them. Just over ten minutes to go.

Henry pulled in at the side of the road and switched off the headlights again. He fumbled in the glove compartment and found a flashlight. Then he got out and inspected the road surface by its feeble beam. It might be possible that the car had picked up mud on its tires from the Rustig Hoek farm track, and that— But there were no tire marks on the road. In the silence an owl hooted mockingly. Henry got back into the car and lit a cigarette. His giddiness was getting worse. He closed his eyes. And when he opened them the miracle had happened.

If Henry had had the foresight to consult the *Dutch Water Almanack* for the current year, he would have learned two facts. First, that the moon would be full on April 9; and second, that it would rise at 21:51 hours. At 21:50 Henry had closed his exhausted eyes on a coal-black sky. When he opened them a minute later a huge bright disk was heaving itself dutifully over the horizon, turning the blackness to silver.

And, clearly outlined against its pale gleam, were the silhouettes of three windmills a couple of kilometers away down the Oosterend road. Henry shouted aloud with relief and started up the engine.

As the car crawled up the road, roaring its urgent desire to be put into a higher gear, Henry's optimism faded. He remembered from some half-forgotten treatise that Dutch water-pumping windmills frequently worked in groups of three, each transferring the water to a higher level, until the third ultimately discharged it into a major canal or lake, whence it could return to the sea. This must be such a set-up; in which case, all three mills would come into operation simultaneously. The mills were about half a kilometer apart, and each could be reached only by a rutted track from the main road. Four minutes to go. No time to visit all three mills. Which was the right one? If he picked it first time, he could just make it. If not . . .

Now he was at the track leading to the first mill. Should he take it or not? What was that? At the intersection of the road with the track a willow tree wept gracefully into the canal, trailing its sweeping green branches in the water. And, caught by a thread among the twigs, something was fluttering in the light breeze—a long, pale streamer.

Henry stopped the car, jumped out, and caught the pale blue ribbon at the very moment when the wind had wheedled it into relinquishing its tenuous hold on the branch. Another moment and it would have floated off down the canal.

The car was up the track inside a minute. Henry scrambled out, stumbled, fell on his injured arm, swore—and ran like a maniac around to the far side of the mill, where the sails faced into the wind. There they were—Emmy and Ineke. Bound and gagged, and more—yes—roped between the posts of the little white fence. Strapped, immobile, in the path of the great sails, like victims on a sacrificial altar.

Ineke first. Henry, his hand shaking, got out his pathetic little pocket knife. Only one hand, damn it. Get the blade open—use teeth. Cut through one rope. That's enough. Drag

229

her out of the path of the sail. Now Emmy—damn this giddiness—God, don't let me pass out now—not before . . . One more effort. One more strand of rope. But it wouldn't give . . .

With a vast creaking, like a giant heaving himself into action, the machinery started. The huge sail, slowly at first, then gaining a terrifying momentum, swung down. Emmy felt the rush of its slipstream on her legs as the strand of the rope parted and Henry pulled her clear.

He said, "Emmy . . ." And began to saw away with the tiny knife at the rope that held her wrists. Before he had managed to cut more than halfway through it, he fainted.

By a superhuman effort Emmy forced her wrists apart, straining unbearably until the remaining strands parted. Then she wrenched off her gag, cut her ankles free, and crawled over to Ineke.

As the gag fell away from Ineke's mouth, she smiled up confidently at Emmy. "I knew our side would win in the end," she said.

18

On Tuesday evening, just before six o'clock, a large and merry party assembled in one of the ingle corners of the big bar in the Hotel American in Amsterdam—large, merry, and somewhat battered. Henry's arm was, of course, still in its sling. Mrs. de Jong wore a large square of adhesive on her temple. Gordon Trapp had a black eye, and Mike Honeyman caused hilarity by his mock embarrassment about the location of the flesh wound that he had received on the *jol*. It seemed that Nightingale had fired just as Honeyman was descending backward into the *jol*'s cabin. The shot had, fortunately, been diverted by Madeleine, who had struck at her uncle's arm and so saved Honeyman's life; but, as it was, he was sitting with considerable care on the edge of his chair. He regarded the whole thing as a huge joke.

Emmy and Ineke were suffering from sore wrists and ankles, and both had caught colds as a result of their damp sojourn under the mill; but even Mrs. de Jong had not had the heart to forbid Ineke to come to this farewell party. The only member of the gathering who was hale, hearty, and unscathed was His Excellency Jan Koetsveen. Fully occupying a bench seat intended for three people, he beamed benignly on the assembled company as he raised his ridiculously small glass of *jenever* in salute.

Everyone seemed to be talking at once, for everyone was eager to tell his own story, as well as to hear what had happened to the others. Gradually, from the babble of voices and the crisscrossing of stories, a coherent pattern emerged.

Honeyman had, as Henry surmised, been lured away from Trapp's London apartment by the La Rue sisters—not a difficult matter in the circumstances. They had turned up, he said, saying that they were friends of Gordon's, had professed great disappointment not to find him at home, and had suggested that Honeyman should come out to dinner with them. He had pleaded lack of cash, whereupon Madeleine had pressed a couple of fivers into his hand, telling him that he could pay her back at any time.

"I thought that was a bit fishy," he said, "but—hell—I'd been away from civilization for a long time and here were these two gorgeous birds positively falling over each other to make much of me. Yvonne telephoned a restaurant—at least, that's what she said she was doing—and came back with the news that there wouldn't be a table free until half past eight. So she suggested that we go to her place first for a drink. I brought along Trapp's bottle of Highland Dream as my contribution."

"Charming of you, I'm sure," Gordon remarked.

"It was a good thing he did," said Henry. "I saw it in Yvonne's apartment and it gave me a good lead on what had happened."

"Anyhow," Honeyman went on, "when we got there, it appeared that Madeleine would only drink wine, and there wasn't any, so the girls went out to the liquor store to buy some. We all had a drink, and then, just when we were about to leave for dinner, Madeleine developed a most precipitate headache and decided not to come with us. She said she would go straight home, and pushed off, taking with her a suitcase of Yvonne's which she wanted to borrow for a trip abroad. Well"—Honeyman finished his *jenever* in one gulp—"don't ask me how, but when you've knocked around the world as I have, you get a kind of sixth sense about dirty work, and, boy, was my sixth sense operating on all cylinders! The whole thing was phony as hell, and I said to myself, 'Mike, old boy, these bits of skirt may not look like thugs in the pay of Mambesi, but watch it.' And a damn good thing I was on my toes. On the pavement outside the house Yvonne suddenly said, 'Oh, Mike, I've forgotten my lipstick. Try to find a cab, will you, while I go back for it?' The next moment I'm on my own, and by one of those odd coincidences a car comes around the corner that very moment and pulls up beside me. Not a taxi, a regular car. And the plug-ugly, the one called Charlie, sticks his head out of the window."

"He gets around, that character," Trapp remarked.

Honeyman went on, "He says, 'Want a cab, sir?' and I say, 'You're no cab,' and he says, 'Private mini-cab, sir.' Then he jumps out, opens the door of the car, and says 'Get in.' He gives me a sort of shove, and I see that it's a gun he's digging into my ribs, a little handbag-size affair, but enough to do damage at that range. Well, as I said, I was ready for him. I'd started my swing before he got the car door open, and I connected with his ugly jaw before he knew what had hit him. I didn't hang around after that. I ran like a springbok around the corner, found a genuine cab, and headed for Liverpool Street Station. With that sort of lark going on, tied up with what Gordon had told me—well—I assumed that the sooner there was a solid stretch of deep water between England and yours truly, the better. I just made the Brittlesea train, borrowed a bike outside Brittlesea station, and a kite from the airfield—plan A, in fact, as I'd often described it to Trapp. What beats me, how did the gang know I was in London? I hadn't seen a soul except old Gordon—I must say, that made me think. No offense, old man, but . . ."

"Yvonne La Rue," said Henry, "is the senior secretary of PIFL—or was. You didn't see her at the office, but she saw you. Heard you, at least. Her office adjoins Trapp's. Of course, she sounded the alarm as soon as she overheard your story. Now, just for the record, why did you fly to Holland?"

Honeyman maneuvered himself into a more comfortable position, saying, "Half a moment. Aunt Fanny is complaining again. That's better. What did you say? Why Holland? About six good reasons, old man. One, it's the first bit of land you hit if you head out to sea from Brittlesea. Two, I've known it all my life. Three, it's flat as a pancake, which makes it good for unorthodox landings. Four—well—hell, isn't that enough for you? Not to mention the fact that Koetsveen was here, and where he was, the action would be. And I'm a sucker for action."

"You are a very remarkable man." Koetsveen beamed. "Ladies and gentlemen, a toast to Mr. Honeyman."

Glasses were filled and emptied.

Mike went on. "Not much to add to that. I brought the kite down in a field near Sneek and hired the *Stormvogel* from an old pal. I brought her to Ijlp, but nothing seemed to be going on, apart from a nice little bit of skirt from the grocery. So I got the local pub to change a fiver into guilders and went to Amsterdam and my aunt. I rather fancy the thought that I did all this on Nightingale's money. I left a message at the American to give Trapp my address, because I had a sort of notion he might turn up. The rest, you know."

"But what happened after Henry and I left you on the *jol?*" Trapp asked.

"I'm dry," said Honeyman. "Grandpa can tell you about that."

"Of course I will tell," said Koetsveen. "There is not much. We brought the boat back to the landing stage at Rustig Hoek, and when I got ashore I found a piece of paper pinned to one of the posts. It was signed Filomeel, and it said, quite simply, that he had kidnaped Ineke and was prepared to discuss a ransom price with me. I was not to go into the house but must take the boat straight on up the canal to the spot where you later found us. It was an old wartime rendezvous we both knew. I must be entirely alone, he said, and must surrender my gun to him before we talked. If I did not obey implicitly, Ineke would die. What could I do? I consulted my good friend, the estimable Mr. Honeyman, and told him that he must go ashore and leave me alone."

"And I told him he was a sodding old fool," Honeyman put in.

Koetsveen beamed again. "Yes, he told me this; and he was right, my friend Honeyman. I said I must fulfill the conditions for Ineke's sake, and then he had the brainwave that he would hide in the water. Just before the rendezvous he went over the side and kept on swimming, hidden by the boat. It was arranged that I would keep Filomeel talking for a while, with Honeyman as an unseen witness who could hear it all and give evidence later on, so that the villain would condemn himself out of his own mouth.

"My signal was to be when I said, 'You win, Filomeel. I can't do any more.' Then the good Honeyman would climb back on board, and we would put up a fight for it. Of course, I could not know that the intrepid Mr. Trapp would arrive also. Nor that Madeleine would be on our side in the end. It is a pity, what has happened to her. She was such a dear little girl, she and her sister both." He sighed sentimentally, brought out a huge white handkerchief, and polished his glasses. "Yes, it seems that until yesterday the girls believed that it was their Oom Willem who had saved their lives, and in gratitude they had always done whatever he asked of them —however irregular."

"Who brought them up?" Henry asked.

"Ah, that was arranged through our good friends the exiled Dutch. They went to live with a widowed lady, a Dutch lady who had married a Frenchman called La Rue. He was killed escaping from France, poor fellow. They hadn't been long with Madame La Rue when Oom Willem sought them out, and after that he kept in close touch. When they grew up, he began to find them very useful for his plans. How much they knew of what really went on . . ." Koetsveen shrugged. "That's anybody's guess. I think the kidnaping of Ineke came as a bit of a shock to Madeleine. I like to think so, at any rate."

"She was a horrid lady," Ineke put in from her mother's knee. "She hurt me."

"I'm sure she didn't mean to, Ineke," said Koetsveen gently. He added, "In any case, it was a fine fight, was it not, my friends? Filomeel will be in the hospital for some time before he is well enough to stand trial." He turned to his daughter. "And you, my little Corry, what is your story?"

235

Mrs. de Jong smiled. "Very short and not at all heroic," she said. "After our visitors had left, Ineke asked if she might go and say good night to Little Annie, and I said she might. I started to get supper, and there was one of my favorite symphonies on the radio. I simply didn't notice the time. Suddenly I realized that the child had been gone twenty minutes or more. I went outside and called her, but there was no answer. Nothing. You hadn't come home, Father, and I was frightened. I telephoned the police in Ijlp, and they said that if there was no news soon, they would investigate. So, of course, when there was a knock at the back door I thought it was the police. I opened the door, and the man—he had told me his name was Van Dam—was standing there. He hit me with something hard." She put a hand to her temple. "I think it must have been a tire lever. Anyhow, I don't remember any more until I woke up in the doctor's office in Ijlp with an awful headache and surrounded by policemen. That poor sergeant; he was so distressed—trying to question me without letting me know that Ineke was still missing . . ." She hugged her daughter, who wriggled and said impatiently, "Oh, *don't,* Mummy . . ."

Trapp said, "And now, Superintendent Tibbett, it's your turn."

"My turn?" said Henry. "I've nothing to tell that you don't know already."

"Nothing? My dear Henry, you've never told me why you suddenly decided that I was not weak in the head after all."

"Oh, just call it—my nose," said Henry, smiling.

"Nose, my foot," said Trapp. "Oh, I've heard all about your famous intuition, but you're not going to tell me that one evening you dismissed me as a harmless lunatic and the next morning you suddenly sniffed the air and decided I was on the track of an international gang. Come on. Tell."

"Yes, you must, Henry," said Emmy. "We all want to know."

"Hear, hear," said Honeyman.

Henry said, "Oh, very well, but it's a bit complicated. It started with one forty-five."

236

"That's as clear as mud, old pal," said Honeyman.

Henry said, "When Gordon first came to see me, I was investigating a sordid little murder, the shooting of a small-time crook in a shady London pub. The murdered man had been working as a kitchen porter, and that took me to Dominic's Hotel to make inquiries. There I discovered a couple of odd facts. The first was that Byers—that was the man's name—had only recently come to Dominic's from another hotel, and that he had no need to carry on with his menial work because he had recently come into money. It began to sound as though he was at Dominic's for some purpose other than merely earning his living.

"Then I found out that Mr. Justice Findelhander had been staying at Dominic's when he died, and that he had just moved into room one four-five. Now, just before Byers died, he was delirious and kept on saying, 'One forty-five.' He was a gambler, and we thought that he was referring to a horse race. He also tried to say 'Philomel,' but my sergeant didn't catch the word properly and thought it was a name, either a girl or a horse.

"At Dominic's I discovered that Byers had been ideally placed to tamper with Findelhander's food tray. The trays all bear the number of the room they are going to, and so, with the change of room, Byers had obviously had the number one forty-five drummed into his head by Nightingale, that is, Philomel or Filomeel. It wouldn't have been good to send doctored food to the wrong room.

"Well, there it was. A bit of 'nose,' a few facts, a coincidence or two. Then I found that the owner of the pub where Byers was shot had been the chief witness at the inquest on Pereira. That clinched it. Madeleine La Rue was staying at the pub and had been going around with Byers—an unlikely combination. Of course, she was acting on her uncle's orders. What I didn't know was how secret information from PIFL meetings was getting out—and to whom? Who was the mastermind? And who had put on a false beard and shot Byers?"

"And the answer was Nightingale," said Emmy.

"The information from PIFL," said Henry, "could only have come from one of the two interpreters—Gordon Trapp or Pierre Malvaux. And Yvonne La Rue was extremely friendly with both of them."

Koetsveen was looking worried. "I am sure that my good friend Mr. Trapp meant no harm," he said.

"Of course he didn't," said Henry, "and neither did Monsieur Malvaux. After all, Yvonne was a senior member of PIFL's staff, and it would not have occurred to them that it was important to conceal the views of the various commission members from her . . ."

Koetsveen said warmly, "That is correct, Superintendent. Our views are not of great importance to the ordinary person. We are not, I hope, a conceited body of men, and in any case, the result of this dispute is of interest only to international law specialists . . ."

Honeyman laughed, and Henry said, "That's where you are wrong, sir, as Honeyman knows. Since the start of the hearings, the Mambesians have begun to dig in the Blue Smoke mountains, slap in the middle of the disputed zone. I don't know what they've found—diamonds, perhaps, or gold, or some even more valuable mineral. It was by then too late to withdraw the dispute from PIFL. So they decided the only thing to do was to win it. They contacted Nightingale."

"Why Nightingale?" Emmy asked.

Henry said, "There are people like him in every great city. The men with fingers in every pie; the men who can fix anything—for a price. As manager of Dominic's, he mixed with diplomats and foreign politicians, with wealthy and influential people in every sphere of life. He was also in touch with certain elements of the underworld—very discreetly, of course. He worked through his grateful nieces most of the time. He established Madeleine at The Pink Parrot, the pub where Byers was shot, and he made his shady contacts through her and through Weatherby, the owner.

"This job, which was undoubtedly proposed and paid for by the Mambesian authorities—although, of course, they'll

238

deny all knowledge and we'll never prove it—as I say, this job was rather out of his line, I imagine. As a rule, I think, he was more concerned with money and vice than with violence, not that he had any moral objection to murder, but it was risky. Señor Pereira was quite simple. Weatherby probably administered the fatal push; the inquest went like clockwork; the money was right; and Nightingale knew that Weatherby would keep his mouth shut.

"Mr. Justice Findelhander was a more difficult proposition. There he was, actually living in Nightingale's own hotel, and suffering from a weak heart. But Nightingale dared not make any move in the matter himself. He had to employ Byers, a thoroughly unscrupulous and unreliable character, who would very likely have blackmailed him later on. Mind you, Byers was contacted exclusively through Madeleine and got his orders from the mysterious Philomel. He had no idea that Philomel was the lordly Mr. Nightingale, but he might have found out later on. Nightingale was taking no chances. Byers was employed; handsomely paid; and then disposed of. Nightingale had to do that unsavory job himself. He chose a disguise which was brilliant in its simplicity—an enormous false black beard and huge dark glasses. Weatherby and Madeleine knew him, of course, but none of the other men in the bar could have described him, even if they had wanted to. He even took care to disguise his voice with a thick accent. He shot Byers and simply walked out, removed his beard and glasses, and strolled back to his office at Dominic's.

"As an extra precaution Weatherby took care to describe the bearded man as small. Then it came to his ears, as these things do in the underworld, that a young man called Peterson, who was in the pub when Byers was shot and who wanted to get well in with the police, was proposing to make a statement to the Yard. Now, this suited Weatherby—outside confirmation of his story would be useful—but he made the mistake of contacting the young man and bribing him to be vague about the gunman's height. Weatherby didn't know that Peterson had already spoken to my sergeant on the

239

telephone and described the murderer as tall. Such a little thing, but enough to tell me that Byers' killer was a tall man, that he was anxious to conceal the fact, and that Weatherby knew him.

"I was still very dense though. I had quite forgotten that murmured word that sounded like 'Phyllis.' It wasn't until Nightingale had the brazen effrontery to check in at the Golden Lion in Ijlp as Mijnheer Filomeel that it all clicked into place and I knew for certain."

Gordon Trapp said, "Filomeel alias Nightingale alias Herbert G. Pierce. He must have known you were at his heels or he wouldn't have bothered to get on the same plane with me and try to persuade me to travel by T-E-E—what was the object of that anyhow?"

"There's a bit of confusion there, I think," said Henry. "He wasn't worrying at all about the Byers affair; he thought he had gotten clean away with it. It never occurred to him that we knew about Pereira and Findelhander. What let the cat out of the bag was the arrival of Honeyman, with his fatal knowledge about the mining camp in the Blue Smoke mountains. So far as Nightingale knew—via Yvonne—Honeyman had seen and spoken to nobody but Trapp, so both must be eliminated at once. Also Koetsveen must have an unfortunate accident without more ado, and Nightingale decided to do this himself. Maybe he had always planned to come to Holland for that particular job. I'm sure it would have appealed to him.

"But, as I said, Honeyman's arrival caused a flutter. Emergency plans had to be made. Mike was lured into a trap from which he extricated himself with commendable speed . . ."

"Where did Madeleine go, by the way?" Honeyman asked. "From Yvonne's, I mean. Not home, I'll be bound."

"No, no. She went back to Gordon's apartment."

"But how . . . ?"

Henry looked at Trapp. "You really should have told me that Yvonne had a key," he said.

Trapp reddened.

"Never mind. Madeleine borrowed her sister's key and a suitcase. She went back to the apartment, put the wedge in the telephone, put Honeyman's knapsack into her suitcase, and departed. She then ditched the knapsack. The object was to remove every trace of Honeyman, so that Trapp would be disbelieved if he claimed to have seen him."

"Why on earth did she wedge the telephone?" Gordon asked.

"Because you were out."

"I don't follow you."

"The girls had hoped to find you and Mike together, and the disposal scheme was for both of you. But you were out, and you knew that you had left Mike in your flat. You might try to contact him by telephone during the evening and realize that he had gone. This might put you on the trail sooner than Nightingale wished. The telephone was therefore wedged, so that a caller would assume that the number was busy and the apartment still occupied. As it turned out, it was a mistake, but I can understand why she did it.

"The main thing we had to do on Friday night was to prevent Nightingale and his amateur shadows from finding out that Trapp had contacted me and been to Scotland Yard —and we succeeded. Nightingale's spies reported that Trapp had been to a night club with friends and had gone back with them to an address in Chelsea for the night. Mercifully, they had no idea who lived at that address. Nightingale himself must have been watching the house in the morning, and despite our precautions he managed to follow Trapp to London Airport and get on the Paris plane with him.

"He must have been taken aback when Trapp told him that he was proposing to catch a train from the Gare de Lyon with only minutes to spare. It gave Nightingale no time to contact his French henchman, who was waiting in Paris for orders. So he tried to persuade Trapp to postpone his departure until the one o'clock Mistral express. That would have allowed ample time to set up a reception committee."

Henry turned to Trapp. "You did very well," he said. "It

was a clever move to let them think you had changed trains, and then, in fact, to melt away in a different direction altogether."

"Melting has always been a specialty of mine," said Trapp with no false modesty, "especially where women are concerned." He sighed. "A pity about Yvonne, but I really don't fancy Filomeel as an uncle-in-law. I shall have to get the lock changed on my front door. However, hope springs eternal," he added as a slim, blond beauty in leopard-skin jeans strolled past.

Koetsveen cleared his throat. It was obvious that he was about to address the group on a matter of some gravity. He said, "Ladies and gentlemen, it only remains for me to thank you all, on behalf of my family and myself, for all that you have done for us. I trust that you will forgive any discourtesy that you have received at my hands, and, by way of a small repayment, I hope that you will accept my hospitality. I have reserved a table at the Amstel Hotel, and when Ineke has been taken home and put to bed . . ."

"Oh, no, Grandpapa! I won't! I . . ."

Koetsveen fixed his granddaughter with an awful eye. "When Ineke has been taken home and put to bed, I hope that you will all dine with me there as my guests. Meanwhile, I raise my glass to each of you. To the charming and heroic Mrs. Tibbett. To the persistent Superintendent, who is as stubborn as I am. To my good friend Honeyman, who tells me the truth about myself. To the gallant Mr. Trapp—Mr. Trapp . . . ?" His voice trailed off in surprise.

And, indeed, Gordon Trapp was no longer with them. He had melted.

Henry was just able to catch a glimpse of him through the window before he got into a taxi with the blond and was whirled away into the sparkling neon heart of Amsterdam.

EPILOGUE

From *The Times*, London, May 24th:

The members of the Commission for Permanent International Frontier Litigation yesterday announced their decision in the Mambesi-Galunga frontier dispute, which has been before the commission for some years.

The commission decided by five votes to four that the treaty of 1876 was no longer applicable and that the frontier line should lie along the watershed formed by the Blue Smoke mountains. This decision has the effect of giving the disputed strip of land to the Republic of Galunga.

Rumors have been rife in well-informed African circles that valuable mineral deposits have been located in the area. It will be remembered that two weeks ago a mysterious explosion destroyed what had apparently been an illegal mining camp in the mountains. Galunga's prime minister has announced that mining operations will begin as soon as possible.

From *The Galunga Mail*, Lungaville, August 28th:

[Advertisement] Wanderlust? Travel fever? The Dakotas and Lysanders of HONEYMAN'S SUPERLUXE AIRLINES will fly you from anywhere to anywhere! Our motto—service and safety! Compare our prices! We operate under license with full government approval. Book now for Christmas!

From *The Times*, London, August 30th:

The Commission for Permanent International Frontier Litigation (PIFL) has been asked to adjudicate in a dispute between Northern and Southern Bimbasi. The affair concerns a fifty-foot-high granite statue of Queen Victoria, which each country claims lies in the territory of the other. Preliminary hearings are expected to last at least three years.

From *The Times*, London, August 31st, Personal Column:

YOUNG MAN, fed up with dead-end job, seeks adventure. Fluent French, Spanish, Dutch, experience of interpretation. Go anywhere, do anything legal. Write Box 1683K, The Times.

ABOUT THE AUTHOR

PATRICIA MOYES, who lives in Holland in an eighteenth-century house, was born in Ireland and has worked as a screenwriter, playwright, and mystery novelist. With her husband, who is an official attached to the International Court of Justice at The Hague, she enjoys skiing, sailing, and traveling through Europe by car. Among her other mystery stories are *Death on the Agenda, Murder à la Mode, Johnny Under Ground,* and *Murder Fantastical*. Miss Moyes has also entered the juvenile field on the Holt, Rinehart and Winston list with *Helter-Skelter*. She is now at work blocking out a new Superintendent Tibbett story.